PATTERN MAKERS

PATTERN MAKERS

by

Sandy Frances Duncan

CANADIAN CATALOGUING IN PUBLICATION DATA

Duncan, Sandy Frances,
    Pattern makers

ISBN 0-88961-138-6

I. Title.

PS8557.U5375P3 1989   C813'.54   C89-094951-4
PR9199.3.D85P3 1989

Cover art: Maureen Paxton
Cover design: Linda Gustafson
Editor: Ann Decter
Copy editor: Angela Hryniuk

Published by *The Women's Press*
229 College Street, No. 204, Toronto, Ontario M5T 1R4

This book was produced by the collective effort of The Women's Press.

The Women's Press gratefully acknowledges financial support from The Canada Council and the Ontario Arts Council

Printed and bound in Canada.

1 2 3 4 5   1993 1992 1991 1990 1989

Parts of *PATTERN MAKERS,* in slightly different forms, have appeared in *TESSERA* 1987, 1989, and in *(f.)Lip,* V.I, #1, 1987

through the memories of Frances and Nonie and Joan

this book is for

Yvonne, Jane, Mirabelle, Kelly, Kirsten, Lisa, Linda, Luanne, Lise, Helen, Barbara, Barbara, Daphne, Betsy, Gloria, Angela, Angie, Martha, Marilyn, Marilyn, Hano, Veena, Mary, Mary, Sheila, Margaret, Jennifer, Elva, Lynne, Lisa, Lynn, Cathy, Kathy, Bonnie, Uma, Eleanor, Eleanor, Sally, Laura, Stacey, Tanya, Alex, Janet, Janis, Jana, Janice, Jean, Jeanne, Jeannie, Joan, Heather, Susan, Leah, Laura, Katie, Pam, Madge, Amy, Libby, Nancy, Nancy, Vickie, Penn, Penny, Chrissie, Tish, Kate, Susie, Jenine, Patsy, Patty, Bobbie, Maureen, Carol, Ricky, Gail, Carolyn, Caroline, Ruth, Betty, Anita, Marlene, Marlene, Shelley, Leanne, Elizabeth, Liz, Beth, Irene, Joanne, Jo-Ann, Audrey, Audrey, Milly, Milly, Thora, Donnie, Donna, Win, Leona, Leslie, Karen, Karen, Kit, Kitty, Val, Rachel, Arlin, Ann, Anne, Anne, Mary Ellen, Kirsten, Kelly—

and for

Pat
who helped to heal the women and make them aware of each other

May the Spider follow us all

IN THE MIDDLE OF THE NIGHT Yvonne opened the refrigerator door and climbed out. She put her right hand to her lower back, rubbed her neck, straightened rather slowly; she had been living in her fridge a long time. The kitchen was lit with cool moonlight, its familiar pattern on the floor, on the wall. So reassuring. Her lips inched into a small smile and she remembered her midnight prowls through the house before she'd moved into the fridge.

Yvonne looked from the moonlight itself to the objects it lit – should have been lighting. She could see no counters, no sink, no table nor oven nor dishwasher; the copper-bottomed pans that hung over the stove were not there either. Her left hand still grasped the refrigerator handle; she tightened her fingers around it for safety. She could hear no house sounds. The fridge was not humming, nor the furnace. Even the clocks were silent. All she could hear was her own blood pulsing up her neck, past her ears. Had something happened to Martin, the children, had they gone away? Had she been living in her fridge too long? Maybe Martin was only redecorating. Reassured again, Yvonne stepped back toward the fridge. Her foot scrunched: sand.

She looked down. The floor was covered in sand, sand had piled up in corners; a few grains fell off the wall. Their little noise made her aware of another noise, so constant it had been only background, but now her attention drew it forward. Upstairs, Martin was snoring.

Yvonne looked back to the moonlight pattern as if staring at it would make the counter, sink, pans reappear, would pull the furnace and fridge motors into action, would clean up the sand. Make everything as it had been, and she could safely climb back into the fridge, having only climbed out to see the pattern. But the sand was still here. Her hand sweat-slipped on the refrigerator door. She let go, wiped her palm on her jeans. Were Martin, the children all right? She took one step away from her fridge, another. Scrunch, scrunch.

Yvonne made herself not run; any hurry would admit her panic and she'd be driven by it. She shuffled through the dining room, the living room – where were the furniture, drapes, pictures, the china swan Janet had given her last birthday? Just rolls and ripples and drifts of sand, chattering like little teeth as she disturbed them. Wanting to scream, but afraid if she started she'd not be able to stop.

One foot on the first stair, then slowly up the rest, Martin's snores increasing in volume. Such a long time since she'd been up here, the backs of her calves ached from even these few steps. John's room closest, then Janet's: the children humped under blankets, asleep. Swept by relief, Yvonne put her hand to the doorjamb, now admitting to herself she had been afraid.

In their bed, her bed, now for a while only his bed, Martin lay on his back, hands crossed on his chest. Familiar pose. Yvonne longed to climb in beside him, warm her feet on his, and look at the moonlight through these curtains, an old familiar view. But each time Martin exhaled in a rattling snore the sand on his chest shifted. Each time he inhaled, one or two grains fell from his moustache into his mouth.

Again she wanted to scream. Instead, Yvonne scrunched over to the bed and shook his shoulder. "Martin, wake up!

8

Everything's covered in sand! The house is a desert!''

He rubbed his eyes, propped himself on an elbow, squinted around the room. "Desert? Nonsense. I don't see any desert. Everything's the same. Go back to sleep.'' He rolled onto his side and pulled the covers up. The last twitch he gave them spewed sand down his neck.

Yvonne crossed the hall to the children's rooms again. "Aw Mum, you're crazy,'' John mumbled. Janet burrowed into her pillow, refusing to wake up. At least there was no sand on them. Yet.

Yvonne stood in the hall, equally positioned between all bedrooms and the stairs, hearing you're crazy, crazy, everything's the same, no desert, nonsense. She put her hand on her chest to keep her heart from leaping through, swallowed against the pressure of breathlessness, of screaming. What to do? How to wake Janet up? Make Martin believe? Or – maybe they were right, maybe she was crazy, no desert, everything's the same. But what about the sand? She could see it piling ever higher in corners, dripping from the ceiling, swirling in some unsourced breeze.

Now panic did run her. She couldn't help it. She knew there was sand. She started downstairs, fighting the scream in her throat. Her foot slipped and she grabbed the railing for support. It crumbled. The balustrade fell away. She looked behind her. The stairs were toppling one into the other and into her shoes. Little moans escaped from the scream in her throat. No way now to go back to wake Janet, to make Martin and John believe her. Jumped the last step and ran into the kitchen—

Refrigerator not there. Nor the walls or doorway she'd just passed through. Nor the window or the wall with the window. Moonlight leaked everywhere, patternless, from the cool round moon high up in the sky, about where the chimney should have been. Yvonne moaned some more, put her hand to her mouth, her stomach heaving into vomit, tightened her muscles against all her liquid viscera. She turned

– climb in, shut the door, everything will be all right—
No refrigerator.

Yvonne looked wildly all around her, listening intently. Nothing she recognized. Only worn and rounded piles of sand, rocky outjuttings, shallow gullies, and a whispering as each grain rubbed against its neighbour. Before her the once familiar yard and park and streets stretched as harsh and uninviting as the moon's surface captured by still space shots.

Yvonne's knees loosened and lowered her to the ground. She put her hand out for support, felt the sand stick to her palm, tried to brush it off, now had sand on both palms. She clasped her gritty hands around her knees, put her head down and rocked—

Alone. Completely alone. No Martin, no children, no fridge – no walls, house frame, foundation. She was nothing, she was aloneness. That tore at her, threatening to suffocate her. She moaned, choked on the gorge banging at the back of her throat; if she vomited, if she let go of anything, there'd be less of her. Already so little, only pain, terrible, terrifying pain. The inside aloneness annihilating her as it sought to join with the outside aloneness. She would blow away like a drift of sand, no corner, no edge to collect in. No boundary.

But she did have a boundary – pain. A hard edge. Pain. Feeling it. Not annihilated.

Yvonne opened her eyes, gritty with uncried tears, found herself staring at the sand surrounding her feet, blowing against her shoes, filling the lace holes; found individual grains to stare at, all the same beige colour in the moonlight. She wiggled her toes, watched the sand shift. With a great effort she lifted her head, re-focussed her eyes, followed streaks of moonlight across the desert. Up there the moon, full, and familiar – not so alone, then.

Yvonne stood up and brushed her palms on her jeans. The pain receded, leaving her dry, dead, like this desert. She looked around. As well as the cold ball of the moon there was another light, a streetlight perhaps or an uncurtained window, perhaps a long way off. People, perhaps help. She looked back once more, hoping – but now not really surprised to see that the view behind was the same as in front. She started toward the light.

&

Yvonne walked for a long time. The light came no closer. Nor did the moon change position in the sky. Each gulley she crossed, each hill she climbed, each flat stretch she trudged through loomed again before her, apparently in the same configuration, like over-patterned wallpaper.

The first paper she'd hung in her white fridge had been like that: green star, pink star, green star, pink star – she'd put blue and white stripes on one wall for variety. This desert needed variety; Yvonne tried to hang up a green star, a pink star, a stripe, but they wouldn't stick. No water for paste in a desert. Thirsty.

The build up of sand in her shoes and her increasing thirst marked the passage of time. But Yvonne didn't want to feel thirsty; thirst could be produced as much by sight of the desert as by any real need. Similarly, there might be no more sand in her shoes now than on her flight down the stairs. Not thirsty.

Wishing there were sounds in this desert, she listened hard, but heard only the scrunch of sand under her shoes, monotonous as the view. She'd put up a mural here, perhaps a lush garden scene, with trees overhanging a path, benches to rest on, and a gushing fountain, some nightbirds, an owl perhaps, to soar by and who at her, who-who—

Who are you? Who do you think you are? Whose desert is this? She shuddered. Let the owl who at someone else—

No one else.

Now only her mouth. Swollen with dryness, it consumed

the desert, the moon, the light. Yvonne tried to ignore it, made herself look at the moon, the light, made herself watch her feet move one in front of the other, one in front of the other, one in front—She was not thirsty. Nonsense. Crazy. No desert. Go back to sleep. Crazy?

Yes, thirsty. She couldn't help it. With that admission, her mouth consumed her as well as the desert. Yvonne was propelled over her flaked lips and into the demanding cavern of her mouth. The uvula hung down like a dessicated grape. The tongue ridges increased and indented and pressed against the roof ridges. She tried to pry her tongue loose. As she did she heard dry sounds, raspings and scrunchings and gratings and dronings: she looked around. All she could see were pillars of teeth, a barricade for her desperately swelling tongue, lined up in rows like ice cubes. If only they were ice cubes—

One pattern overlapped another. Her teeth became ice cubes. Beads of moisture formed on them, then dripped and gushed, bathing her whole mouth. Her tongue and roof ridges sucked avidly. Now the cubes became a huge block of ice that melted fast in the heat, squelching the dry, scary sounds as water flowed down her throat. She pressed against the side of her mouth, hung on to a molar-shaped cube to avoid being swept away, and watched her uvula high above fill and swell, felt its surge of pleasure, of relief.

As Yvonne moved out of her mouth a grin stretched her lips, no longer flaked and cracking; what relief, what happiness, to have thirst quenched. Magic teeth, she'd never known. Of course, perhaps she hadn't been thirsty in the first place, just thought she was. To have magic teeth that turned into ice cubes really was crazy. So, she was crazy, she didn't care. Not thirsty any more.

Yvonne moved back into her mouth and her teeth shifted into ice cubes again, drops of water—

Outside again. She didn't want to wear the magic out, if that could happen. Grinned again: she could do it when she

12

had to. Definitely crazy. Didn't matter, crazy or not, how it happened, whether she was really thirsty or thought she was—

Yes. It did matter. She had been *parched*, and now she wasn't and she'd quenched her thirst her own way. She looked around at the moon – let the desert go on!

The desert was going on, unrelieved by cacti or lichen or, in the moonlight, even by colours the sun might have shown. Was the light any closer? She should have reached the river long ago. Perhaps the geography had changed as well as the landscape, or perhaps the river had filled with sand. Walking through such fine sand strained her shins and thighs; she was unaccustomed to walking after her long time in the fridge. Her feet dropped to a shuffle that trickled more sand into her shoes, but took less energy. Hands in her pockets. Wished she'd grabbed her purse before the fridge disappeared, felt unclothed without it swaying gently from her shoulder. No credit cards, no identification – at least no owl asking who?

Trudge, trudge, trudge, trudge. Yvonne peopled the desert with her mother and father, Martin, the children, but their faces blew away like swirls of sand. She tried faces of friends – she didn't have many; in the fridge she hadn't been set up for entertaining—

Why into the fridge in the first place? Defrosting it one morning, throwing out limp celery and a jar of chutney that had grown something pink on top, washing the sides and racks and crisper. Noticing, really noticing, the clean, cool, enticing precision of its white interior, had just climbed in. Such relief. Out before the children came home for lunch, but after that, spending more of each day in the fridge, until that was where she lived. Martin and John and Janet had adjusted well. So well that Yvonne had sometimes wondered why she hadn't climbed into the fridge before.

Wished she hadn't got out tonight. Comfortable there, especially after she'd moved in her favourite chair. Food

13

within easy reach, no sand in the fridge, no pain, all that white, precise protection—

Her refrigerator! Here, in the desert! A few metres ahead, its left-opening door slightly ajar. Light leaking out in a crack toward her. The light she'd been following? Climb back in. Make her house reappear around the fridge, build walls and roof again, stairs, place the children sleeping in their beds. Martin snoring again.

Yvonne stumbled into a run toward the fridge. One toe nearly onto the crack of light from its door – the fridge receded in front of her. Faster. The fridge accelerated, its light, its door staying the same unobtainable distance in front. Oh no, had to get closer. Touch it, had to touch it, feel its smooth, cool enamel, grasp its handle—

Faster, breathing harder, gasping, her lungs, her chest, aching, her heart pounding, all of her tearing. Sobbed, put her hand to her mouth again, stifling the sob into moans. Not waiting for her, her fridge, not waiting for her, she was all alone. The pain was back. Cracked, crazed with pain, she would crumble into little bits and blow away like the sand.

"No," she whimpered. "No. No!" Shouting now, she took her hand from her mouth, and shook a fist at the refrigerator. "NO!"

The distance between them increased. Still shaking her fist, all of her still shaking, still panting. But the pain receded, as the fridge had. Her heart and breathing slowed toward comfort. "You won't have me, won't have you!" she yelled.

Now other refrigerators appeared beside the first, some with doors open, some closed, some with separate freezer compartments and frost-free signs, left-opening doors and right, yellow and bronze and green and white, lined up like department store appliances. Yvonne laughed, immediately covered her mouth, and looked, out of habit, to see if anyone had noticed. But of course she was alone. Only the moon – and the light, still ahead.

A deep breath. Walking again. This time the fridges did

not move in front of her. As she trudged past each one, she flicked her finger at it, and fridges fell to either side with a sound like thunder. Bang, bang, bang, bang.

&

Bang! Her forehead bumped on something hard. Ow! Rubbed the bump, put her hands out, stretched her palms against whatever she'd bumped into, stretched her arms to either side, could get no measure of it – a picture of the moonlit desert and the moon in the sky behind her. Her outstretched palms grabbed her outstretched palms. Stared at a woman made small by the desert and the moon. Too fat thighs, lines spreading from the corners of her eyes. Hair needed a good combing.

Yvonne sighed, slumped against herself. To have walked all this way only to be confronted with all the way she had walked, all the desert behind her, to have been brought – hands to hands, nose to nose, hips to hips – face to face with herself. She had hung no mirrors in the fridge.

Yvonne stared at her eyes – blue, into her eyes, could not see far in, tried to pull open the door behind her eyes, tried to topple the fridge that was in the way – opened her mouth and looked in – moist, rosy pink in this beige desert – looked at her teeth. She watched as she made her teeth into ice cubes, as water flowed from them, around them, over them, over her lips, drops spattering the mirror—

The light she'd been following was at such an angle she couldn't have seen it and its image simultaneously.

Again she started toward it: a streetlight, the pole bent so the lamp hung down from an ornate, curving, wrought iron, art deco support. She expected fog and a crowd: long-skirted, hat-brimmed women; men with curving meerschaums and their hands behind their backs. Surprised by a rose in the umbra of the light, a single rose on a stalk so tall that the flower bloomed only half a metre below the lamp. A red rose, fully opened but not yet fading, with a single drop of moisture on its petal. She bent to smell the perfume and saw the stem of the rose surrounded by a white veil: many moth-wings in a cobweb.

Yvonne shook the stem. Holes appeared in the veil as the dry dead moths fell to the ground. Through the holes she could see a large, hairy, black spider. She hesitated, then shook again. Such a beautiful rose didn't need a spiderweb, and she was in no danger. Spiders when disturbed, scuttle off to baseboards, or in a desert, under rocks.

This spider, disturbed, rose up on its legs until it was eighteen centimetres outspread and let go of the stem. It jumped directly at her. Landed on her shoe. Scuttled up her pantleg to her thigh, across her belly, down her other leg and onto the sand. It turned to look at her and crouched down, shrinking its eighteen centimetres to nine.

Yvonne's stomach rose into her throat. She gagged, shuddered, and brushed furiously at her leg, still feeling the crawl of the spider. Now she straightened and, keeping her gaze on the spider, backed away a step or two at a time. Why had she shaken the rose?

The spider waited until the distance between them was five metres, then started after her. Yvonne speeded up, turned so she could walk faster. The spider darted forward as well. Running; the spider broke into a scrambling gallop. Yvonne ran faster, tripped, fell down hard on both knees. Couldn't breathe. Gagging and panting, she closed her eyes and knelt there, too tired to stagger up, expecting at any instant to feel the hairy tickle of the spider crawling up her leg, over her buttocks, onto her back.

Then she did feel it, the crawling sensation, jumped to her feet and shook all over. She shrieked and shrieked, high, harsh sounds that arced across the desert and cracked the mirror. The shrieks split and multiplied and returned. Mirror fragments fell all around. Geologic faults in the desert opened to their sharpness like skin to a scalpel. Surrounded

16

by unbearable screeches, a tapped underground river of sound, Yvonne fell down again under the weight and pain of the sound. Slammed her hands over her ears. Curled up with eyes still closed, still feeling the crawling sensation on her skin, anticipating a bite on her jugular vein, hunching her shoulders for protection.

A long time curled on her side, muscles as taut as she could keep them, until they screamed and relaxed of their own accord. No choice but to continue to relax, still with her hands over her ears, trying to shut out the shrieks and sounds that screamed – like her muscles – inside her brain. Where was the spider? On her? Had it disappeared? Had it really been there? Did she really want to know?

No. Just lie here, eyes closed, shutting out the desert, the spider, the sounds, forever. Like being in a fridge, lying here, muscles aching, stomach hurting, so tired, but then – Yes. She had to know. And lying here, her arm asleep under her, one knee numb where the other dug in, was not like being in a fridge, she no longer had a fridge—

She opened her eyes, looked around, raised her head, looked around.

The spider, sitting five metres away, combing one hairy leg with another. Sitting five metres away. It had apparently not moved. Crazy. Dummy. Stupid. Had not come closer, had not crawled over her. This time.

Now the spider felt Yvonne looking at it, stopped its grooming and stared back: a blonde-haired stocky woman, fullness of lips, of breasts balanced by full hips, agitated, pleading eyes. In the shared stare grew fine lines, tendrils, wisps, webbing – snap.

Now Yvonne saw the moonlit mirror-sheared abysses zig-zagging darkly to their own pattern, sensed the bottomless-ness of them. She staggered up, backed away. The spider followed. Drove herself into a run, desperate to get away, but where were the edges? If she fell in – which was worse, the abysses or the spider? Slowed, stopped. The spider stopped as well. She was right on the edge of an abyss, toe of one shoe sticking over. Black like a pencil line on the surface; who knew how it opened up beneath? If she swayed forward she would fall in.

She screamed. That action tipped her backwards. Threw herself farther backwards, and the spider turned to follow as she moved in another direction. She struggled to keep panic under control, swallowed against it, abysses everywhere, a black line – there. No, there. Now over here. Cracks in the earth like deep crazing, nowhere was safe. Made herself stand still, feeling the turgid heaviness of silence in the abysses, the – nothingness. A swirl of sand blew into a crack making an almost-sound, a felt sound: thousands of teeth grinding. No longer controlling her panic, Yvonne had to run. Saw the spider poised between two of the jagged splits, ran toward the spider, past it, away from the cracks in the earth. The spider turned and scrambled after her.

&

Fatigue flattened Yvonne's terror and slowed her to a walk. So tired she felt dizzy, might faint. Be a relief, wouldn't have to keep her attention on the unpredictable crevasses or the apparently predictable spider which, each time she checked, followed at a constant distance of five metres. Might stumble forever through a moonlit desert split by abysses, followed by a large, hairy spider. Magic teeth weren't enough. She needed a place to rest – if she fell asleep what might the spider do? The abysses?

Imperceptibly the sky turned a luminous eggshell pink, then blue. Yvonne watched the sun roll over the horizon. Her mood lighter, she glanced back and was glad the moon still shared the sky. Soon it and the sun were equally balanced.

She looked at the spider, a more awesome, revolting sight

now she could see it clearly: hairy, with curving mouthparts, eyes on stalks. She shuddered. As the sun drew colours out of the desert, the abysses' edges closed into scribbled lines across the ground. Still, Yvonne was careful not to step on one.

On the horizon was a jagged outline. As she came closer she saw there were three trees, two douglas fir and a cedar, their trunks surrounded by salal and salmonberry. Yvonne hurried, smelling the moist vanilla of sun-warmed vegetation. Dove into the shade, pushed through branches to the centre where a small spring seeped under mossy rocks. She breathed deeply, could not get enough of the spring-growing, earthy scent, knelt, shoved both hands in the water, spring-cold, rubbed them, and washed her face. The spider? She looked up. Five metres away, under the cedar.

Yvonne collapsed onto the ground, untied her shoes and emptied the sand. Enough to make a little pile, dull beige, unthreatening in this lushness. Pulled off her socks, stretched her toes. Salal and bits of grass tickled. Behind her was a large grey-green rock; she leaned back, sighed, wiggled into comfort, amazed and grateful for an oasis, a hiatus, found her eyes closing. She fought them open; how much closer would the spider come if she slept?

"You're rather heavy, you know."

Yvonne registered the voice, a contralto or tenor, woman or man. She did not move, but tightened every muscle, flicked her eyes in both directions. A voice?

"I said, you're rather heavy."

Yvonne sat up, looked around, leaned back again. She was alone, she knew it, just tired. Wasn't hearing voices a sign of craziness? Nothing here but this rock and salal. The spider – did it speak? It was still over by the cedar, crouched down, watching her.

"Will you pay attention! You're leaning on my back and you're too heavy!"

Yvonne leapt up, looked around. Hadn't she endured

enough in the desert? Now voices? Answering voices was really crazy—

Still, she whispered, "where are you? Who are you?"

"Oh really! I'm right here!" An irritated voice.

Yvonne watched legs protrude from the rock. A head protruded. It slowly rotated to face her. A very large turtle, well over two hundred pounds, blotchy grey-green shell, identical to a lichen-covered rock. Its head was not strictly a turtle head although it did have a long upper lip that could be mistaken for a beak, and its eyes were widely set. Its freckles looked turtlish, but from the top of its head sprang short, curly red hair. It was also able to smile, which it did briefly, in greeting.

"A turtle?" Yvonne covered her mouth with her hand, but not before a giggle escaped. Disappearing houses, fridges, magic teeth, mirrors, spiders – now a turtle?

"If you continually state the obvious, we are not going to get along too well. If I look like a turtle, then I must be a turtle. Is your pet there well-trained? I'm not partial to spiders. If he gets too close, I'll bite him."

"It's not my pet. It's sort of – following me." Both looked at the spider, back to each other. Yvonne sat down again, this time with her back to a tree, and curled her arms around her knees. Her eyes level with the turtle's. Mascara. Eye liner. Lipstick. Really crazy! "Is this where you live, Turtle?"

"Don't call me Turtle. Just because I look like a turtle and therefore must be a turtle, I do not have to be addressed generically. I have a name. Jane. And no, I don't live here, I'm just sojourning. I was looking for some other turtles, but I seem to have lost the ocean. Glad you dropped by, I was getting lonely, not that I can say the same about your friend."

The spider had climbed halfway up the cedar and was busy with its back legs.

"Not partial to it myself," Yvonne replied. Then, "didn't know turtles were afraid of spiders."

"I'm not afraid. I'm cautious. There's a lot you don't know about turtles. There was a lot I didn't know."

"Oh – you weren't always a turtle?"

"Heavens no, I just woke up one morning and looked in the mirror and there I was." Jane laughed – bitterly, Yvonne thought. "Ed didn't even notice."

"Oh, a woman!"

"The obvious again. Of course I was a woman. Do you think a man would turn into a turtle? He wouldn't risk his dignity. And children can pretend to be turtles. Only a woman—" Jane went into a spate of head-shaking that rattled the wattles on her neck. "Women turn into all sorts of things. A neighbour of mine woke up to discover she was a gerbil and before she could do anything, her son took her off to kindergarten for Show and Tell." Yvonne started to laugh, swallowed it at Jane's frown. "It wasn't so funny in the end, she was eaten by a dog."

"Oh." Both stared in front of them, contemplating the dead gerbil. Yvonne asked, "weren't you shocked when you turned turtle? What did you do?"

"It was a bit of a surprise –"

Yvonne looked at her sharply – surprise? – replayed Jane's tone, her arched eyebrow – bit of a surprise.

"– I just reorganized the house on a lower level and got used to it. Women can get used to anything. Though Ed never did. Of course he never really noticed, so I don't know if he would have – gotten used to it, if he'd noticed." Jane paused, pushed at some salal with her flipper. "It was hard to climb up to my desk though, I had to type on the floor. How did you get here? This oasis isn't on the tourist route."

Yvonne propped her chin on her knees. "Got out of my fridge. Disappeared. Everything disappeared. Met the spider by a rose bush. It started following me, then the mirror made abysses—"

She frowned at her sentence hissing like a disconnected hose. The words were weak, incomplete, did not truly

21

describe, like Jane's bit of a surprise – what was she doing having a conversation with a turtle anyway? How did turtles put on eyeliner? Yvonne looked up. "Exhausted. Would you keep your eye on the spider? Make sure it doesn't come closer?"

"What am I supposed to do if he does, batter him to a pulp with my flipper? Challenge him to truth or consequences at fifty paces?"

Yvonne smiled. "Find out it's identity. Are you sure it's a he?"

Jane wiggled her upper lip. "No. What do you think?"

"It?" Yvonne looked over. The spider had spun a thread and now dangled from a cedar branch like a black plumb-bob.

"Nothing's an it in the animal kingdom, not above an amoeba."

"It. He." Yvonne turned back to Jane. Both said together, "she?"

Jane wiggled her flipper forward. "That could be. Arachne, Charlotte, Spiderwoman were all famous female spiders. Besides, Freud considered the spider a female image, not that I approve of Freud, those poor women he thought were hysterical. He'd probably consider me a conversion case and try to convince me I'm not a turtle."

"Aren't you," Yvonne chuckled, "a conversion case?"

Jane glared. "That's not funny. And it's off the topic. Possibly the spider is another woman."

The spider did not move a leg, let alone turn around.

Yvonne prodded the salal with her toe, patted it with her hands. Satisfied there were no rocks or more dangerous denizens, she curled up on her side. "Something different about this spider." She closed her eyes, opened them again. "Jane? About Ed not noticing? Know what you mean. Martin didn't notice the house turn to sand."

Jane looked at her, away quickly and down, and Yvonne saw the planes of her face loosen into sadness. Jane glanced

22

back, gave her a tight smile, said, in a brittle cheery tone, "that's the way it is then, isn't it."

Yvonne closed her eyes. Shortly, her fuzz of sleep was penetrated by Jane's voice. "The most I can do is wake you if the spider charges. I'm not very brave." Then she mumbled, "About noticing? Thanks."

&

When Yvonne awakened it was dusk. Immediately she wondered if what she thought had happened had really happened, but Jane's shell was directly in her vision. It was true, she was in a desert oasis with a turtle and a spider.

In the muted light Jane was a series of curves. Her back curved, her flippers curved outwards, her head curved in another plane, and her eyelids, now at half-mast, formed the farthest forward curve. Even the plates of her shell repeated the curving pattern.

Jane turned her head, and Yvonne saw a web-like glistening on her face. Had the spider crawled over Jane, over her? Disgust closed her throat. Jumped up, stumbled, had to grab the tree for support. Every muscle in each leg protested her sudden movement. "Oh – too much walking." Saw the spider, still suspended from the cedar branch. The web on Jane's face – tear tracks. "What's wrong?"

Jane had withdrawn her head, emerged now, seconds later, all tears vanished, mascara neatly restored. "Nothing's wrong. The spider's been hanging there the whole time. I think it slept too. Maybe it does everything you do."

Yvonne watched the words issue from Jane's mouth in florescent yellow, purple, hot pink, lime green, then pop with the shimmer of soap bubbles in sunlight. She rubbed her eyes in case they were fogged with sleep. "But you were crying?" Yvonne tried again.

Jane moved her flipper in a motion that would have been a shrug had her shell been looser. "Who, me? Oh, no. Well, not much. It's nothing."

23

These words shone and popped more slowly. Yvonne saw a small naked child curled up in the shell, arm bent to hold a plastic soap blower to parted lips. "What's the trouble?" "There's no trouble." Pause. "What could possibly be wrong when you don't know where you are and don't know what direction to go in? What could possibly be wrong in spending the rest of your life in a six metre square containing three trees, a giant spider, and a woman who asks questions? Especially since I as a turtle have such a long life to look forward to! Why nothing in the world could be wrong!"

Yvonne looked around. Douglas firs and cedar were preferable in an oasis to palm trees and cacti; a spring of water and salal for a mattress. Bigger than her fridge. Jane was quite right, nothing wrong with the oasis. Yvonne smiled, then pushed against the tree to stretch her calves and hamstrings.

"For goodness sake, is your brain frozen? Look around! I can't move more than three steps in any direction! I can't leave because there's no water out there, it's only here, and anyway I don't know where the ocean is! I need to find some turtles so I can learn how to be one. Not just any turtles, sea turtles! In case you haven't noticed, I have flippers, not feet! I've never belonged anywhere, but this is the worst! A turtle in a desert! Just try swimming through a desert!"

Jane plopped her chin on the ground. Tears glistened on the salal.

Yvonne took a step and, wincing at her stiffness, touched Jane's shell. Familiar desperation. She would have liked some help or comfort when the fridge disappeared. "Not going any particular place. Help you find the ocean. We'll head west. Has to be there someplace." Maybe Jane could help her with the abyss, the spider.

Jane sniffed. "W-E-L-L —"

Yvonne watched the word take shape, become the largest

well in the world, all bricked around. Peered in – black and heavy and dry, rustling with – fear? doubt? Farther in, the damp mustiness of mildew and phosphorescent sparks of rot. Whatever water the well contained was not fit to drink. Maybe Jane couldn't help her. Maybe she should continue alone.

"– let's not be hasty. It's pretty comfortable here. There might not be an ocean the way everything's changed, or we could search forever and not find it."

"Suit yourself, Jane. But if you don't try you'll never meet more turtles." Might as well go to the ocean. Might as well have company.

"Well, maybe you're right. That's logical. I could stay here my whole life and never see another turtle. I guess you're my last chance." Jane sniffed, tried to smile, ducked inside to again repair her make-up.

Yvonne put on her socks and shoes, stood up stiffly, stretched some more. A breeze swayed the spider back and forth on its strand. Perhaps it would like to stay in the oasis. Relieved she and Jane were going together; safer with two. Safer, with a turtle?

To loosen her leg muscles, Yvonne walked to the edge of the oasis. The sun a red ball balancing on the horizon. Its beams picked muted pinks and blues and bronzes out of the black desert, inched long washes of shadow toward her – an abyss, erased by shadow to a dotted line, still there.

Blood beat up the side of her neck, her chest tightened so she couldn't breathe. If the abyss opened and she – or Jane – fell in? Just a line, maybe they could jump it – turtles can't jump.

She had a large Pink Pearl eraser. Running into the desert, she rubbed desperately at the line, and when she stood up, only an indentation remained. Eraser dust mixed with the grains of sand. Watching that, Yvonne calmed, placed the Pink Pearl in the desert like an offering. She wouldn't tell

Jane about the abyss. No point worrying her.

"Are you sure we should be leaving?" Jane asked. "This might be the only oasis there is, the only water."

"We have to try –" Yvonne hesitated, then blurted, "can give you a drink."

"How can you give me a drink? You don't have a canteen."

"My – teeth – uh – turn into ice cubes." She watched Jane sneer disbelief. "Know it sounds silly." Why not go on alone, or stay here?

"It sure does! Do you expect me to believe that? You're crazy!"

"Perhaps. Perhaps." Yvonne's rawness again abraded. "But if so, what about you?" They glared at each other. Jane shifted her eyes first.

"Here, show you." Yvonne moved her head closer. Important that Jane believe her.

"Demonstrate elsewhere, please." Jane pulled her neck into her shell, her face tight with disdain.

Yvonne leaned over and drops of water appeared on the salal. "Saliva," Jane proclaimed.

Yvonne straightened, swallowed, placed her hands on her hips. "If you won't believe, you'd better stay here."

Jane wriggled her lips, rolled her eyes, considering. Yvonne's cheeks were mottled with intense conviction. "I'm sorry, I didn't mean to hurt your feelings. It's just – hard to believe. Please do show me."

Yvonne sighed loudly and leaned over Jane's shell. Water splashed coolly, ran down her flippers. Jane stuck her tongue out, caught drops like snowflakes. She licked both front flippers. "That's phenomenal! I'm sorry I doubted. How can you do that?"

"Told you, even if it is crazy. My teeth turn into ice cubes and they melt."

"Yes, but how? It's not just fantastic, it's miraculous!"

Yvonne smiled, relieved that Jane accepted her teeth, yet also frightened. Sharing the magic of her teeth made it more real, but what was it? And if Jane could accept it, was it crazy? Which was scarier – crazy or not-crazy? "Glad you think it's okay. Seemed like a miracle in the desert – so thirsty. Don't know how it happens – you know if others can do it?"

"I've never heard of anyone. You must be a witch." Jane returned her smile. "And it's more than *okay!* Though it probably has a biochemical explanation that we don't know." Jane licked the last drops off her left flipper. A real miracle woman – perhaps.

Looking beyond the shade to the hot sun, the dry sand, Jane could feel her shell steaming, herself being cooked within it. Yvonne was again stretching against the tree. To get to the ocean they would have to cross the desert. Oh, do let her be a miracle woman!

Jane waddled to the spring where she drenched herself and drank as much as she could hold. "Just in case," she said with a tight-lipped smile. Her stomach sloshing and gurgling, she lumbered after Yvonne into the full glare of the sun.

&

Beyond the oasis was a ridge. At the top, Yvonne turned to wait for Jane, slowly ascending, her flippers spewing sand to each side. Turned in time to see the douglas firs and cedar begin to topple. As they collapsed onto the salal the edges of the oasis folded in. The lips of the abyss she thought she'd erased were eating it.

At the horror on Yvonne's face Jane turned too. "Now we can't go back! What if there isn't another oasis? We'll boil to death! I can feel it already!"

Yvonne stood absolutely still, concentrating on the desert through the soles of her shoes, willing herself not to jump, not to run, until she'd located the rest of the abyss.

A spurt of water geysered up from the spring like a burp from the mouth of the desert. In midair the water turned

27

to sand and stayed an upright pinnacle. Beside it a black blob stretched and straightened.

Yvonne watched the spider scuttle toward them, felt a flare of rage they hadn't eluded it, yet strangely relieved that it was coming too. She bit each word. "Don't panic. There'll be other oases."

Jane encapsulated her fear in caustic cynicism. "You can't assume if there's one oasis there'll be others. You can't assume there's an ocean and we'll get there. Your logic is faulty. Even if you do have magic teeth!"

The spider had stopped five metres away, waiting. The sole line of the abyss seemed to be behind them. Yvonne started forward again and Jane slithered beside her. They walked on silently for a while, across a rock-strewn plain. Yvonne looked back; yes, the spider was following, no, the abyss was not. "Let's assume there are other oases so we don't bumble about in this desert with that spider forever."

Jane glared at her. "No way. Seeing is believing. Show me an oasis. Show me an ocean, thank you."

"Can only try."

It took Yvonne a minute to realize Jane had challenged her, and that she had accepted the challenge. She frowned at the turtle waddling beside her, her head bobbing in time to her flippers. Jane moved too slowly. Yvonne stepped out in front-she'd like to walk away. Couldn't show her an ocean if an ocean wasn't there, but she could assume that the ocean was to the west – where it had been all her life – and if they continued in that direction, they would find it. That would show her.

Jane watched Yvonne walk away, and wanted to shout, don't leave me! What had she said to make Yvonne mad? It was just a conversation, wasn't it? *Show me*, just a way of speaking. "Yvonne? Could you please give me a drink? Yvonne?"

Yvonne stopped to watch Jane lumber up, her face pleading and trying not to show it. Just Jane's way, Yvonne

28

thought. Don't know her very well. She leaned over Jane and made her teeth gush water, and Jane's shell steamed in the heat. Yvonne put her face in the cloud of vapour which condensed on her. She licked off the drops and replenished the water supply.

"I didn't mean to make you mad," Jane said finally. Yvonne smiled and shrugged, continued walking. Jane found she was trembling, took a deep breath. "I didn't like it when you walked away on me, Yvonne!"

Yvonne looked at her. "Oh?"

"No!"

"Wouldn't have left you."

"How did I know that?" Jane glaring at her.

"You have to trust."

They walked up another ridge in silence, and at the top, saw more ridges. Jane thought of undulations left by some gigantic ebb tide that had taken all the ocean with it. *Trust* reverberated; how to respond?

Yvonne walked along self-righteously – how could Jane think she'd leave her? Though maybe alone would be easier – this was one slow turtle – Yvonne laughed. "Look really funny if anyone could see – a woman spitting on a turtle's back and it steams and a spider's following them—"

Jane smiled. "Does it want a drink, do you think?"

They both looked behind. The spider had paused, legs outspread, five metres behind, as it seemed to do each time they stopped.

"Not giving it anything!" Yvonne's throat tightened into the gag she'd felt in the night.

"Well, it probably conserves what moisture it needs," Jane offered. "Don't you think it's odd it's following – like a dog?"

"Shoo! Go away!" Yvonne made flapping motions. The spider continued to stare. She got caught in the stare, grew into the stare, into fine lines, tendrils, wisps, webbing – snap.

Jerked her head around, rubbed her eyes, looked at Jane.

29

"If it wants to follow us that's its problem."

&

They continued to climb ridges, Yvonne toiling up one side and leaning back to balance down the other, walking slowly because her muscles were stiff and tender. But walking slowly kept her close to Jane who huffed and grimaced. Her flippers could not get a purchase in the sand, and, on top of ridges, she had a moment of being balanced on her undershell while she scrabbled over with her flippertips. The spider stalked along behind. Desert stretched in each direction unrelieved by oases, and they kept passing sand columns – or sand columns passed them; it became difficult to tell what was moving – perhaps they were standing still, the desert creaking by on a giant conveyor belt.

"It's too bad you didn't spend time in the oven, you might be able to provide food too." Later Jane asked, "what did you do in your fridge all the time?"

Yvonne considered. "Interior decorating? Painting, wallpapering, coordinating – moved things about."

"It's not a big space to work in. Didn't you feel cramped?"

"No. You can get things perfect in a small space. Got it so perfect when the door was closed you couldn't find it." Yvonne laughed. "A good decorator knows what really goes with what – say green stars with blue stripes—"

"Didn't you get lonely?"

"Too busy. Interior decorating is demanding."

"Cold?"

"No. When Martin came in he said it was cold, but –" She shrugged. "And the children –" A sudden pang; Yvonne paused while Janet and John's faces flashed by, "– maybe they didn't stay still long enough."

"How did you fit in a fridge anyway?" Jane's curiosity had intensified. Yvonne felt she was being interviewed.

"How did you turn into a turtle?"

30

"But why a fridge? Why didn't you decorate the rooms in the house?"

"Why a turtle? Why not a horse or three-toed sloth?" Exasperated, Yvonne looked down at Jane. "Being in a fridge was like turning into a turtle except you carry your room with you. Need any decorating help?"

"Oh, you couldn't get in! I don't have extra room inside, just enough for my make-up kit and a small mirror." The very idea – Jane pulled her neck in defense.

"Ultra private, eh?" Yvonne teased.

Jane returned to her topic. "I don't understand why you didn't freeze in the fridge."

For some paces Yvonne mused. "Don't either. Guess my body adjusted. Never thought about it."

"Was Martin mad when you moved into the fridge?"

Yvonne laughed a small laugh. "Martin was always mad. Wasn't Ed, when you turned turtle?"

"He didn't notice until we had to go to his staff party, then he was. I'd have embarrassed him." Yvonne gave a laugh of recognition; Jane looked up in surprise, then laughed too. "Have you ever noticed how women laugh when they think something's hopeless?"

"No, hadn't – you're right! It's all they can do."

"We can do."

We, Yvonne thought and nodded. She smiled at Jane, felt stirrings of excitement, friendship. "How long did you stay – after your – conversion?"

"About a week. At first I couldn't believe I was a turtle. I kept looking in the mirror. Of course I knew I couldn't reach anything and I couldn't sit at my desk – I'm an academic, religious mythology, so I have to sit at a desk. Then I got desperate to find some other turtles. And I started craving seaweed. I even cooked dulse, but it didn't taste right, bought at a supermarket. I have to have sea grasses. I don't know what they taste like, but I know that's what I need. I crave them, just the thought keeps me going."

Yvonne felt cooled by Jane's tone, could see brown bumpy seaweed under water, long strands of kelp and bright sea lettuce. "Want nothing like that," she announced, to her own surprise.

"Nothing?" Jane dissolved her contemplation of sea grasses, considered. "You must want something, everyone does."

"Nothing can think of. You're lucky to know what you want. Martin used to open the fridge door and shout, 'what do you want? What is it you want?' Drove me crazy. Could only think: more wallpaper."

Jane heard the flatness of Yvonne's tone, the sadness of her words. She didn't know what to do, but wanted to do something. Balancing on three legs, she put her right front flipper on Yvonne's toe, awkwardly patted it. Yvonne stumbled at Jane's unexpected motion, and her foot sprayed them both with sand. They chuckled, without much mirth, and Yvonne said, "laughing women again?"

To talk to Jane, Yvonne had to walk with her head down. She was surprised when she looked up and saw they were approaching a low cliff. She pointed it out to Jane who probably would not have noticed, so close to the ground. Its face was in shadow, but as they drew closer they saw a dark spot, a hole, a cave. The sun was high overhead and they were hot and tired. Jane asked what time it was. Yvonne looked at her watch: "noon."

"Is that all? I thought it'd be more like five or six!"

"The sun's still at noon," Yvonne observed, "though we have been walking forever. This watch doesn't work very well."

"Why do you wear it then?" Jane's tone testy.

"Oh – a present from Martin – a long time ago. We'll set it for seven-thirty, that feels about right."

"You can't change the time according to how you feel!"

"Why not?" Yvonne asked. Jane couldn't answer.

A slight slope up to the cave. They peered in. Cool and

dark, the cave opened out behind its entrance. Yvonne said, "shall we? For a rest?"

"There might be snakes or – "

"Bears," Yvonne finished. "We can shout."

"Hello in there, whatever you are, get out!" Jane felt so ridiculous her voice cracked and they both laughed.

Yvonne stooped to enter first, put her hand up in case she bumped the roof, and straightened slowly. She flared her nostrils for bear or snake scent, but the cave smelled comfortably old and dry-earthy. Jane watched her, then pulled her head into her shell and flippered carefully across the sundark threshold.

"You stay out!" Yvonne shouted at the spider who had three legs in. It paused and rotated its eyestalks at her.

"Oh, let it in, there's plenty of room." Jane's voice was muffled.

"How do you know in your shell? Don't want to share a cave with a spider! Ugh!"

The spider folded its legs and crouched down. Half of its body was in sun, half in the dark.

Yvonne felt the heat of sudden anger at this – insect! How dare it keep following her, how dare it do everything she did! Wanted to kick it, step on it, squish it. Breathed hard through her still-flared nostrils, tried to look around.

The spider waited until her back was turned, scrambled quickly in and over to the back wall. At the sound, Jane stuck her head out, thought, good for you, and gave the spider a small smile. She waddled about, exploring. The space was perhaps three metres by five, and quite smooth and round, no stalactites hanging down, stalagmites sticking up.

Yvonne explored too, ignoring the spider now, except for a grimace of recognition, then lay down close to the door, her back against the wall. Jane finally settled in the middle of the cave and stretched out her head, legs, tail to their full length. She looked like a hide-covered coffee table.

Yvonne put her hands behind her head and stared at the

roof. "If this were a fridge, could put sky wallpaper up there, with a moon, maybe half-full, and three or four stars, not too many. Don't like over-statement."

Fatigue vibrated Jane's every muscle; she was sure her flipper-tips were twitching. "I hate wallpapering, all that paste and dirty water, I did it once. White walls, that's what I like. Spacious and clean." More tired than she'd thought.

Now it was night. A moon hung full in the sky. Yvonne welcomed it back, but was glad she was in a cave with Jane. Three stars surrounded the moon. A gap and then more stars, and more stars. Stars everywhere, moving closer and closer together, forming dyads and triads and quartets, clustering, making groups of light as bright as the moon – and over there another moon and then another and another – Yvonne shivered and her heart fluttered arhythmically. "Too many! No! Go away! Just one moon! A few stars!" She rolled over toward the wall, clasped her arms across her midriff, and tightly closed her eyes.

&

When they awoke it was again light. The spider sat on the ledge outside, its back legs folded, front extended, watching Yvonne, waiting. How close to her had it crawled, how long had it been watching? Sleep was so private, she'd never thought it fair to watch a person sleep. "Time to get going," she said to Jane.

Jane groaned. "Every part of me hurts. I wouldn't have believed a shell could hurt."

"You'll limber up. My legs don't hurt today."

Jane thought Yvonne uncompassionate, glared as she rotated laboriously toward the doorway. Yvonne saw the look, returned a small smile of amused sympathy.

"Good morning, Spider, you look like you want us to get going – is it morning?" Jane asked Yvonne. "What time is it?"

34

"Seven-thirty."

"That's the time it was last night. You're right about your watch."

Yvonne led the way down from the cave, glanced back – a nice cave, sorry to be leaving. "What time would you like it to be, Jane?"

"Bed time." She laughed, then groaned; every part of her complained at having to move.

"Bad time?"

"No, I said bed time, oh. Wrong time."

"Over time." Yvonne laughed.

"Out of time. That's what we are," Jane said, "out of the time of your watch, anyway. The sun's more like noon again."

"Out of time in the other sense too? Let's hurry, get out of this desert."

Jane waddled a fraction faster. "Maybe there isn't an out. Maybe it goes on forever."

"Don't say that!" Yvonne's tone sharp. Her fear as well. No abysses just now; ridges, dunes, gulleys, and blowing sand.

"I'm amazed there's so much desert. You'd think we'd hit some mountains or the ocean soon. Where did it all come from?" Jane looked up at Yvonne. "Did you make it up and we're going around in circles?"

"What would you make up a desert for?" Yvonne shoved her hands in her pockets, rolled a loose thread between her fingers, rolling up her irritation. Jane was so suspicious, so – complaining. "We're not going around in circles – we pass different things. You're too close to the ground – your view is limited. We haven't seen that before." She pointed to a rectangular, box-like object, a long, flat hill perhaps, perhaps a ridge or mesa.

"Maybe not that one," Jane conceded, "but the topography does have a repetitive similarity. Except for a notable lack of oases. Which, my dear, you assumed we'd find."

Yvonne made an exasperated tongue click. "Don't rub it in."

"I'd like to rub it out. The desert." Yvonne thought of the Pink Pearl eraser she'd left behind, but Jane meant the sand in her eyes, nostrils and mouth. She tried to spit. "Would you please rinse me off." Yvonne did, had a drink as well.

When Jane could see again, she said, "I take back what I said about circles. We must be making some headway. That hill is much closer now."

Their path, which they defined by walking on their shadows, was angling them toward the hill or ridge, so now instead of its being to their right, it was ahead of them, and they would pass by its farthest corner. "At least we won't have to climb it," Jane said, noting its change in position.

"Did we speed up? It's a lot closer suddenly." Yvonne thrilled with excitement.

They saw divisions now in the perpendicular plane of the ridge, vertical lines or cracks, and the occasional horizontal one. Beside each crack something shone in the sunlight, and their eyes hurt in the brightness of it. They stared at the ground, lifting their heads only to check their progress, Yvonne shading her eyes as she did so.

Now for each step she and Jane took toward the ridge, it seemed to have moved three steps toward them.

As the distance between them and the ridge narrowed, the ripples and heaves in the sand flattened into some sort of pattern: wallpaper or floor tiles or a picture of blown sand. It looked bumpy but felt smooth and Jane slithered faster. "What's going on here?" Her voice high with sudden fear.

Now they were one hundred metres away, now fifty, and now they saw it was not a ridge—

Yvonne took another step, dragged her foot, stopped. Her lips parted, she breathed in rapturously, let it puff out. "Fridges," she formed, but only the fragment of a whisper escaped.

"Oh god! No!" Jane retracted every bit of herself so fast her shell bumped on the ground. She was awash with terror, it was flooding inside her shell, drowning her, she couldn't move, couldn't look. They'd walked toward these refrigerators, they should have gone the other way – so many, an army, lined up with sides abutting, the sun reflecting off each handle, each nameplate. They'd never get away. Fridges – *Yvonne! Oh No!* Jane peered out.

Yvonne had drifted ahead. Between her and the appliances the sand rose in wafts and swirls, all brightly coloured. The air was filled with a low humming that hurt Jane's ears, but also compelled her to listen.

One refrigerator lurched forward with a four-cornered swaggering motion, and Jane shivered at its menace. Didn't Yvonne see it? What was she doing? The refrigerator's door swung open, revealing a blue interior. Now a bronze fridge with separate freezer compartment staggered forward, and then a very old, round-cornered one, its enamel yellow with age.

Yvonne took a step, another step. The coloured swirls of sand parted in front of her to make a path, and the humming intensified. The first fridge lurched closer. Its door opened more, exposing egg racks, butter dish, ice cube trays, shelves neatly positioned. Its light was on, a glow from the rear, and the control dial almost shone, its roundness emphasizing the strict angularity of every other line.

"Yvonne! Stop! Come back! Don't go any closer! They'll kill you!" The humming drum-rolled lower, more loudly, steadily, as the line of fridges behind the first three tramped toward Yvonne. Jane extended her legs and flippered forward as fast as she could, cursing her shell, the fridges, Yvonne, cursing.

At Jane's voice, Yvonne turned somnambulently. Her slightly parted lips curved in a small smile, and around her eyes were rapture, adoration, excitement. She raised her hand, palm outward, waved it twice, either a pat or a benediction. "They've come for me, they want me, see how they're shining? We belong together. Never should have left."

Jane blinked with doubt, yet was soothed by Yvonne's tone, her conviction, compelled to believe her almost against her will. She looked toward the leading refrigerator now three metres away, a fridge, so innocuous, so bland, so familiar, promising relief from the glaring sun, the dry, gritty sand. Maybe there'd be one for her as well.

The light shifted for a micro-second, an invisible cloud in the way of the sun – or perhaps Jane blinked again – and she saw the colours fade out of the sand; saw the hard, cold, unyielding enamel of the ranks behind the three foremost fridges; saw the old, round-cornered one shudder, open its door wider in a malevolent grin. Everything was as before, except the shudder skipped over the sand and into her shell. She was shaking, trembling, cold herself.

"No! Stop! You'll be trapped forever! You'll die! Yvonne! You said you'd find me the ocean! Come back! Now! Please!"

But Yvonne took another step toward the fridge whose door swung wide in welcome.

"Oh Yvonne!" Jane started to cry. She couldn't do anything, what could a turtle do? Couldn't open a fridge door – they'd take Yvonne away, she'd never see her again – alone. She'd be alone in the desert, they'd both die. "Yvonne!"

A scrabbling, scuffling noise behind Jane, beside Jane. She thought it was another fridge, pulled in her legs and neck. Panic screamed her. But the scrabbling passed by. The spider reached Yvonne, grabbed her around the thighs with its two front legs, bit its mouth down on her shirt. Yvonne's scream echoed Jane's as the spider pulled her away, swung her around and threw her across its back. It staggered under her weight. Yvonne's dangling arms and legs obscured the spider from Jane's view. The refrigerator's light dimmed, its door half-closed, and it lurched toward them. But the spider was galloping away, Yvonne bouncing on its back, still screaming.

Jane slithered nearer to the refrigerators, drew in her head, closed all her apertures, held her breath. A mighty crunch that reverberated even in her teeth, a thud, and shock of pain. Jane gasped, dimly registering Yvonne's screams fading in the distance. She opened her eyes and peered around. The fridge had toppled over her, lay on its side in the sand, hinges broken so its door was askew. She pulled her head in again, wished she could wipe the tears that tickled her face, and waited for the rest of the attack, waited for her shell to be cracked by the fridges' heavy corners, waited to become a vulnerable, naked pulp, waited—

Silence. Her fatigued muscles relaxed. She forced them tense again. Silence. She opened her eyes, peered out. The lead fridge still lay in the sand, a discarded, used appliance. The others had turned and were marching back the way they'd come. Only the old one lingered, its humming faint and mournful; soon it too turned to join the battalion. Jane watched them gain distance, shrink, close up and become only a desert ridge. She looked in the opposite direction. Yvonne and the spider a bump on the horizon.

Jane hurt all over. She'd be a mass of bruises – this was too much, deserts, fridges, of all things. She sniffed, wiped tears off her cheeks with her flipper, then found herself looking at it: mottled grey-green liver spots; had she aged, being a turtle? She extended and spread her fingers – webbing between each one and no thumb, but she'd learned to hold her eyebrow pencil between the first and second finger. She'd awakened to discover she was a turtle, and so she wanted to be a turtle, didn't she? Find other turtles? Right. The ocean. Right.

Then it hit her, as hard as the fridge. She was alone. Yvonne and the spider a small bump on the horizon. Nearly over the horizon. She ran after them – no, she slithered, waddled, panting with the effort of moving 250 pounds of shell on flippers through slippery sand, crying, "don't leave me, I'll die," swearing in frustration, "come back, wait for me," raging, "how dare they run away like that," crying, "I need you, you said you'd find me an ocean," raging again with the sadness and frustration.

Now a pencil line grew out of the ridge, galloped across the desert after the spider and Yvonne. As it passed Jane, growing darker, pressing deeper, part of her mind registered *geologic fault*, and she moved farther away where the sand was firm. She waddled on, panting, thirsty, sweating, knew her mascara had run all down her cheeks, she must look a sight. The line caught up to Yvonne and the spider, a widening, deepening wedge-shaped vee behind its leading point. Jane watched it eat the ground from under the spider's right legs. Jane watched Yvonne fall over the lip, waddled on, watched the spider scramble back to safety, waddled on. She wanted to run away, wanted to plop down and hide in her shell. She waddled on, sweating with renewed terror, waddled as fast as she could to the spider. Joined it looking down.

Down. Down. Nothing. Total silence. Jane looked at the spider, back into the abyss. Her throat hurt with dryness of thirst, of panting. She tried to swallow, looked back to the spider. Its eyestalks were fully extended, rotating wildly. One eye seemed to look at her. She yelled, "Yvonne? Yvonne? Yvonne!"

"what?" A faint, far away reply.

"Are you all right?"

"what?" Faint, expressionless.

The spider was moving its back legs in a crazy sort of dance – spinning, Jane realized as a thin thread extruded. The spider turned, crawled up on Jane's back, leaped off the other side, and under her. She understood, braced her flippers, peered over the edge as the spider launched itself down. Increased pressure on the strand. Jane slowly backed away from the edge, thinking of horses roping calves. She collapsed on the sand as the spider – with Yvonne – appeared over the lip of the abyss.

40

Yvonne's face smooth and white as fridge enamel. Jane reached out a flipper to touch her, hesitated, drew back. The abyss was shrinking, perhaps the hot sun was shriveling it. It was shriveling her. The spider dragged Yvonne over, nudged her onto Jane's shell. Jane smiled at the spider. Its eyes, no longer rotating, held still on hers. "Thank you," she said and began crying. "You're wonderful. You saved her. Let me give you a ride too."

The spider deliberately took one step back with each of eight legs. Jane waited a moment, but it was waiting until she started, so she did. Perhaps it hadn't understood what she'd said.

&

Jane moved very slowly over the hot sand, under the hot sun, under the weight of Yvonne. Was she unconscious, Jane worried, she felt like a dead weight, wished she'd wake up and give her a drink, she felt so thirsty, exhausted, used up. Jane plodded on and on, looking no farther ahead than her front flippers swimming through sand and was nearly in the oasis before she noticed it.

Gratefully she plunged through the sparse outer fringe of lodgepole pine to the centre—

Was that? – could that – be running water? Had to be—

A waterfall splashed down a rocky overhang to make a small deep pool surrounded by grass, buttercups and cottonwoods. Jane shrugged Yvonne onto the grass, slithered down the bank and into the water with her mouth already open. Gulped and gulped, let the water pour down her throat, and not until her thirst was quenched did she relax into the sensations of coolness, wetness on her sun-seared skin, her shell. She dove down to the muddy bottom, saw rocks and fish and weeds, felt the confident speedy motion of her flippers. She swam around the perimeter of the pool with her eyes just above water, and could see how the grass

41

grew at the edge. Inches tall, it towered above her. Ants crawled around the roots, and skater bugs skimmed the water's shaded surface. At the far end of the pool, blue and white chicory bloomed beside a rotting log. Desert receded into memory as Jane relaxed and cooled.

Eventually she felt well enough to turn her attention to Yvonne, who, she realized as she swam back, was lying on the grass, crying. The spider dangled from a cottonwood branch that curved over the waterfall, refreshing itself in the spray.

Yvonne stumbled to her feet. Her face contorted, her eyes swollen and red, tear streaks on her cheeks. She picked up a clump of mud and hurled it at the spider. "Hate you! Hate you!" A shriek ending in a wail. Her shoulders slumped and she sank down to the grass, curled up again and sobbed.

The missile had not hit the spider. Still, it resignedly pulled itself up its strand until it was hidden in the leaves.

Jane yelled, "the spider saved your life! Twice! Aren't you being a little ungrateful?"

Yvonne turned on her. "Oh shut up! Don't care! Didn't ask to be saved! Didn't ask for any of this – desert, abyss, my fridge to disappear – get a chance to go back, that damn spider stops me! Want to go home—" The pain was tearing her again, couldn't stand it, she sobbed and sobbed, didn't care who heard, didn't care ungrateful, didn't want a life—

"You climbed out of your fridge that night. You did it, no one else did." Jane's tone was firm – she had battled down her anger – and concerned. "You'd be a meal for a fridge by now if it weren't for the spider, or still at the bottom of that geologic fault. You got out of your fridge and now here you are and, as you said, we just have to go on." She paused, added, "stop thinking about what you've lost, concentrate on what you can create."

"Oh shut up," Yvonne repeated but with less anguish. "Know what happened, don't need your preaching, you just want me to find you an ocean, no one cares about me don't

42

know what to want want my fridge—"

A small, curled up Yvonne sobbed and sniffled and wailed. Jane swam back and forth beside her, not knowing what more she could do than watch the grass grow and the water fall down the rocks, watch the cottonwoods bend over the pool and the buttercups rise up around Yvonne. As she swam she noticed that everything around them was lush. Eventually the only sounds were the water falling into the pool and the rustling of leaves in the warm breeze. Yvonne slowly stood up, undid her vest and shirt, pulled off her jeans, pants, shoes and socks, curled her toes over the edge of the bank, and half dove, half fell into the pool. When she surfaced and pushed the hair out of her swollen eyes, Jane was grinning at her.

Yvonne searched her face, her eyes, for anger or forgiveness, feeling drained and tired and still sad. She cleared her throat. "What was it you said, 'concentrate on what you can create?'" Jane nodded. "Guess this is the way it is then, isn't it?"

"I guess so." Jane smiled again. Slowly Yvonne smiled back.

They floated in circles pushed by the current. Yvonne placed her head on Jane's back, felt Jane's flipper against her thigh, looked at her own toes straight out in front, couldn't remember when she'd last cried, felt peaceful and pensive now. The overhanging trees had grown enough so the spider dangled closer, and Jane and Yvonne watched it sway in a small circle, its one strand creating a prism in the spray.

"You don't really hate the spider, do you?" Jane asked, hoping not.

Yvonne stared at it. Didn't know how she felt, but could find no hatred. "Guess not," she finally said. "And you should be thanked – both of you."

Later, Yvonne washed her clothes and hung them to dry on the branch, helped Jane wash her hair. But she had to

43

push Jane out of the pool; the bank was steeper to clamber up than to slither down. They lay on the grass while the sun warmed them, and Yvonne combed Jane's hair, fluffing the curls with her fingers.

"The old fridge? It was a McClary –" Yvonne sighed.

"– like my mother's." Jane twisted to look at her, raised an eyebrow. Yvonne returned the look, blinked against a sudden stinging, sighed again: an acceptance. "Not *like. Was* my mother's fridge. We recognized each other." Jane inched closer, patted Yvonne's leg with her flipper.

A sudden wind twisted the branches and the leaves on the branches. Yvonne stilled her hand on Jane's hair. They looked at each other, toward the wind. The spider was blown in a wild arc over the waterfall, then it scrambled up its strand. Wind tore at Yvonne's hair. She grabbed her drying clothes before they blew into the pool, and lurched against Jane.

Down a road beside the waterfall rolled a rotund object pushed faster and faster by the wind. The object screamed, a roly-poly on wheels, its screams torn away by wind. Yvonne held her half-dry clothes in front of her and fumbled into her shirt. Jane pulled her neck into her shell, braced her flippers against attack, against her terrified heartbeats.

At the foot of the hill the object flew off its vehicle, somersaulted once and splashed into the pool. As suddenly as it had begun, the wind stopped. In the silence, Yvonne and Jane stared at a vacuum cleaner hose and an overturned skateboard, two wheels still spinning.

&

Yvonne waded into the pool, gathered the roly-poly up and half-carried, half-dragged it out of the water. She glanced at Jane's astonished, fearful expression, matched it with her own as she laid the torso on the grass: a red-dressed woman, no arms, no legs, unconscious. Yvonne checked that she was breathing, stroked the hair out of her eyes. No arms, no legs? A movement caught her eye.

Over there, two green skirted, green masked men were setting up a portable operating table. They arranged their instruments beside them, scapels, saws, hammers, drills – an amalgam of surgical, dental and carpenter tools. Now a nurse started toward Yvonne and the torso. Yvonne stumbled into her jeans, yanked up the zipper. She stood protectively in front of the torso – but was the nurse coming for *her?* Would they operate on *her?* Closer came the nurse, no need for the mask around her neck: her smile reached only to her cheek muscles, blue eyes remaining vacant. The doctors turned from their instruments, made a final adjustment to the table legs.

Yvonne put her fists up, but the nurse, still smiling, ducked around her, and reached for the torso. "No!" Yvonne grabbed the nurse's shoulder, shook it. "Get out of here! All of you!"

One of the doctors threw a scalpel like a dart at the spider. Severed its strand. The spider thudded to the ground, lay still.

"Hey!" Jane waddled over to it. "Cut this out, Yvonne!"

"Okay, all of you! Get out of here!" The doctors, nurse, table, instruments disappeared, leaving the scalpel as the only evidence, glinting in the sun beside the spider's curled, motionless form.

Jane breathed on the spider, bent its legs gently in and out. "It's not dead, just stunned. That's lucky for you, Yvonne! This is your fault!" Angry enough to accuse, irresponsible, but stopped herself. Enough hurting. She picked up the scalpel, a folding one, stored it with her make-up kit. "You didn't have to hurt the spider!"

Yvonne contritely agreed. "Didn't mean to. Should have saved the nurse though."

45

"You can't save everyone." Jane's eyes widened. "At least you're admitting you created that scene, that it was your reality!"

Yvonne frowned, wished Jane weren't staring at her like that – hard like that. Shrugged, looked at the woman on the grass. "Only wondering if she'd lost her arms and legs in surgery – and so – maybe did create that scene." She glanced at Jane and pointed. "But did not create her!"

Jane was surprised at how great her relief was. She hadn't expected Yvonne to admit it; Ed never admitted anything, always stuck to the same story. A gush of warmth for Yvonne. "Thank you for saying that."

"What? Didn't create her?" Yvonne, sulking, knew that wasn't what Jane meant, knew Jane would say –

"That you did create the other scene."

– and she wanted Jane to not say any more.

The woman on the grass moaned and her eyes fluttered under their lids. Yvonne sat down beside her, wondered about taking her wet dress off, but decided the sun was hot enough. She concentrated on the woman's light brown hair, pleasant, slender face, smooth skin, straight nose squared off at the tip, concentrated on the way the planes of her cheeks sloped into her jawline and down her neck to her clavicle, her chest, keeping her eyes on what was there, not allowing them to stray to what was not, to the shoulders, the hips. Yvonne caught Jane's eye and winced.

Jane, crouched by the woman's right shoulder, grimaced in acknowledgement. She knew of no ailment or disease or accident that would make a woman look like this. The red tee shirt dress hung over empty sockets; Jane remembered her childhood dolls: when one limb fell out its mate did too; they'd been held in by rubber bands. With arms and legs this woman had been tall, probably willowy.

Large grey eyes opened, focussed on Yvonne, on Jane, closed as if trying to make sense of Jane, opened, looked from Yvonne to Jane again. The woman arched her spine, stretched her chin back and bumped the top of her head on the ground. Was she having a fit, Yvonne wondered. "Help me up, please." Barely controlling desperation, the woman's tone commanded and pleaded. "Push on the small of my back. Thanks." Yvonne put her other hand in front to keep her from over-balancing. Upright, the woman relaxed a bit. "Where's my skateboard?"

Yvonne brought it over, lifted the woman on to it, and draped the vacuum cleaner hose around her neck. The woman grabbed it in her teeth just above the metal end and, by moving her head, propelled herself toward a tree. Jane kept her eyes on her flippers waddling after the skateboard; Yvonne crossed her arms, felt her breasts pressing on them. The woman manoeuvred to lean a shoulder socket against the tree. When Yvonne sat down beside Jane, they were all about the same height.

"The last thing I remember is flying into that." She jerked her head toward the pool. "Thank you for saving me – was I unconscious for long?"

"Not long. What would you say Jane – three, four minutes?"

"You're the one with the watch." Jane was trying not to stare at – or not avoid looking at – the torso. "How are you feeling?" she asked, apparently of the skateboard's left front wheel.

"A little damp, and I must have bumped my head." She raised her shoulder as if she'd touch her head, had she a hand. "But okay, considering. Mirabelle's my name."

Amazing grey eyes – Yvonne introduced herself and Jane. "She's a woman, not a turtle. Mean, she's a turtle, but she's a woman also."

Mirabelle paled. "Don't Move! There's a very large spider behind you!"

"Oh good!" Jane turned, smiled at it. "Are you recovered now?" It had squatted down, its eyestalks firmly fixed on Mirabelle. At Jane's question, it rotated one briefly to her, back to Mirabelle.

"You know it?" Mirabelle asked Jane.

"Oh yes. It's been following Yvonne."

"How awful!"

"On the contrary, that spider has saved her life – twice. It's her spider."

"Willing to share it." Yvonne glared at Jane.

"A turtle. A spider." Mirabelle shook her head in disbelief. "You look normal, Yvonne. How do you fit?"

"Oh, lived in my fridge. The mistake was getting out." More bitter than she'd intended. Eyebrowed an apology at Jane, smiled.

"She also can't seem to say *I*. Says me and my all right, but not *I*." Jane hadn't noticed the eyebrow.

"Can't ? Never knew that!" Yvonne blushed, naked, mortified. Blinked against the sudden sting of tears. Cruel of Jane to mention it in front of a stranger. Why no ? Where was it? Both Jane and Mirabelle looking at her.

"Oh, I thought you knew," Jane said in surprise. "I'm sorry."

"Maybe if you practise –?" Mirabelle offered tentatively.

"Oh well. Doesn't matter. Don't care." Lying, of course. A blank in her throat. Shrugged again.

"Well, that's us." Jane turned back to Mirabelle. "What happened to you? Were you born like that? Or were they amputated?"

"No, they just fell off—"

Jane guffawed, then scrabbled into her shell. Horrible to laugh, but it was like her doll. "I'm sorry." Her voice muffled. "I didn't mean to be rude. I was thinking—" Her head emerged, new lipstick, blusher. "Do carry on."

"Well, Christmas is a big deal in our family, I have children –" Yvonne nodded. "I hit the stores when they open and don't leave till they close – anyway, it was a day like that—"

She shifted against the tree. Yvonne said, "would you be more comfortable in some other position?"

"It's okay, thanks – anyway, I was going into the department store and right at the entrance was the Salvation Army man, you know with his plastic bubble and tamborine thing with jingle bells and I always give, so I got out a dollar and pushed it through the slot. The man smiled and said 'Merry Christmas' –'' Mirabelle glanced at the pool, became as still as the pool. Yvonne and Jane waited. ''– Just as I was leaving I looked into the Salvation Army bubble and there was a little finger lying on top of the bills and coins – took me a minute to realize it was mine –'' She looked down and slightly to the right. Jane and Yvonne thought they could almost see the arm and hand from which the finger would have been missing.

''That was the beginning, then things kept piling up, the school concert, girl guides, the car pool, bake sale, then a neighbour got sick and I looked after her children, then canvassing for the heart fund, the cancer fund, the united appeal, then my husband's car broke down – just little things, doesn't sound like much, but there wasn't enough of me to go around, and each time I seemed to lose something.''

''Didn't it hurt?'' Yvonne asked.

''Not really. Sort of a tug when each thing came off, no blood – that was a blessing – I hate blood. It was all a nuisance. To be honest, it worried me a bit – but it didn't *really* bother me – like, I could adjust so it became normal. My husband helped me in and out of bed.''

''Sounds dreadful! What happened then?''

Mirabelle looked away, began to blush. ''Well – I woke up one morning and realized I didn't have much more to lose. My hair was going, my hair – a woman's crowning glory and all that – and then – my husband's very attached to my – breasts—''

''Aren't you?'' Jane asked. She hadn't heard 'crowning glory' since she was a teenager – how could the woman have put up with so much?

''Not the way he is. And they're about all I could lose

without dying. I figure I need the rest of me – what's left – aren't I entitled to it?''

It sounded like a genuine question; Jane and Yvonne looked at each other in amazement, back to Mirabelle. Yvonne said, ''of course! You're even entitled to keep your arms and legs!''

''Mandatory equipment,'' Jane added, ''even if they're flippers.'' Mirabelle appeared only half-reassured, half-believing.

''Then what happened?'' Yvonne prompted.

''I don't exactly know.'' Mirabelle's voice was so low and hesitant, Jane and Yvonne leaned closer. ''My neighbour asked me to babysit and I said 'no'. I was as polite as can be, I didn't want to upset her, but she got mad anyway and I guess I got scared. I hate people being mad at me—

''But I didn't know what to do, lose my hair or have people mad at me, so I thought I'd better figure it out. I got on my son's skateboard and with that vacuum cleaner attachment I can push myself along pretty well except –'' Tears in her eyes. She blinked, looked over at the spider, toward the pool. ''– I feel a little helpless. I don't have much control – especially downhill. I might have drowned if you hadn't been here.''

To say the least! Yvonne replayed wading into the pool, this time with a shudder. She glanced at Jane, who said, more matter-of-factly than she felt, ''well, we were here, so you didn't.'' Jane thought she'd never seen anyone so helpless – no arms, no legs – and yet not helpless – a skateboard, a vacuum hose, smiled with admiration, and asked, ''where?''

Mirabelle started. ''What do you mean, where?''

''Where is here? Where are we? Do you know? We don't. Out there is a desert, we just crossed it. Is this an oasis? What's up that road? More desert?''

''I don't know about deserts. There's more of this back there – trees, you know, forest, and then some houses. My house.''

"An ocean?"

"That's much farther on. This is the Interior—"

Jane snorted. "No wonder you keep decorating with fridges and operating rooms, Yvonne! The Interior!" Mirabelle looked at both of them, puzzled. "She was an interior decorator," Jane explained.

Yvonne smiled enigmatically, stood up and stretched. She glanced at the spider, walked a few steps out of the shade, clasped her hands behind her back. Do ? If so— She placed the end of a rainbow faintly up the waterfall. Turned back, caught the spider rotating its eyestalks from the waterfall to her. So she had a speech impediment. At least she could make pictures.

Turned to the others. "That's west, up there?" Mirabelle nodded. "No desert?" Nod. Yvonne raised her eyebrow at Jane: invite her along? Jane glanced away, then back, and smiled yes. "Would you like to come with us?" Yvonne asked. Mirabelle shifted on her skateboard, rubbed her cheek against the hose.

"Where are you going?"

"To find the ocean," Jane snapped.

Mirabelle closed her eyes, sighed. "I don't really want to go back yet. But I should. I feel so guilty—"

"Why?" Jane asked.

"I took off. I left. Though I did leave a note, I don't want them to worry—" Mirabelle looked from Yvonne to Jane. A woman who lived in a fridge. A turtle. A spider. She sighed again. Tired. Uncomfortable. If she fell into another pool –

"Maybe I could come a little way. I did leave a note—"

"Is the spider ready to travel? I'm not going until it is." Jane waddled over to check.

"Oh good grief." Yvonne tapped her fingers against her thigh.

Then, with Jane balancing on the ends of her flippers, Yvonne manoeuvred the skateboard under her and hoisted Mirabelle on Jane's back. She wound the vacuum cleaner attachment around Mirabelle's neck like a slipped laurel wreath and kept her hand on Mirabelle's shoulder so she wouldn't fall off Jane. They progressed up the hill to the top of the waterfall and rolled along the path beside the stream. Jane looked behind for the spider. So did Mirabelle, and then Yvonne found herself having to check. There it was, toiling its customary five metres behind.

&

The path wound through a forest of pine and poplar, over arid ground sprinkled with needles and last year's leaves. Billowy clouds occasionally obscured the sun and deepened the shade. The path was smooth and the skateboard rolled along with minimum effort. Jane steered with her front flippers and Yvonne, as well as balancing Mirabelle, provided the momentum. All three found travelling this way so much easier than on previous days that they were lighthearted and Jane began to hum. Shortly Mirabelle snorted, a combined guffaw and sneeze, put her head to an angle as if she'd cover her mouth, had she a hand. The snort grew into laughter.

"I was thinking of *The Wizard of Oz*. It was one of my favourite books when I was a child. I read it to both my children. You could be Dorothy, Yvonne, since you're pushing us, and the spider's Toto tagging along behind. Jane and I, we're the Tin Woodman and Scarecrow –" Jane snorted derisively and Mirabelle's voice faltered. "– of course we don't have a Cowardly Lion – I just mean, we're off on a journey of some sort –" she laughed at herself before they did, "– and of course there won't be a Wizard—" Her voice trailed off as she wished she hadn't said anything – they'd think her so silly.

But Yvonne's tone was serious. "He wasn't much use in the book. He didn't do wizardly things."

"Just another weak man you can't depend on! He had a whole institution set up for his own protection!" Scorn

52

dripped off Jane's lips like excess saliva. Mirabelle was relieved it was for the Wizard, not for her.

"What institution?" she asked.

"The Emerald City! The Wizard fooled the citizens into believing he was great and powerful so he could believe it himself! Study institutional systems sometime the way I have! Politics! Religion! Education!"

Mirabelle and Yvonne looked at each other, both feeling Jane's bitter tension.

"I was just thinking –" Mirabelle backtracked, uncertain. "I didn't mean to get you riled up." She looked fearfully at the top of Jane's head, and added, in spite of herself, "it would be fun to meet Glinda – the good witch."

Yvonne said, "can't see how this is like those books. This path isn't a yellow brick road though like it better than the desert." She hippety-hopped a few steps and sang, a tone flat, "'we're off to see the wizard, the wonderful wizard of Oz.'" Mirabelle turned and gave her a grateful smile.

"Still, it makes me mad, weaklings pretending they're strong," Jane acknowledged in a calmer tone. "But you mean a quest, don't you, Mirabelle? A search?" Jane peered around and Mirabelle nodded. "I can tell you, in most quests the hero, if he's a man, knows what he's searching for – unlike us. The holy grail, for example. Of course, it's not so easy nowadays. All holy grails or relics have been properly identified and stuck in museums. Now they have to create their own to search out—"

"Like going to the moon?" Mirabelle interjected, but Jane had warmed to her topic.

"I think chasing about for an object takes the emphasis off the process, and the object becomes more important than what's involved in locating it – the life the hero is living, if you will. It's the same with the holy grail. At some point in history the grail itself became the symbol, not the fact it was a vessel and vessels are built to contain something. So when did the container become more important than what it was created to hold? When was the emphasis taken off the contained, the original, life-giving power? And the answer to that, my friends, is: when the power of the goddesses had to be diminished so patriarchies could rule. And –"

Mirabelle and Yvonne could barely control their laughter. Yvonne made hitting motions over Jane's curls. "Sounds like you've done a lot of lecturing, Jane."

Jane's head snapped around. Saw their amusement, frowned. "Oh, was I lecturing?" They nodded.

"But it was very interesting," Mirabelle hastily assured her. Jane looked from one to the other and slowly smiled.

"Is that why you turned into a turtle?" Mirabelle asked. "Because everything's so complicated to you?"

"I don't know, nothing's that simple." Jane laughed. "Maybe everything is simple but people complicate it. Maybe I was trying to simplify. What's more basic than a turtle?" Her tone had become sardonic, but in a minute she brightened. "I can live a hundred more years as a turtle than I can as a woman. When I started studying basic Theology before I specialized in Myth I wanted to be a minister but they weren't ordaining women then. I fought that for a while, but I gave up. I guess I didn't believe enough in the resurrection. I want to live now, for as long as possible." She shut her eyes and her voice dropped to a whisper. "I'm scared of death."

The skateboard and Yvonne's feet made no sound on the path. Leaves hung still in the absence of wind. No squirrel rattled a branch. No bird sang. Even whispered, Jane's statement resonated firmly in the cavern of bush, echoed in their ears and minds.

"I'm only scared of dying," Mirabelle offered. "Of taking a long time to do it, bleeding and hurting – but maybe it doesn't hurt any more than losing my arms or legs did."

"I'm scared of Death," Jane elaborated. "Of the Void. Of total nothingness, of being abandoned. Of what might be

or might not be. I want to stay with what I know as long
as I can."

"You've studied too much." Mirabelle's tone sharp.

"Or not enough." Jane continued ruefully. "I always feel
I'm a failure. Whatever I do isn't good enough, wherever
I am I don't belong so I'm going to find a group of turtles
and study how they do it and live 150 years. Turtles are long-
lived, you know."

Yvonne said, "young, scared of having stitches – ever.
Used to think about it and break out in a sweat and shiver
and cry and then when stitched, wasn't as bad as
thought it'd be."

"Death isn't like having stitches," Jane stated.

"No, but maybe the principle's the same."

"Is that why you moved into the fridge?" Mirabelle asked.
"You thought things were worse than they really were and
didn't want to face them?"

"Oh, who knows. Ever know as much about yourself as
about others?" Yvonne laughed, looked at the trees beside
the path. A cloud had covered the sun; momentary dusk.
Her face became wistful.

"Younger,   wanted to be an artist, create a whole new
way of looking at the world, have others share my visions.
Everyone was very nice about my paintings, my mother and
Martin thought how lovely – said everyone should have a
hobby, but they didn't think – and guess   didn't think
also – that painting was serious. They thought it shouldn't
interfere with the business of living. 'Very nice, dear', my
mother always said. But she didn't really look. Lots of people – maybe most people – never really look."

&

Absorbed in her own thoughts, each silently let the path
lead her in a slow curve. They barely noticed the sun touching the tops of mountains that now surrounded them,

55

became aware only when its light was abruptly extinguished. The moon balanced on one high peak and, as their eyes adjusted to the whiter, dimmer view, they saw the outline of a log cabin ahead. Just then, lights went on in the windows and smoke started drifting out of the chimney. Ten metres in front of the cabin a path of crushed stone began. To the right was a large fenced garden.

Yvonne pushed the skateboard. Jane dragged her flippers for brakes. Caught between their two motions, Mirabelle tottered precariously. "Help!"

Yvonne steadied her, kept both hands on her shoulders as they contemplated the cabin. "You live near here, Mirabelle. Do you know the owner?"

"No."

Jane laughed, "that's like saying, you come from the city, do you know Sybil? She drives a truck."

"You know what mean. Shall we see if they're hospitable?"

"Might as well," Jane said. "If you want to."

"Most folks around here are friendly." Mirabelle felt a beat of nervousness.

Yvonne put her fist up to knock, but the door opened before she could touch it. They paused on the threshold, registering both that and the sound of a string quartet, a very good recording on a sophisticated sound system. Kindling crackled under two huge logs in the fireplace, and a table was set for four.

"Hello!" Yvonne shouted. "Are we intruding?" No answer. She glanced at Jane, at Mirabelle. The kindling crackled, the quartet progressed to the next movement, delicious smells emanated from the kitchen.

"An enchanted cottage," Mirabelle whispered as her nervousness increased. "We'd better be careful."

"Now that is silly. You'll be saying it's the Three Bears' house next! The owner's in the bathroom or out back looking at the moon. Hello!" Jane yelled.

56

Yvonne stuck her head farther in. "If the owner's not around the law of the North applies. Use what you need and replace it when you go."

"Yes, but this isn't the North, it's the Interior." Jane liked precision.

"Oh well, same thing. It's rural. Come on." Yvonne pushed the skateboard over the threshold.

"Maybe we should just leave?" Mirabelle rubbed her cheek on the vacuum attachment, couldn't get her teeth around it.

"It's okay." Yvonne started to close the door, nearly cut off the spider's back leg. It dashed in and she jumped back. "Damn insect!"

"Arthropod," Jane corrected, watching the spider settle in a corner near the fireplace. "I don't know why you don't like it. It's very nice and predictable for a spider, and it likes you. Did you know there were spider goddesses in Hindu, African and Amerindian mythology?"

"The original spiderwomen?" Mirabelle looked around, expecting the owner to appear, to tell them angrily to leave.

Yvonne slammed the door. "It's attached itself without even asking! Don't feel free. Always loathed spiders, especially big hairy ones, and don't like being followed, but there doesn't seem to be anything   can do about it!"

"You could tell it to go away," Mirabelle offered, "not that I want you to."

"Tried that." She stared at the spider crouching in the corner, staring at her, then frowned. Had she? Smacked her lips in disgust, turned –

"Oh!" Yvonne put her hand to her throat. "A quintet, not a quartet! Never was musical!"

The others followed her gaze. The music was not coming from a stereo, but from five penguins arranged in a semi-circle opposite the fireplace.

"This is too much, Yvonne! You're getting quite out of control!" But Jane was grinning.

"Honestly! Didn't do this,   don't think." She frowned

at the penguins in confusion, then shrugged and smiled at Jane.

With a flourish of crescendos, the penguins ended the Beethoven, shuffled their papers, poised their bows, nodded at each other, and launched into Mozart. The cellist towered over the rest from its perch on a high stool.

"If you didn't do it this cottage really is enchanted," Mirabelle breathed ecstatically. Yvonne lifted her off Jane's back while Jane got off the skateboard, then placed Mirabelle back on it. From that height she could look the first violinist in the eye. She smiled at it.

"Penguins," Jane murmered, waddling closer to them. "How far to the ocean?" she asked, glancing at them all.

"Don't interrupt, please. Wait till they finish playing." Mirabelle looked around the room again, including the spider in her smile. "I guess the owner really isn't here," she announced, and allowed herself to relax.

Yvonne noticed a computer on a low table, green print flashing on its screen. She read aloud, "Welcome. Make yourselves to home."

"How nice," Mirabelle effused. "Music and a welcome message. All that's missing are flowers."

The computer's screen flashed: *flowers are outside where they belong! But pick them if you must!*

"No, no. It's fine," Mirabelle said hastily, looking to Yvonne for reassurance. "I didn't mean to sound ungrateful. We don't need flowers."

The penguins flourished the end of a movement. Jane repeated, "how far to the ocean, boys?" The cellist plucked a string, tightened a peg. "Is the ocean nearby?" Jane smiled.

"Maybe they don't speak English," Mirabelle said.

"Maybe they're not boys," added Yvonne.

"Yes, that's a point." Jane's excitement soured toward frustration. "You can't tell with penguins – penguins can't even tell, they drop pebbles in front of each other for courting. She addressed the quintet in a formal tone. "Please tell me

58

how far the ocean is." The first violinist picked up its bow, about to start the next movement. "Where is the ocean? – Ocean?" Jane yelled, "où est la mer? Wo ist den ozean?" Her flipper tapped the floor in extreme impatience. She repeated the question in Hebrew. "Tcha!" She smacked her lips disgustedly, turned back to Yvonne and Mirabelle. "Are they ever dumb!"

"The strong, silent types." Mirabelle laughed. "But they're very good musicians."

The logs had caught fire and the crackling was quieter. The penguins resumed playing. Beside the table stood an ice bucket chilling a bottle of champagne. A buzzer sounded, switched off. The computer flashed: *your dinner is ready now*.

While Jane hoisted Mirabelle onto a chair, Yvonne brought plates and dishes from the kitchen, set broiled rainbow trout, spinach linguine, parsleyed baby carrots, and a tossed salad on the table. She opened the champagne.

"What a wonderful meal!" Mirabelle swallowed a spurt of anticipatory saliva as Yvonne deboned her trout. "I wonder who cooked it – and I wonder who the fourth place is for."

"The spider, of course!" Jane's plate with linguine and most of the salad was before her on the floor.

Yvonne looked around. The spider had backed into a corner near the bedroom door. It regarded them, but made no move. "Don't want it at the table while   'm eating! The thought makes me sick!"

"Shh, you'll hurt its feelings," Mirabelle said. "There, there, Spider, she didn't really mean it."

"Did too." Yvonne closed her eyes. The corner empty. Polished floor extended unlittered to the baseboard. Not even a dustball.

"Well at least feed it," Jane insisted. "It can have my trout. Poor trout, happily swimming around, then next thing, the pan." She shook her head sadly, a piece of lettuce forgotten in her beak.

"Have some more champagne," Mirabelle coaxed. "Don't think about things like that. Let's be happy and cheerful. If this *is* an enchanted cottage and we're about to be shoved in the oven or turned into toads, we might as well enjoy the meal."

Jane retorted, "you're the one who thinks the most dire thoughts, Mirabelle! Even though you tell us not to!"

"Oh I just want everyone in the whole world to be happy," she giggled fizzily.

Yvonne put a plate with the last trout on the floor. "It can eat this, but you give it to it, Jane.   'm not giving it a thing!"

Jane shoved the plate toward the spider. It ran out of its corner and leapt on the trout, began tearing out chunks with a grinding sound like wasps pulping wood. "Hungry, weren't you?" Jane observed, and Yvonne pulled her chair around so her back was to the spider.

After they'd finished eating, Yvonne cleared the table and put the dishes in the dishwasher. No sooner had she closed the door than its cycle began. She watched its lights flash, its dial move, listened to its comfortable sloshing and chugging, and wondered if the house were run by all the appliances collectively or if the computer were in charge. The coffee maker had made the coffee and three mugs sat beside it. All she had to do was pour. And get the milk.

Yvonne contemplated the fridge, avocado to match the stove. She preferred white. She'd had no need to get anything out for dinner – hadn't thought about the fridge until now. A separate freezer section, automatic ice cube dispenser in the door, right opening. The largest size of fridge, a Westinghouse—

Around the slosh, slosh of the dishwasher, Yvonne could hear strains of music and Jane's voice. Maybe no one took milk in after dinner coffee. She didn't. She could ask, or she could say there was no milk – but the computer would probably correct her. Just a fridge, she told herself. Not her fridge. Not a phalanx of desert fridges. An appliance to serve her. She yanked the door open.

"MAKE UP YOUR MIND BEFORE YOU OPEN THE DOOR! YOU'RE LETTING ALL THE COLD OUT! YOU CAN'T BE HUNGRY! YOU JUST ATE! DON'T STAND THERE WITH THE DOOR OPEN! ELECTRICITY COSTS MONEY! GET OUT OF THE FRIDGE! DINNER'S IN HALF AN HOUR. YOU CAN WAIT! WHO ATE ALL THE LEFTOVERS? SHUT THE DOOR!"

Yvonne did, backed away, shaking, slopped the coffee into the cups, picked up the tray and rattled it to the living room.

"My mother's in the fridge," she whispered.

"You mean it runs in your family?" Jane.

"Tell you, my mother's in the fridge. Heard her."

"Put the tray down," Jane ordered. "We'll go see."

"Maybe we should leave her alone." Mirabelle looked worried.

Jane pressed, "your mother can't be here. You said she was dead. Oh, will you dry up!" The last was to the penguins, but they played on.

Jane started to the kitchen. Mirabelle prepared to roll off the sofa, but Yvonne picked her up. "Open the fridge door," Jane commanded. Yvonne hesitated then, at the expression on Jane's face, did, just a crack.

"SHUT THE DOOR! MAKE UP YOUR MIND BEFORE YOU OPEN THE DOOR! DON'T STAND THERE WITH THE DOOR OPEN—"

Yvonne slammed it. "See?"

"Sounded like my mother." Jane's laugh had a touch of horror.

"Open it again, Yvonne. Go on," Mirabelle urged, twisting a bit in her arms.

Yvonne reluctantly did so. "WHO ATE ALL THE LEFTOVERS? SHUT THE DOOR!"

"It says the same things," Mirabelle observed, thinking,

61

definitely an enchanted cottage. "Open it wider."

"MAKE UP YOUR MIND BEFORE – YOU CAN'T BE HUNGRY, YOU JUST ATE! – DINNER'S IN HALF—"

"A mechanical voice," Mirabelle continued. "You just think it sounds like your mother. Could have been me, I was always telling Dick and Sally to get out of the fridge. Not a bad idea to wire the fridge to say it. Saves your vocal cords." She smiled at Yvonne, at Jane. Both of them looking as if they wanted to believe her, but couldn't. Yvonne opened the door a crack. "– LETTING ALL THE COLD OUT! DINNER'S—"

"Grab the milk this time." Mirabelle started to laugh, and finally Jane joined her. Yvonne did not. Mirabelle said, kindly, "it's okay, Yvonne, don't be scared, this is a wonderful enchanted cottage—"

"You've made," Jane finished.

Yvonne flared, "do you really think   make up things to scare myself with? What do you think   am?" They both stopped laughing and looked at the floor like chastised children.

"Sorry, Yvonne. I didn't mean to make you mad," Mirabelle mumbled.

"You didn't," Yvonne said, but plunked her down on the sofa not too gently, poured the coffee. Jane finally muttered, "just a joke," and poured cognac into warmed snifters. The penguins moved into modern jazz.

"Should we offer them anything?" Mirabelle finally asked.

"The computer doesn't say to," Jane pointed out. Yvonne was looking at the spider who had rolled onto its back, extended its legs and gone to sleep.

&

Much later Yvonne asked if anyone wanted a third cognac. The jazz and previous cognacs were so mellowing that Jane, her chin outstretched on the floor, and Mirabelle, propped pillowlike in the corner of the sofa, could only mumble replies through small, contented smiles. The computer flashed: *would you like your bath drawn now?* continued flashing since no one could move to respond. The door crashed open. In tumbled two men. After they tumbled they somersaulted, and after they somersaulted they bounded; they leaped and vaulted and careened around the room, whooping and chortling. The spider flailed all its legs until one touched the wall and it could push itself over. It furiously began to spin. The computer printed: *is this your entertainment committee?* but no one noticed except the penguins, who put their instruments in their cases and rolled up behind a barricade of music stands.

"What the hell's this?" Jane yelled, balancing on the ends of her flippers. She rotated her head between the intruders and Yvonne and Mirabelle, and the now puce coloured wattles on her neck shook with rage. "They can't barge in like this – get out, you assholes!"

"Maybe they live here." Mirabelle had somehow managed to make herself smaller – a crumpled, unfluffed pillow.

"No way! This is our cabin! They can't barge in and take over!" Jane banged a flipper. "Who the hell do you think you are?" The men paid no attention. Jane turned to Yvonne, saw large staring eyes in a white face.

Starting on her skull, in her skull, white spilled over her head and down, inside and out, slowing thought, fading images, clogging sound, weighting limbs, making motion impossible. The room was white, a tin of paint spilled over the whole scene so it was blanked, nullified.

Jane still raged enough puce, crimson, cerise, to tint Yvonne's white to pink at least, yet no one paid attention. Yvonne sat still, painted, her fingers still around her snifter, the men still acrobatted, the spider spun. Only Mirabelle, a pillow dented by many heads, unable to move without help, responded. "I agree with you, Jane, I wish they'd leave, but there's nothing we can do. Maybe they need a place to stay like us. They seem friendly, anyway."

"Don't be so damned agreeable, Mirabelle! They're intruders and we don't have to be intruded upon!" But Jane looked from Mirabelle to Yvonne to Mirabelle – without them she could not maintain her fuel line to action. Her shell lowered to draw in her legs, her tail drooped, and her chin came to rest on the floor, lower lip flaccid in a pout.

The men stopped in the middle of the room and began tossing four balls back and forth with increasing speed and velocity as if trying to outdo the other. They simultaneously pulled out sticks and balanced balls on them while tossing others in the air. The first man pointed his stick at the second and the ball flew off it, bounced on Second's head. First caught it again on his stick.

"Show offs," Mirabelle whispered.

"Reminds me of my graduate seminars." Jane's voice was as flat as her tail.

Now Second balanced both balls on the end of his stick, rotated it vigourously. First put his stick in his mouth, positioned a ball on each end and bent over backwards until his hands touched the floor. Second climbed on First's stomach and put his stick behind his ear. He threw the balls up until they bounced off the ceiling, caught each one. It seemed neither man would miss.

Yvonne yawned, air drawn in only to her uvula.

Second got off First's stomach and they both stood up. "Any of you girls like to try? We'll show you how, course it's difficult, takes a lot of practice, we can't guarantee you'll never miss."

Mirabelle looked at Yvonne, at Jane. "No thank you."

First raised his eyebrows. "Guess they're not convinced we're good enough to teach them." They took off their shoes, lay down on their backs and spun the balls on the soles of their feet. They pumped their legs until the balls were flying around the room.

One ball bounced against the ceiling only inches from the

spider. "Watch out!" Jane yelled. Mirabelle and even Yvonne looked up. The spider had spun a large web, nearly as dense as the one on the rose stem and like then, was difficult to locate in the web's opaqueness.

At Jane's admonition, the men sprang up, deflated their balls, folded their sticks and stored them in their pockets. "Got anything to eat, girls?" First asked hopefully.

"No." Yvonne, flat. The paint had no gloss when dry.

"Nothing? You'd think they'd feed us after that show, it was one of our best." Second started toward the kitchen.

"There is no food left. And we are not girls." Jane.

"I guess you're not," First laughed. "You are a turtle." He covered his mouth with his hand, mock-whispered toward Second, "turtle soup?" Then, "just joking," to Yvonne.

After the first glance, both men had kept their eyes averted from Mirabelle; she was grotesque, no arms, no legs, an inflatable pillow propped on the sofa. Now she said, "can't you rustle up something, Yvonne? It's not neighbourly not to feed people."

"No, it's not," Second said.

"And we did perform for you," First added.

"We didn't ask you to," Jane said. "You barged in. Barge out the same way."

"These gals are not very grateful. Maybe we should go find someone who appreciates us." But First had straddled a chair. Second banged cupboards, opened drawers and the fridge. They heard it chattering at him, cut off in mid-scold.

Mirabelle saw Jane's obdurateness, and felt confused. Feeding people was a nice thing to do, wasn't it? Wouldn't these people be nice if they were fed? Her right thumb itched; she tried to scratch it – no fingers, no thumb – didn't make sense—

First said, "what are you girls doing out here in the wilds all by yourselves?" He was looking at Yvonne, but she, still painted, didn't notice.

"Having a good time until you came along," Jane replied.

65

"And we're not all by ourselves, we're together. And for the second time, we are not *girls!*"

"Oh come now, you're not that old." He smiled slowly at Yvonne, had not taken his eyes off her. "Didn't you like our little performance?"

"No," Jane said. "I found it downright boring and intrusive – you think that because you can juggle balls anyone will stop what they're doing and be delighted to watch you! Well, we're not!"

But she might as well have said nothing; her words hovered over him like a cloud he could ignore, once he'd first acknowledged its existence with a tilt of his head, denied it by winking slowly at Yvonne.

That wink pushed a button somewhere in the room. The lights dimmed to a cool blue glow and a large bed descended from the wall. The bed had a blue satin quilt and matching sheets turned back. Above it on the ceiling appeared a mirror. Very faintly Yvonne heard strains of: *You made me love you, didn't want to do it.* Her chest rose, collapsed in a deep sigh. Bits of paint flaked off. Beside the bed now a pool of water, slowly expanding, its surface langorously rippled. Tall bullrushes waved at its verge. Yvonne uncurled her legs, stood up, brushed her hair off her forehead with the back of her hand, tightening her pectoral muscles. She floated over, dragged her fingers through the pool, lay down on her back on the bed, left arm under her head, a tiny smile on her lips, and accepted the slow closing of her eyes.

Second returned from the kitchen, lounged nonchalantly in the doorway, hands in his pockets. First got off his chair, took a step toward the bed.

Jane remembered the refrigerators. Furious and scared, she lumbered around the sofa, positioned herself between First and the bed, and bared her teeth. The spider peeked out of its web, its legs bent to pounce. Mirabelle didn't know what to do. Her absent thumb still itched. She thumped off the sofa and rolled across the floor to the computer, pushed the control button with her chin. Instantly the light changed from pale blue to red and the computer printed: *look up!*

"Look up Yvonne!" Mirabelle yelled.

First was nearly at the bed. Second had shoved himself off the doorjamb, was crossing to the other side.

Far too slowly for Jane or Mirabelle, Yvonne opened her eyes, tilted her head, looked up. The mirror did not reflect her lying on a blue satin quilt, did not reflect the pool surrounded by kind bullrushes, the pool's surface reflecting the reflection of Yvonne in the mirror. No image at all of Yvonne.

The mirror showed ropes and chains and piercing objects, bound girls with smiling lips and vacant eyes, breasts with claw marks, thighs bulging from blood pooled by tight garters, fire and ice and every imaginable sort of whip, bull whips and cats o' nine tails and riding crops and billy clubs, whips with lashes at the end or marlinspikes, some deceptively feathery and some for bludgeoning.

Yvonne screamed, leapt off the bed. Her scream broke the mirror and the shards fell down to slash the bed and splash into the pool, instantly shriveling whatever they touched. Bed and pool were annihilated.

Yvonne crouched with her back against the wall. On flipper-tips Jane stalked toward the men. "Get out right now! You don't belong here! We don't want you! Get out this instant before I bite your legs off!"

First looked at Second with a puzzled frown. Second shrugged. "You've got the wrong idea. Just having some fun. We're perfectly nice and trustworthy."

"Get out!"

The men looked from Jane to Mirabelle to Yvonne. When they reached the door they soft-shoed a few steps and twirled their hands in the air. But their performance lacked enthusiasm.

Jane padded over to Yvonne, laid her head in her lap.

Mirabelle kissed Yvonne, and one long strand from the spider web wafted down and rested – without Yvonne's knowing – on her hair.

&

In the morning Yvonne awoke first. Saw Jane still enshelled on the floor, then turned over toward Mirabelle. Nothing but a greyness – the spiderweb must have fallen down. Pulled her hand away, one finger had nearly touched it, and slid out of bed, her throat tight with disgust. That grey mass, that substance, that shroud. She backed away and looked around; the computer had printed: *good morning*. In the corner the spider lay on its back, legs tightly furled, one strand of the web still attached to its abdomen. Yvonne nudged Jane's shell, looked toward the bathroom, hoping to hear sounds of the shower, the toilet, anything to indicate Mirabelle was there and not, as she feared, under the web. Silence, except for a caucus of crows outside.

Yvonne nudged Jane's shell harder, reached toward the web on the bed, breathed deeply. She ran into the kitchen, came back with a wooden spoon; with this she poked at the shroud, trying to find Mirabelle's face, to pull the web away from her mouth, afraid she'd already suffocated.

As she touched the web with the spoon it parted lengthwise like a run in a nylon, then across the middle until the web was divided in four, and as she poked, the four parts collected at Mirabelle's shoulders and hips and the web ran down into these parts.

Holding the spoon in front of her like a lance Yvonne backed away from the bed. She put her other hand to her mouth in case her scream escaped. Some web continued from Mirabelle's left side across the bed and the floor to the spider.

Mirabelle opened her eyes, smiled, saw Yvonne's look of horror, amazement. Yvonne shakily extended the spoon, wanting to scrape the web away, and pulled at the nearest

68

arm. It wafted up then flopped back onto the bed. "Ouch. What are you doing?"

"Did you feel that?" Yvonne did it again.

"Of course I felt it – oh! Ahhh!" Mirabelle leapt off the bed and instantly folded onto the floor. She shook herself all over, then pushed up on her willowy, floppy hands and feet, bent her legs until semblances of knees took her weight.

Yvonne banged on Jane's shell with the spoon. "Will you wake up!"

Mirabelle crawled to the bed, lifted her arms onto it so her hands, which were only tendrils of her arms, could grasp it. She tried to haul herself up like a striving baby, but her new limbs had little strength. "Help me," she said to Yvonne, shoving up on her knees, trying to pull with her hands. Yvonne stepped forward, held out her hand, immediately withdrew it, gagging. She could not bring herself to touch that webbish substance.

Jane's head emerged. She saw Mirabelle, she thought she saw Mirabelle, but there were long grey gossamer appendages attached to her body, one of which led to the spider. She withdrew her head, re-emerged with the scalpel, knowing now why she had kept it. Sliced the strand still attached to the spider and, freed, the strand retreated to Mirabelle's left foot. Jane wedged her shell under Mirabelle's buttocks, heaved. Mirabelle tottered up, legs wide spread, hands grasping the mattress, a baby's first steps.

All three stared at each other. Yvonne's horror faded to astonishment. Jane's face shone with a sense of miracle. Mirabelle's flaccid facial muscles matched the softness of her limbs.

"Look at me." She tottered, took a step, wobbled, put a hand to her face, missed and hit her hair, laughed through her tears. She dragged the right foot in front of the left, wobbled again, moved the left foot forward and Yvonne got behind her to catch her if she fell.

Mirabelle flopped in a semi-circular line from the bed to

the wall, put a hand out, wobbled back. "I'll get the hang of it again." Her laugh was moist with tears. "I can't believe it," she said, for all of them.

Then she saw the spider. She tottered over, put one hand on the wall for balance, scooped it up. She held it against her breast in an arm that was turning pink as blood vessels flowed down from her body. She straightened so she could hold the spider in both arms. "Thank you, thank you," she crooned, rocking it to and fro, not knowing tears were on her cheeks.

The spider twitched a leg, another leg, lay still again. Mirabelle sat down and placed the spider in her lap so it could feel her thighs as well, also turning pink with blood. The spider moved its legs in unison, inward, outward, perhaps in time with its breath, with her blood. Mirabelle stroked its tummy with one long finger, stroked each leg in turn, placed her palm upon its head. Finally she turned the spider over and stood it on its own legs. They watched it scrabble to the corner, turn around so it could view them – its accustomed place.

&

"We better be going," Yvonne said, having washed the spoon and returned it to its drawer.

"Do we really? Why?" Mirabelle walked back and forth in time to the music, picking up objects and putting them down, trying out her new limbs. The penguins had taken up their instruments again at exactly nine o' clock, were now playing a little morning music.

"We just do. It's not a journey if you stay in one place."

"I don't want to leave." Jane planted her flippers obdurately. "We have everything we need here and the computer says we're welcome. We'll make sure the door's locked so we're not broken into again."

"Yeah," Mirabelle agreed.

"No! We can't stay. Don't know why. This is someone else's place —"

"Whose?" Jane demanded.

"Someone's. Don't know whose. Just know it's not right to stay. Besides, you said you need to find the ocean, remember?"

"There are penguins here which means a turtle can live here. When I figure out how to communicate with them they can tell me where the ocean is. I can go there and come back here—"

"No!"

"– or you can create an ocean, Yvonne. You did pretty well with that pool last night—"

"No!" Everything getting red and jagged for Yvonne. The penguins juggled balls, the abyss was talking to her mother – why wouldn't they understand, why wouldn't anyone help – "No." Her hands were shaking up and down, rapidly. She tucked them in her armpits and noticed the spider sitting by the door. "Look. It wants to go."

Mirabelle gushed, "aw, the spider." Both Jane and Yvonne had to smile, had to again look at her walking, picking things up.

Jane resumed, "Yvonne, I accept that you are making this all up. I accept that it's your reality. Okay. But it's perfect right now. You can stop. You've got us here and we can manage here. You've done a great job. You don't have to do more."

Yvonne considered. Considering pushed the red jagged bits into background like mountains in an old cowboy movie. "That pool wasn't salt water.   can't make enough salt water for an ocean, no matter how hard   cry – try," she corrected.

Jane pondered too. Her flippers were planted foursquare to her body. She looked at the penguins, at the table, looked back to Yvonne. "I don't know whether to say this or not –" she breathed deeply – "I'm struck by how easily seduced you are." She met Yvonne's sudden glare. "You made the

71

bed last night. You lay in it. And those fridges." She shook her head. "Some of the reality you create is dangerous. You need Mirabelle and me and the spider."

Shards of fear in her stomach. Yvonne ground them smooth with anger. "Want me to say thank you? Thank you."

"No, I don't want thank you – and we should thank you – no, I just worry about you. It's safe here. Let's stay here."

"Yeah," Mirabelle agreed.

Jane continued, "do you seduce yourself?"

"Huh?"

"You create those scenes and move into them so easily—"

"Did not create those men! Not the abyss or the spider – or this cabin! A quintet of penguins, a talking fridge, for goodness sake! All   bloody well did is get out of my fridge! Now that was safe!"

"Frozen."

"Safe!"

"Frozen."

"Safe! And you're a bloody great turtle to talk!"

In the space of their glares the music swelled; they turned to find all the penguins staring at them. "Shouldn't fight in front of the help," Jane snarled, and Yvonne started to laugh.

Mirabelle toddled over, plopped herself on Jane's shell and wrapped her arms around Yvonne's waist. Yvonne stiffened against recoiling from their webbiness, made herself try to relax. She had clothes on; they weren't touching her skin.

Mirabelle said to Jane, "if we go on a bit farther you might find the ocean, and you can always come back here if it doesn't work out."

Jane gave her the look of someone betrayed. "How come you're so anxious to go?"

"I'm not anxious." Mirabelle blushed, glanced around the room, at the spider by the door. "I just – want to walk down the road," her voice dropped to a whisper, "on my own – my new – legs."

"Oh great." Stiff-flippered, Jane strode forward. Yvonne

hauled Mirabelle upright before she fell. At the wall, Jane turned. "Seems I don't have any choice."

"You do." Yvonne realized she was angry. "You can stay here. Alone."

"That's no choice."

"Though   don't want you to."

"Nor do I. Please come." Mirabelle disentangled herself from Yvonne, wobbled toward Jane, held her hand out.

"Yes. Please." Yvonne felt like pleading, couldn't plead. "As Mirabelle said, you can come back here. It's important to go on. Don't know why."

Jane sighed loudly, wriggled her nose and lips in painful acquiescence. "Oh well."

Mirabelle beamed into a grin, flapped a hand on Jane's head. Which Jane retracted part-way, glowering at the floor.

Silence hung tense and heavy for some minutes. Yvonne looked around. They had to go. She wished she knew why and could explain. Such a comfortable cabin – remembered feeling grateful for the cave – how long ago –? "Want to take the computer? It's so useful."

"If you didn't create this cabin that's called stealing!" Jane turned her glower in the computer's direction. It flashed: *would you like your bath drawn now?*, the leftover no one had responded to last night. "Oh well, type yes," Jane hissed.

Immediately they could hear water running in the tub. "See how useful it is?" Yvonne said, but Jane was already slithering toward the bathroom. "It's the rule of the North, whatever you find, you can use."

"You can use it but not take it," Mirabelle clarified. "And you know this isn't the North, it's the Interior."

"All the more reason. Besides, we'll just be using it in a different place."

Mirabelle raised her eyebrows at Yvonne. She was holding a Hummel figure, her fingers becoming her own. "Why not ask the computer if it wants to go? I brought my children up to be self-directed."

"Good idea. How old are your children?"

"Thirteen and fifteen."

"So are mine. Girl and a boy."

"Mine are a boy and a girl."

They looked at each other. The computer turned the tap water off. "Tell it more cold," Jane yelled, and Yvonne typed it in.

"What's your husband's name?" Yvonne asked.

"Martin."

"Hmmm. So was mine. Is mine." A minute of staring. "But you live around here,   don't."

"Martin's a common name – well, fairly."

Yvonne turned back to the computer, typed: would you like to come with us?

Wait. Searching. Answer unavailable.

"You know computerese, Mirabelle? Doesn't make any sense to me."

"Type: list."

"My software is user friendly," Yvonne read to Mirabelle who was attempting an arabesque. "We want to use it and it's friendly."

"It's probably okay then – but to be sure, get it to justify – ow!" Mirabelle's knees buckled and she hit her chin on the coffee table. "Just when I think I'm getting the hang of these, they do something to prove I'm not." She rubbed her chin. "Ask it how you hook it up again before you unplug it."

Jane emerged from the bathroom, untowelled and dripping. "Ask if it's battery-operated too." But it was too late. Yvonne had pulled the plug – which was more than Jane had done.

&

Yvonne loaded the computer on top of the skateboard and, helped by Mirabelle, hoisted Jane on top. "We're really off now," she said, pushing the skateboard onto the road.

74

Mirabelle slunk along beside. Slinking seemed to be Mirabelle's best motion.

Jane cast wistful glances at the cabin until they could no longer see it and finally said, "at least I'm at eye level again. I was tired of looking at your knees, Yvonne."

"Insulted! What's wrong with my knees?"

"The mud on your jeans is distracting – though my view'd be widened now – I'd have your knees to look at, Mirabelle."

All three looked at Mirabelle's legs, then her arms, skinny, unhumanly grey-tinged, each ending in five tendrils which, when she was not concentrating on them, tended to float or flap in the breeze, as if volition, determination and desire strengthened them into bones and tendons.

"How is it to have arms and legs again?" Yvonne asked.

"Oh, wonderful! And – weird. When I think about it I feel like I'm walking on stilts, and I get scared and want to shake them off –" she shook her arms, feeling their weight drag at her shoulder sockets "– or run fast to get away from them."

She laughed. "When I'm not thinking about them they feel like mine, like a new crown for a tooth you know has been made for you but doesn't feel like yours yet," another laugh. "Then when I'm thinking about them another way, I'm so grateful and so lucky I almost cry. You don't know how wonderful it is to move freely again." Tears in the laugh. She looked behind at the spider.

"Is this the height you used to be?"

"I don't know – I used to be five-seven."

Yvonne looked her up and down. " 'm five-four. Say you're closer to five-nine now."

"Oh?" Mirabelle re-felt being so small on the skateboard, shuddered, felt herself expand to include her new arms and legs, expand with gratitude. "I don't mind being taller."

"Too bad the spider didn't have a better sense of proportion," Jane commented. "Your appendages are rather wraith-like."

75

"Shh." Mirabelle looked back at the spider. "I'm so grateful I don't care how long it spun them."

"For." Yvonne saw Jane and Mirabelle's puzzled expressions. "How long it took to spin them," she elaborated. "One word changes the whole meaning."

The sun shone directly on the path from a cloudless sky. Few trees provided shade. Yvonne unbuttoned her quilted vest and rolled up her shirt sleeves, wishing she had on shorts.

"I wonder if the penguins are still playing," Mirabelle mused.

Yvonne thought. "They stop playing when there's no audience and they weed the garden. They're the general caretakers – left them the vacuum attachment –"

"Some present," Jane said.

"– though in the evenings they play chamber music for their own enjoyment, even if no one's there—" Jane and Mirabelle were laughing at her. "Well, you asked," she finished defensively, knowing that right then, the penguins, all wearing straw hats, were thinning radishes.

"But how did they get to the cabin?" Jane inquired. Mirabelle added, "how will they manage without the computer?"

"Do you have to know all the details?" Yvonne's voice rough. Cleared her throat. "Can't you just accept that they were there – or if you have to know more than you saw, can't you make it up yourselves?"

"I suppose so –" Mirabelle started, but Jane cut her off.

"No. I want you to tell me. It's your story." Yvonne frowned, tightened her lips, but said nothing. A cloud of confusion inside.

The hard-packed dirt road followed the banks of a stream that wound around soft hills, green-fuzzed in the distance. Cottonwoods overhung the gravelly stream and the air was messy with their blowing pods. Birds warbled invisibly and a breeze cooled the air. Their progress stirred up a roll of dust. Mirabelle saw the spider more than five metres behind, waited for it to approach and scooped it up in her arms. When she caught up Yvonne shuddered at the way Mirabelle had the spider wrapped close to her chest. It draped assorted legs over her arms with every appearance of contentment.

"It was having to breathe our dust," Mirabelle answered Yvonne's expression. "It's still tired from spinning my arms and legs. I owe it a lot. You can't imagine how wonderful it is to be able to walk again, to scratch my own nose, to feed myself, to not ask for help." She bent her head over the spider, stroked its back with loose-jointed fingers.

"Just keep it away! Can't stand to look at it this close!" Yvonne kept her head toward the stream, and the muscles in her neck became taut with the effort of not looking, repulsiveness having its own fascination.

Around a bend and cradled between two hills, they came upon an apple orchard all pink and white in early bloom. Sheep grazed beneath the trees and with their white coats, not yet shorn, they looked like fallen clouds. Yvonne thought the aspect paradisical, the blue of the sky and stream, the green grass emphasizing the pink-whiteness of the blossoms, the sheep, the clouds.

They stopped. Yvonne and Mirabelle lifted Jane off the computer. "I'm allergic to blossoms, I get hay fever and eczema!"

"Really? We won't stay long then—" Yvonne was cut off by Mirabelle's giggles. She tried to cover her mouth, hit herself in her ear. "Sorry, Jane, I just had a vision of your shell covered with red bumps – a turtle with eczema!"

"It's not funny! If it gets in my shell, how will I scratch? Hay fever makes my nose drip and I have enough trouble blowing it ordinarily, you should remember –!"

"I'm sorry I laughed." Mirabelle was truly contrite.

"I'll stay in here, that should help." Jane submerged herself in the stream until only her eyes and red hair protruded, glared balefully once or twice, then loosened her umbrage in the delight of the scene.

Mirabelle and Yvonne sat down and the spider curled like a cat on a sunny rock. They could not get enough of the sight of the orchard, were far enough away to see its whole aspect stretching up the hillside, yet close enough to hear the bees hovering over individual blossoms. Yvonne and Mirabelle breathed deeply, commented on the smell of the air, fecund with sun-warmed growing grass and apple blossoms.

There were no other orchards around and no habitation, just the pale green hills stetching up on either side, their rounded tops, darker with lodgepole pine, forming the horizon.

Eventually Mirabelle said, ''this is so beautiful, but it's a shame it's spring and not fall – then we could eat the apples.''

Yvonne smiled and continued looking at the orchard.

Slowly the blossoms loosed their petals. One, two, three fell to the ground, lazily blown in circles by the breeze. Others joined them and the air became a pink and white petalstorm hiding branches and tree trunks, covering the sheep and grass. Some petals wafted across the orchard, across the stream, into Yvonne and Mirabelle's laps. Some landed in the stream and were carried down to stipple Jane's shell.

When the blossom storm subsided, the tree trunks hung green and thick with leaves. Dandelions grew up around the trunks, the sun shone hotter as the breeze dropped, and shorn sheep slept on the grass. The hills around the orchard turned brown under the sun, their forested tops a darker green in contrast. The women watched the apples grow, watched the leaves shrink as the sun blazed, watched the apples turn from green to gold and red, watched some early leaves curl off the trees. Soon the branches dipped lower with the weight of their apples and the tree trunks seemed thicker and squatter. The first few apples fell among the sheep who eagerly reached out their necks. The sun was lower now behind the brown hills and, to the dark green forest, aspens gave a golden contrast. Yvonne turned to Mirabelle. "Is this what you wanted?" Mirabelle nodded; she was crying. "It tears at my heart the way the seasons go by so quickly – like seeing your life pass all at once." Yvonne touched her shoulder and stood up. Mirabelle followed her to the stream. Jane's back made a convenient stepping stone. They crossed the grass, climbed the fence, watched a startled garter snake disappear, and reached for the closest apples. There were Gravensteins, Rome Beauties, Spartans, Transparents, Cox's Orange Pippins, Early and Late McIntosh, Red and Yellow Delicious all on the same trees, all ripe at the same time. Yvonne and Mirabelle ate four each, then picked tender ones for Jane. The spider climbed a tree and wrapped itself around a particularly delectable Delicious.

"Sometimes, Yvonne," Jane said when she was full as well, "your artistry is perfect. If you keep this up, we'll have no problems."

"Oh, do you really think   created this?" Genuinely surprised.

"Of course you did. You've switched from interior decorating to exterior. You've been having a few problems – the fridges and that geologic fault, and the jugglers last night – and you did admit you conjured up the operating room."

"Weird you saw that. Just thinking about it,   thought." Yvonne had a puzzled frown. "Can't take the credit, if so, would have edited out the spider—"

"Then I wouldn't have any arms or legs!" Mirabelle added more calmly, "I don't think I can agree with Jane. You didn't make me appear on my skateboard, did you?"

"No, and   didn't turn you into a turtle, Jane. You want someone to be in charge, to take care, and you've decided that person is me. But you got to that oasis yourself.

And   can't carry you. Can only push you."

"Hmmm." Why was her heart beating so hard? Didn't need anyone to take care of her, what nonsense, could take care of herself – but the drinks in the desert –? Jane rested her chin on the grass. She began to sneeze.

&

The road continued to follow the stream around tree-clad hills. After they had listened to the birds, and noted the patterns of sun and shade, and named the trees they knew, the natural beauty had a certain repetitiousness. Yvonne's lower back was tense from pushing Jane on top of the computer; she kept straightening and shrugging. Jane had her eyes closed, her eyeliner particularly thick and heavy today.

Yvonne glanced at Mirabelle who was watching her finger-tendrils float in front of her with a wistful expression. Mirabelle caught the glance and smiled. "When I was a child and we were traveling, my father would tell stories. I love stories."

She sure does, Jane thought. All those *Oz* stories – no one ever told me stories – just lies: grow up, work hard, do what you're supposed to, everything'll be okay, you'll be taken care of— She snapped her eyelids open, turned her head. "Tell us a story then."

"I didn't mean me!" Mirabelle flicked fearful eyes away from Jane. "You tell a story – or you, Yvonne."

"Your idea."

"Me and my big mouth." Mirabelle's arms waved as she tried to clasp her shoulders. She still bobbled as she walked; her slither got caught in potholes and she stumbled. She wanted to change the topic, wished someone else would, couldn't and felt breathless, longed for— "My father told really exciting stories he made up, they'd go on for miles, and I never got tired of the stories or of traveling."

80

"Tell us one of them." Jane's tone was coaxing.

"I can't remember any. And anyway, I can't tell a story the way he could."

"Did you tell your children stories?" Yvonne asked.

"No."

"Why not?"

"I can't. I read them stories, but I've never made up one myself." Mirabelle blinked back tears. Sitting on the couch, Sally on her lap, warm and baby powdered after a bath, Dick pressed against her side, the sleepy heaviness of him, his cowlick sticking up as it dried— She sighed and it caught like a sob in her throat. "I can only remember fairy tales, Cinderella, Sleeping Beauty, The Poor Little Match Girl – I never read that to my children, I couldn't have without crying, the poor thing, shivering all alone in a doorway – I liked Red Riding Hood."

After her first glance at the struggle on Mirabelle's face, Yvonne had looked back to Jane's shell, but saw instead John and Janet at the kitchen table, swirling fingerpaint on large sheets of paper, rainy afternoon, was she baking cookies? Before the fridge—

"Tell us a story, even Red Riding Hood," Jane encouraged. "Just make it different. Don't let the grandmother get eaten by the wolf."

"But that's the point of the story!" Mirabelle stared at her – green eyes, they were – caring? Why did she wear so much make-up?

Jane looked away. Too vulnerable, Mirabelle shouldn't let herself. She cleared her throat, hardened her tone. "It's time some of these stories had a different point. For centuries now that old woman's been eaten by the wolf and silly Red Riding Hood – silly *vain* Red Riding Hood – hasn't done a thing but ask it about its teeth! I mean, anyone old enough to walk through a forest by herself should be able to distinguish a wolf from a woman! Anyway, what was a sick old woman doing out there in the woods alone? And why did

81

they need the woodcutter to save them – or her, depending on the version?''

"You are so hard, Jane.'' How can she change moods that fast? It hurts – "Fairy tales are one of the safe things in the world. They're cozy and comforting, they've gone on for generations, and they're history, they tell the way the world is. Why must you ruin it?'' Mirabelle ended on a painful bleat. *Ruin. Ruin.*

"They never comforted me. They've always scared me, the way the stepmother turns into a witch and poisons Snow White –''

"Always liked witches,'' Yvonne interrupted Jane.

"– why are stepmothers like that? And all those victims, Rapunzel, Cinderella, and the girl who had to guess Rumpelstiltskin's name – and happily ever after, that's the biggest lie of all!''

"But they all end that way, they have to!'' Mirabelle wrung her new hands. "A fairy tale has to start *Once Upon A Time In A Land Far Away* and end *They Lived Happily Ever After!*''

"That's right, get them as far away as possible, make them as unrelated to reality as possible! They're lies! They're more than lies, they're crimes!'' Jane had gone into a spate of headshaking. She moved her flippers in a motion that would have speeded her through water, but, perched on top of the computer, only created a breeze.

Yvonne mumbled, "how come they're lies? Who wants to tell us lies? What's the difference between lies and stories?'' She looked up, wishing she could see Jane's face. "Aren't you hoping for a *happily ever after* with the ocean, Jane?''

"I am not!'' Was she? "I just want to be in my proper medium!'' Didn't she? Yvonne shrugged, but Jane could not see it.

Mirabelle didn't want Jane and Yvonne to fight even if Jane was hard, even if she was difficult to convince. "All right,

I'll try to tell a story and try to give it a different ending, but I don't know if I can. I'm not very clever, not like my father.''

Both Jane and Yvonne looked at her and sighed, very loudly, very pointedly.

&

"Once upon a time in a land far away," Mirabelle grinned. "It's my story!" Yvonne and Jane laughed. Jane reached out her flipper and touched Mirabelle's hip.

"A little girl lived in a castle with her mother and father. Her grandmother lived in another castle, across a field and a river and a woods. The girl's name was Red Riding Hood–"

"I knew it would be this story!" Jane's flipper-nudged Yvonne.

"–because her grandmother had made a cape with a hood out of beautiful red satin and the girl wore it all the time. It was too small for her now, tattered and frayed, and she had to pin it at the neck because the button wouldn't reach the hole, but she still wore it everywhere over her jeans and tee-shirt."

Yvonne laughed. "There's reality, Jane!"

"One day Red Riding Hood wanted to visit her grandmother. She begged her mother to take her but her mother had to go to the bank to cash her pay cheque and her father had a meeting so Little Red Riding Hood said, 'I'll go alone. I'm big enough now.'

"Her mother thought maybe she was but wasn't exactly sure. She told Red Riding Hood to keep her eye on the smoke coming out of the castle chimney so she wouldn't get lost and said she'd pick her up after she'd gone to the bank and supermarket and collected her father from his meeting." Mirabelle's tone was becoming assured. Jane crossed her front flippers, balanced her chin on them.

"Red Riding Hood climbed down the winding stone steps, crossed the courtyard, and lowered the drawbridge all by herself. It was so heavy it bounced when it hit the ground but still she did it. Across the moat the grass was green and the birds were singing and the orchard was in bloom and bees buzzed about and two deer passed by. She smiled at them and they dipped their heads in reply. Oh, I forgot, she was riding her pony, she'd saddled it all by herself. It was a kind pony, all white except for brown splotches on its rump and nose.

"Red Riding Hood loved her pony and she also loved her doll. She had to go to her grandma's today because her grandma had made her doll a cape just like hers out of the same red satin. Red Riding Hood didn't want her grandma to make her a new cape, which she'd offered to do frequently, so she'd made one for the doll.

"Little Red Riding Hood galloped across the pasture and slowed to a trot when she came to the woods. She was scared of them. They were deep and gloomy and overgrown. Her parents kept phoning the woodcutter to clear the path but he was difficult to get hold of. She wished the path were straight enough to gallop, but it was narrow and twisty and full of roots. When she reached the deepest, scariest part she rounded a bend and came upon – a wolf! Her pony reared and tried to run back but Little Red Riding Hood held on.

"'Little girl!' the wolf yelled. 'Help me! I can't get this thorn out of my foot. See how swollen it is?' He held up his paw which was red and oozing. Red Riding Hood's fear changed into feeling sorry for him.

"'Don't you help him,' her pony said. 'It's a trick, he's going to eat you up – and me too. Let's get out of here.'

"'No he won't, he's hurt, we have to help him.'

"'We'll gallop to your grandmother's and send help. Your mother always says to do that – don't take a chance, say you'll send the police.'

"'Oh fiddle, don't be a chicken!' And with that Red Riding Hood dismounted and approached the wolf.

'"Ha Ha!' The wolf grinned. His teeth were yellow and green and cracked and broken and slavering. 'You should listen to your pony, little girl. It *is* a trick. My foot might be sore but it's not that sore! Now I *am* going to eat you up!'

'"Red Riding Hood stared as the wolf limped closer and closer, blood oozing from his paw, saliva dripping from his lips. She was so scared she could have turned into jelly right there on the path, but instead she grabbed her doll in both hands and bashed the wolf on the head. 'OW!' The wolf growled and fell over. Red Riding Hood hit him again. 'No you're not' bash 'going to eat me up' bash 'and not my pony either!' Bash. The doll was solid, unbreakable plastic.

'"Told you so,' the pony said as Red Riding Hood climbed back on.

'"Now it just happened that grandma was in bed with the woodcutter. They had arrived at a delicate point in the proceedings when they heard the drawbridge clank down and the pony clatter over the cobblestones.

'"It's my granddaughter!' Grandma pushed the woodcutter away. 'I'd forgotten she was was coming!'

'"So were we,' the woodcutter said, putting his hands to his groin in disgust. Nevertheless, he got out of bed and ducked into the closet just as the bedroom door opened.

'"Grandma, grandma, there's a wolf with a hurt paw who tried to eat us up and I bashed him with my doll but she's okay—'

'"I told her he was dangerous. I told her not to dismount.' It was a righteous pony.

'"What are you doing in bed in the afternoon? Are you sick?' Red Riding Hood asked.

'"Just a little congested, dear. I'll be all right in a while.' Grandma reached for her peach-coloured negligée. 'Why don't you go to the kitchen and see if Cook is baking? We'll worry about the wolf later. And take your pony with you!' It was also a nosy pony. When the door had closed Grandma whispered, 'coast's clear' and the woodcutter came out of the closet. Grandma had been carrying on with him for years, ever since Grandpa ran off with the scullery maid which meant Cook had to do the washing up as well.

"Shortly, Red Riding Hood appeared with a slice of cake for herself and camomile tea for her grandmother. 'Oh, I should have brought two cups,' she said, seeing the wood-cutter in bed as well. 'It must be a very catching congestion.' However, Grandma's cheeks were less flushed and her eyes looked more alert.

"Red Riding Hood went back to the kitchen for another cup of tea and more cake and they all sat on the bed eating and drinking and not worrying about the crumbs. Grandma gave Red Riding Hood the cape she'd made for the doll and a hat for the pony, also out of red satin, with attachable ear pieces for winter. The pony had complained about his ears getting cold.

"Eventually Red Riding Hood said, 'we've forgotten about the wolf. What are we going to do?'

"'Phone the Animal Shelter,' Grandma said, but Red Riding Hood shook her head. So Grandma and the woodcutter got out of bed and got dressed and the woodcutter collected his axe and chainsaw and they all went into the woods.

"When they got to the path, Red Riding Hood reached down for her grandmother's hand. The woodcutter was astounded at how overgrown the path was – what with one thing and another, he'd not been there for some time. He turned on his chainsaw, and clipped branches as he walked.

"Around the bend they came upon Red Riding Hood's mother and father crouched down with the wolf looming over them. It appeared that the wolf had them in his power and the woodcutter charged up with his chainsaw at the ready.

"'There you are!' Mrs. Red Riding Hood yelled when she saw him. 'We didn't know what had happened to you! Will you do something about this path right away?'

"The wolf was sitting quietly with his paw in Mr. Red Riding Hood's lap. The first aid kit from the car was beside them on the ground and Mrs. Red Riding Hood was taping the end of gauze around the wolf's paw.

"The wolf cringed when he saw Red Riding Hood. 'Keep her away from me! She hits!'

"'You tried to eat me up!' Red Riding Hood had hold of her doll, the reins, and her grandmother's hand. 'Why are you helping him?' she asked her parents. 'He tried to eat me up!'

"'Did you really?' Mrs. stilled her hand on the gauze.

"'I was only teasing. I wouldn't have really, my foot hurt. It's much better now,' the wolf whined, as Mrs. Red Riding Hood stood up.

"'You had better get out of here,' she said in her stern, firm tone. 'We don't want you around.'

"'That's for sure.' Red Riding Hood held her doll up. The wolf cringed again and limped off without saying 'thank you'.

"'And don't come back! If I ever see you near my family again, I'll shoot you!' Mr. shouted after him.

"They all went back to Grandma's castle for dinner. The next day the woodcutter cleared the path so well that the sun shone on it, and bluebells and bleeding hearts grew up. Red Riding Hood was no longer scared to go through it and she lived happily ever after – more or less."

&

"What do you mean you can't tell a story!" Jane declared. "That was excellent! I'm glad Grandma was having a good time."

"It wasn't as good as my father would have done."

"I liked what you kept of the original, the wolf's teeth, and Grandma in bed and Red Riding Hood thinking she was sick –" Yvonne nodded, laughing. "– I thought all the elements worked better and the heroine had her own power."

"So you lose the magic." Mirabelle heard herself sounding despondent. Tired; her hip and shoulder sockets ached. She blinked back a few tears, sniffed. "Fairy tales are supposed to be magic. And they have to be overdone, they can't be what happens day to day the way we live, three women travelling through the Interior."

"I feel guilty," she continued after a pause in which Jane and Yvonne shared a glance, "like I've done something wrong telling it differently. If we re-write the fairy tales, what's there to hang on to? What's left of the past? There's no history to stand on. I feel in a vacuum of now, no past and –" She was shivering, wrapped her spiderweb arms together. "– I don't know where we're going so there's just here and now."

"Exactly," Jane said. "There is just here and now. Just you here at this moment. Anyway, fairy tales are not history."

Yvonne frowned. "Think they are."

"They're not considered so. They're not included in the history books."

"That's different. The stories we tell shape us and history's a story." Yvonne looked at Mirabelle wrapped up in her own arms, her own pain. She offered, "for me, the *you here right now* contains all the past and the projection of the future. It's comforting knowing it's all right here with us." She laughed, a little self-consciously.

Mirabelle smiled wistfully. She wished Yvonne's trying to help her feel better worked.

Jane, staring ahead from her perch on the computer, did not see the glances. She continued, as if into a vacuum of where they were going, "it wasn't any good for you before, when you believed fairy tales the way they'd been told for generations. You lost your fingers, remember? And your arms and legs and you were losing your hair."

"Really, Jane! I think you over-analyze! That was my problem, it had nothing to do with fairy tales. Fairy tales

88

comfort me, they're a link with the past, like going to church when you're small and being given a lifesaver during a sermon you don't understand. They're being looked after by your parents or looking after your own children, they're when everything's all right –'' She started to cry. Yvonne reached out to touch her, but Jane still didn't notice. She just moved her flippers excitedly.

''I know there isn't any white knight, Mirabelle! No one's going to rescue you and parents eventually die and before they do you have to look after them! A woman has to grow up and look after herself and fairy tales don't tell her how to do that! They tell little girls to go to sleep for a hundred years until they're kissed by the prince and then they're enslaved for the rest of their lives!''

''It's called love, not enslavement! God, you're hard, Jane!''

Yvonne heard the whine in Mirabelle's voice, agreed that Jane was hard – all those plates of shell, armour, what was being protected in there? Jane was the only one not walking; *she* was pushing her, taking care of her.

''I don't think it's love when the woman's passive, when she can't choose! She might be looked after but that's what she trades for being controlled, for having no individual power!''

Mirabelle felt breathless with the conflict, but had to continue. ''You're a great one to talk, Jane, you in that giant shell! You sure you're talking to me? Not to yourself?''

''No need to get personal. I know we've all been damaged.'' Her tone did not agree with the words. Yvonne saw soap bubbles popping brightly.

''Personal is exactly what we do have to get.'' Yvonne thought she was inviting Jane, but then she felt the truth of what she'd said, wondered what it meant for herself.

Jane paused to banish a wisp of fear, continued to Mirabelle, who was wiping her face on her forearm, ''I think that after a woman is rescued she resents the rescuer—''

''You resent me?'' Yvonne interrupted.

"Of course not! I was talking about men!" Familiar anger, preferable to fear.

"And women – stepmothers and witches."

"Not true." Jane pulled in her legs, her tail. Said quickly, "I thought this was an intellectual discussion?"

Yvonne took her hands off Jane's shell. The harder she pushed the more obdurate Jane became – what was the point?

Jane looked around in surprise as the skateboard coasted to a standstill. "What are we stopping for?"

Yvonne rubbed her lower back, quite sore – was she getting her period? Rubbed her abdomen, bloated, tender. "Walk for a while. Tired of pushing you."

Jane heard her irritation, allowed them to hoist her off the computer. She studied both their faces – Mirabelle crying? What had she done wrong? She felt contrite, a little scared. "Was I going on again?" Slowly, they both nodded. Jane looked down at her flippers, had a sudden image of how her feet had been – though these flippers would have been her hands. She wiggled their tips – her old fingers. She looked up. Yvonne's face, Mirabelle's higher up. "I'm sorry." To both of them. And to Mirabelle, "I hope I didn't hurt your feelings."

Mirabelle smiled and shook her head. "It's okay. And now it's your turn to tell a story."

&

They were walking three abreast at Jane's plodding pace. Mirabelle's arms were not strong enough to push the computer on the skateboard, so Yvonne continued to do it, but the load was much lighter without Jane, and her backache eased to a dull, diffuse nag. Mirabelle waited for the spider and picked it up again. It was not tired, Yvonne was sure, and decided Mirabelle liked holding it. As long as she kept it away from her—

"Okay," Jane announced, "I've got a story. Here goes. Ready?"

"Ready," Mirabelle agreed, "but please start it properly."

Jane looked up at her slyly. "Once upon *many* times—"

"Oh Jane!" Mirabelle made a kicking motion and Jane pretended to duck. They all laughed.

"Once upon many times there was a bunch of boys who charged around the countryside looking for something magical – okay?" Yvonne and Mirabelle nodded. "Sometimes the magical thing was a grail or a bit of shroud or a begging bowl or even a bone or stone – but let's just call it a cup. Okay?" More nods.

"Now this cup had been lost for centuries and many apparently good but actually death-causing deeds had to be done before it could be won. As the telling of the tale went on over generations, the cup got larger and more valuable and be-jewelled and ornate and magical and sought. More boys charged around killing others and rescuing maidens, and they called themselves knights and warriors and kings and sirs, and they developed lances and armour and spears and eventually guns and bombs and the Cruise missile. In the process they did some good things I suppose, certainly saw a lot of country, we needn't talk about those things because they're all written down.

"Anyway, there was always a woman. She might be sitting by a stream looking young and beautiful so the knight'd fall in love with her, or she'd be weeping and wailing and tending some other hurt knight, or she'd be a hag with jagged teeth and wispy hair, all bent over. The woman was the guide or signatory for this cup so the boy would recognize her immediately whatever her form. She'd tell him how to find the cup but in some obscure way so he didn't quite understand. You got it?"

Yvonne and Mirabelle said, "yes."

"Now here's this woman sitting by a stream and along comes a knight in armour on a huge horse and she knows by his lance and shield that he's a fine fighter, and she says 'good sir, if you do such and such you'll find the cup.' The knight goes off and does such and such and gets so caught up in doing it, it takes him years to remember he's looking for the cup. In the meantime, more boys have passed by the stream and met the woman and they're all killing each other for the opportunity to find the cup and be famous.

"One day the woman says, 'to hell with this! I'll do it myself!' She goes up to the nearest bunch of knights and says, 'stop fighting and follow me. I'll show you where the cup is and we can all share it!'

"They trudge up to the magic castle or hidden hill and the woman makes the knights put down their weapons and take off their armour. They stand around in their jockey shorts feeling embarrassed and probably chilly but they follow her into the castle or cave or wherever. She tells them to sit down and they do, cross-legged on the floor.

"They watch her lift the cup off the pedastel or shelf and turn around, holding it level with her breasts. The knights gasp in awe at its beauty. Some even faint when they see it, for it is encrusted with valuable gems, has huge handles, is made of the most precious metal, and covered with unique and illegible inscriptions, every possible symbol women and men have used since time began.

"The woman looks at the knights looking at the cup and she smiles as one by one the jewels fall off. The boys in the front row reach out to grab them but they crumble like old teeth under their touch. The inscriptions blur and the handles shrivel so she must grasp its stem and layer by layer the precious metal vanishes and the cup becomes smaller and smaller, until it is the size of a soup bowl. Now they can see it is made of amber perhaps or jade, a round shape that grows warm and glows in her hands.

"The woman tilts the bowl towards them and they can see it contains liquid. As they watch, the contents increase as if the bowl were being filled by magic. The contents reach the lip of the cup and dribble over. Drops of blood hit the floor but, instead of disintegrating like the jewels, where each drop falls, a woman stands. Soon the cave is full of girls and women, some young, some old, some pale and blonde, some dark-skinned, with curly hair and straight, some with wings on their backs. And the women are dressed in costumes of different ages, from raw bearskin to purple punk.

"The first woman smiles, and sets the cup back on the shelf. She says, 'you boys made the cup more important than its contents. So now you can stop killing each other.' And to the women she says 'welcome Sisters. Your absence has been conspicuous.'"

"She can't say that!" Yvonne declared. "It's a cliché!"

"Oh well then, she says, 'welcome Sisters, we've missed you'." Yvonne smiled.

"And so they all got married and lived happily ever after," Mirabelle finished with a teasing smile.

"Not necessarily!"

"Why didn't the woman let the blood out of the cup ages ago if she knew where it was?" Mirabelle asked. "Why did she wait till now?"

Jane twisted her head as if shrugging her shoulders. "She got caught in the story herself. She liked sitting around telling the knights where to go – at least the stories told her she liked it. They were exciting stories – it's as you said, she wanted to be rescued, to live happily ever after. She wanted to believe it could work that way and so she colluded."

"So she's at fault as much as the men?"

Jane sighed. "I don't like to think that."

"You have her put the cup back on the shelf, Jane," Yvonne noted. "It can all continue the way it has."

"Hmm. So I did. Perhaps I'd better change that."

"But all those women did get out of the cup and maybe

93

they're around somewhere." Mirabelle laughed and stroked the spider. "Maybe one of them is my new Red Riding Hood!"

&

"Now it's your turn for a story, Yvonne."

"   'm –"

Jane continued, laughing. "Though I'm not sure this isn't all your story!"

"– not feeling very well," Yvonne finished in a whisper.

Mirabelle and Jane stopped and turned, instantly concerned at Yvonne's white face, drops of perspiration at her hairline. She was clutching her belly with one hand, rubbing her lower back with the other. "Can we rest for a while?"

Apprehensively, Mirabelle asked, "what's wrong? Are you sick? Do you have a fever?"

"Something you ate?" Jane offered. "The trout perhaps?"

"I ate it too, and I'm fine – so did the spider," Mirabelle stated.

Laboriously, Yvonne collapsed under a cedar tree. Mirabelle placed the spider on its legs, reached out to help her, but Yvonne wriggled until her back was against the trunk. The spider crouched down, staring with fixed eye-stalks.

"Cramps?" Mirabelle asked. Yvonne nodded, rubbing her lower belly. Mirabelle reached out again, this time to stroke Yvonne's hair. Yvonne pulled away from her webby finger-tendrils, saw Mirabelle's flash of hurt. But she could only concentrate on her increasing pain. She moved her head back and forth against the tree, realized she was panting.

" 've not been – feeling well – since we left the cabin – thought my back was – sore because of – pushing Jane, then thought – getting my period – now, if – didn't know better –" she looked at them with large eyes, gave a scared laugh, "   'd think   was in labour."

Jane and Mirabelle glanced at each other. Mirabelle bit the

inside of her cheek; Jane's face was corrugated with worry. "You don't look pregnant," Jane observed, trying to sound matter-of-fact.

Yvonne slipped down to curl up on her side. She moaned, ended it panting. " 'm not." A spasm seized her. Moaned again. "There's no" pant "way   can be."

"A miscarriage?" Mirabelle stroked the hair off her forehead.

Pant "can't" pant "be – oh!"

"I guess you are," Jane observed. "Your water's have just broken. Oh oh, it's not water."

Mirabelle's face was nearly as white as Yvonne's. "What are we going to do? We don't have any hot water, any cloths." Her voice breathless.

Jane waddled closer. "We'll manage." Hoped she sounded more confident than she felt. "You've had babies and I used to be a midwife. Remember Yvonne's teeth, one thing she has is lots of water."

Yvonne had undone her jeans; now Mirabelle helped her take them off. Jane crouched down so Yvonne had her shell for a support.

"Keep panting," Jane instructed, "until you feel like pushing."

"Different – from my – other – births – sharp, something's too sharp. Ow." Mirabelle held out her hands and Yvonne grasped them, squeezed, noticed what she was doing. They felt webby, mildly sticky, felt – okay. Blood, not amniotic fluid on her thighs.

"Oh dear." Jane tried to not feel scared, tried to remember about hemorrhages.

Yvonne made her teeth gush water to wash the blood away, shivered with fear. The spider inched closer, only a foot away now, continued to watch. Yvonne closed her eyes, and tears squeezed out. Mingled with the sweat on her cheeks, neck, fell onto her shirt. When she looked again, everything was filmed – an unfocussed lens – except for the

95

spider. Something – an expression – on its face reassured her.

Then she was drawn inside, could feel from inside her outside hands rubbing the skin on her abdomen, could feel her uterus bloated, swollen, so sensitive to pressure – felt the stretching, pulling, opening of her cervix, her vagina, felt sharpnesses against her cervix, scraping down her vagina – too dark inside to see, could only feel inside, from inside she tried to smooth the way with her hands, pushed the walls of her vagina apart to make room, protected its surface with her hands, with her arms, from the scraping of the sharp birth object, aware of rustlings, stirrings still in her uterus, used her outside hands to pluck whatever baby from her vulva.

Trembling, all of her, Mirabelle rubbing her lower back with one hand, supporting her shoulders with her arm. The solid warmth of Jane to lean on, her head turned around, her eyes soft and worried.

Mirabelle looked up, saw the softness in Jane's eyes, smiled. She'd always known it was there. Somewhere.

An uncontrolled fountain of water gushed from Yvonne's teeth, and she rinsed what she had born in its spray—

Paper. A ream of paper. Blank. White. Manuscript size. Her terror grew, and the shivers became shakes, she was still gushing water, and now inside her uterus the flutterings, the ticklings increased, and she was shaken from inside as well, the flutterings vibrated down her vagina like little burps of air, poof poof poof and exploded into tickles at the exit—

Words. All sorts of words, some large, some small, some snake-like ones that wiggled off into the grass, some fat and pink like baby angels or exotic birds. These ones flew away. Others dissolved in the fountain spray from her teeth. The air was full of words like soap bubbles or like moths, the ground was covered in wiggling, writhing words like snakes and worms, words hung from the branches overhead, nesting birds and sleeping bats.

Yvonne closed her mouth, stopped the gushing of her

96

teeth. She'd never seen so many words. She didn't know there were so many, such beautiful words, the ones clinging to the trees shimmering multi-coloured in the sun, the ones on the grass webs of light. And to think she'd had them in her all this time! Yvonne cradled her paper to her breast and, with more joy than she could remember, watched her words cavort and gallivant, meld and flow apart. They were happy to be free, she could see.

Languidly, she stretched out her hand to touch some words as they spiraled by, but they eluded her fingers. Jane snapped at words as they circled past her beak and tried to put her flipper over those wiggling on the ground. Mirabelle chased back and forth like a butterfly catcher. More urgently now, wanting to hold all that she had birthed, Yvonne stretched out the paper. But the words avoided it, avoided Jane's and Mirabelle's attempts to catch them, teasingly tormenting their new mother. Soon all the words had flown or crawled away.

Yvonne cradled the paper to her breast, sobbed, rocked back and forth, rocking the paper, rocking herself, sobbed. Sore, battered inside, she'd used too much water, felt dry, hardly enough for tears – and now, sobbing wordlessly, the bereavement of a stillbirth. She rocked the paper against her breast, as blank as she was empty inside, why had they gone away, did they not love her, she had born them all this time, had born them—

Still, a birth.

Mirabelle had her arms around her, Jane was rubbing her back. Yvonne opened her eyes, blinked the tears off her lashes, saw her blood-streaked thighs, looked up.

The spider crouched in front of her, holding something in its two front legs – a word. A very little word. Yvonne held out the paper and the spider placed the word upon it. AM. She stared at the word on the paper, felt herself smiling at it, smiled at the spider – then realized her left hand was clutched around something hard – she opened it. I lay there, thin and solid. She put it on the paper too, and held it out for the others to see. **I** and **AM**. Below them, curled like a question mark, clung a wiry, dark blonde pubic hair.

&

They rested, entwined together, for some time, looking at the two words on the paper, feeling the loss of the vanished words. Yvonne, her head propped on Jane's shell, Mirabelle's arms still wrapped around her, closed her eyes. She felt the emptiness, the soreness of her uterus, yet was still awed by giving birth. Mirabelle, holding Yvonne so tightly she wondered if their bodies had melded together, felt her own uterus contract in sympathy, and rejoiced that Yvonne was no longer rejecting her touch.

Jane could feel the heavy warmth of both against her shell; she rested her head on Yvonne's shoulder. A strand of Mirabelle's hair tickled her face and she wrinkled her nose to dislodge it. As Jane looked at the spider sitting motionless at Yvonne's feet, a wave of awe swept over her. Now she understood why the spider had followed Yvonne from the desert. "You *are* a real miracle woman, Yvonne." Jane's voice tender. "Not just magic teeth, but giving birth like that too. What was it you said earlier – something about getting personal?'"

Yvonne sighed deeply, opened her eyes, looked toward Jane. "I didn't think you'd heard me."

"Say that again!" Jane and Mirabelle in simultaneous excitement.

"I didn't think—" Yvonne held up the paper, whispered to it, "I, I, I." Her throat and mouth full of sound. She laughed through tears of joy, patted Jane's flipper, Mirabelle's arm.

"You have your **I**! You gave it to yourself," Mirabelle whispered. "Jane, you'd said it was her turn to tell a story."

"So I did. But I didn't think— What a – personal story."

98

They looked at the paper in silence. Yvonne sighed bleakly. "I don't want to sound ungrateful for **I** and **AM** and the paper, but – why didn't the other words stay too?"

Jane moved her head on Yvonne's shoulder. "I don't know."

Mirabelle gave her a comforting squeeze. "At least you know they're around somewhere. They'll come back when they need you. Children always do."

"But what about when I need them?" Yvonne felt so bereft new tears leaked out.

"Well, yes." Mirabelle stroked Yvonne's hair. "I guess you'll have to search for them. Jane and I can help."

"I can't tell stories without words." Yvonne sobbed hard.

Jane shifted her head. Her tone became less tender. "You've been managing pretty well, Yvonne. Wallpaper, fridges, operating rooms, cabins, and so on."

"I want my words! All my words! I want to tell stories in words! *My* words!"

"At least you can say that now," Jane observed. "*I* and *I want.*"

"There, there," Mirabelle patted. "We'll look for them. At least you have two. That's two more than you had before – do you think the AM refers to the spider since it found the word, or to you since you birthed it?"

"I don't know. Maybe both of us." Yvonne's tone quieted as her desperation eased. She looked at the spider who was cleaning its front legs, and closed her eyes in a momentary thank you. **I** thank you.

But Jane wasn't right about stories without words. Wallpaper – someone else's patterns. The fridges, the operating room – nothing lasted. With words she could make her own patterns, with words she could save her patterns, her pictures, for later – why had they left her?

Yvonne struggled against soreness to sit up. She saw tenderness on Jane's and Mirabelle's faces, and tried to smile. "Thank you. **I** thank you." Her eyes filled with tears again.

"Aw shucks, t'waren't nothin'!" Jane aped a vaudeville tone, crossed her eyes and stuck her lips out, then gently flicked Yvonne's leg with her flipper. Yvonne smiled, blinked away the tears, and tried to remember how happy she'd felt watching her words in motion.

Mirabelle gave her another hug, and unfolded her legs to stand up, but she'd been sitting too long. Yvonne stood up first, and held out her hand. Jane got behind and pushed. Eventually they had Mirabelle upright, wobbling toward the path. Jane smiled, thinking of an ungainly heron with arms.

When her gait was steadier, Mirabelle returned. "How are you feeling?" she asked Yvonne.

"Sore and tired and – messy. But okay." Yvonne looked at the two words on the paper, clasped it again to her breast, then passed Mirabelle the paper to hold. Yvonne washed herself, rinsed off her jeans, flapped them dry in the breeze and stepped into them. She held out her arms for the paper. Mirabelle laid it gently in them.

"Shall we away?" Yvonne invited, taking up her position behind the computer.

"Do you feel well enough?" Mirabelle inquired.

"If we go slowly." She laid the paper on top of the computer and looked around the birthing place as if to memorize it: only a spot of dampness on the needle-brown ground under the cedar tree. The words had not returned. She hoped they would be happy, sighed and pushed the computer onto the path.

Jane started to giggle. She put her flipper up to her mouth, overbalanced, and her shell crashed onto the ground. Her giggles grew into guffaws and whoops. Yvonne and Mirabelle and the spider looked at her; she seemed hysterical. "I can't help it," she laughed, "reminds me of, I have to tell you, oh it's too funny for words!" That started a fresh spate.

"Tension," Mirabelle fell into step beside Yvonne. "Births sometimes have that effect."

Jane waddled fast to catch up, still snorting and chuckling. "I'm sorry, Yvonne, don't think I'm being facetious, it's just – remember that neighbour of mine who turned into a gerbil?" Yvonne nodded. "She had a neighbour who gave birth to birds – five of them, two robins, a canary, a duck and crow. Her obstetrician fainted right over the delivery table so the nurse had to finish." Jane was laughing again.

"I knew someone who knew her!" Mirabelle shouted. "Didn't her husband sue her for breach of promise?"

"Were they," Yvonne giggled too, "breech?"

"I don't remember that, but she had to bring those birds up without any help. The crow talked back and stole things, and when they'd finally flown the coop –"

"Empty nest syndrome?"

" – she missed them so much she built a nest in a tree in her backyard and sat there waiting for them to come home."

"Did they?"

"Nope. Finally the authorities hauled her off to the mental hospital, poor woman."

"All she wanted was her children, didn't matter who they were or what they looked like." Mirabelle was nearly in tears. "I don't think it's funny at all. I bet they never went to visit her either – did they?" she asked Jane.

"I don't know." Jane wasn't laughing any more. She finished defensively, "like a lot of stories, it's only funny until you think about how the woman must have really felt."

"Yeah." Yvonne looked down at her paper.

Jane waddled closer to peer at the two words. She shook her head in amazement and raised one eyebrow. "Babies." Her tone was sardonic, but her smile tender.

Mirabelle had paused to scoop up the spider. She said to Jane, "a turtle, a gerbil, and a woman who had birds. By any chance, were you living near a zoo?"

&

"Girls! girls! Oh grrr-ulls!" The three women froze, darted looks at each other, leaned closer together. Jane pulled her

101

head halfway into her shell. Involuntarily, Yvonne and Mirabelle turned. Leaping toward them through the forest were First and Second.

"Oh no!" Mirabelle clutched the spider and looked around for escape. The path bisected a grassy, dandelioned grove; the nearest trees were metres away. She grabbed Yvonne's arm with her free hand, could feel Jane's shell pressing against her leg. Yvonne unbuttoned her vest and shirt, shoved her paper against her breasts, re-buttoned just as the men drew up. Panting and red-faced, they wiped sweat off their foreheads with the backs of their hands.

Jane had withdrawn completely. Now she realized she couldn't leave Mirabelle and Yvonne; she stuck her head out belligerently and planted her flippers. Her tail lashed back and forth as she glared at the intruders. Yvonne crossed her arms over her breasts, shifting so the paper no longer dug into her rib. The spider struggled free from Mirabelle's grasp, scrabbled across the clearing and up a fir tree. Mirabelle felt deserted. She, like Yvonne, wrapped her arms tightly around her, feeling the strain in her shoulder sockets. The three of them, all touching, formed a phalanx beside the computer and watched with stony faces as the men juggled smiles over other fast-changing expressions.

First exclaimed, "you sure got a strange pet, girls. Hey!" He nudged Second. "She's got arms and legs now! How'd you do that?" addressing Mirabelle directly.

"One of those things," she mumbled at the ground, wiggling her fingers in her armpits. Yvonne shifted closer for support.

"Get on your way now!" Jane's teeth were clenched.

The men looked at her, at each other, at Yvonne and Mirabelle who were also glaring, at each other again.

Second jammed his hands in his pockets. "Thing is, we're sorry about the other night."

"We don't care! Get going!" Jane snarled.

"Made a mistake," First continued to Yvonne, "intentions all honourable and so on, you know, heh heh." He rocked back and forth on his heels. "We ran to catch up with you. To apologize. Also—"

Second broke in, "we'd like to make it up to you. Come with you."

"Offer our services. For your protection." First flourished a mock-bow.

Yvonne, Mirabelle and Jane looked at each other, rolled their eyes, tightened their lips. Yvonne pressed her arms against her paper for reassurance, safety. "We are doing just fine by ourselves."

"The only protection we need is from you!" Jane clipped each word, lashed her tail for emphasis.

"Thing is," First said, "we really mean it." He looked at Second, who nodded. "There's things we can learn from you girls." He had a moustache.

"That's too damn bad." Spittle sprayed through Jane's teeth. "We don't want you along. And we are not *girls*!"

Second had a fringe of beard on his jawline. "It's danger-ous for you girls out here alone. We owe it to you." He pulled a ball out of his pocket, rubbed it on his shirt, twirled it between his fingers.

"We mean it. Believe us. You have to let us make it up to you for last night." First's tone was sincere, so was his expression. He grabbed Yvonne's arm for emphasis.

"Take Your Hand Off Me!" She shook free, stalked toward the trees. Mirabelle followed. So did Jane, glaring over her shell.

"Come on, let's get going! Right now!" Jane had a fierce, disgruntled frown.

At the fir tree Yvonne turned. "How far could we get before they caught up again?"

"They did apologize. We have to be kind." Mirabelle unclasped an arm, wafted it around. The spider dropped from the tree and crouched down like the black spot. She leaned over and patted it.

"We do not have to be kind, Mirabelle! They haven't been kind to us. They're not even hearing us! They only want to come so they'll feel better! And so they'll have an audience!" Jane's cheeks had bright red blotches. "I don't want them coming with us, Yvonne! Under any circumstance!"

"They might turn out to be nice," Mirabelle offered. "People can change. You have to allow them that."

"I don't give a damn! You are too softhearted for your own good – for our good! Remember your arms and legs, could be all your hair this time!" Mirabelle sighed at Jane's glare.

"Okay, Jane. You're right. We won't let them come with us." Yvonne had been watching the two men. First had one hand on Second's shoulder, was gesticulating with the other, an intense discussion. Second glanced toward them; catching Yvonne's eye, he looked quickly back to First. Yvonne's lip curled in a smile of recognition. *Girls* over here, *boys* over there – high school—

Hands in their pockets, the men sauntered across the clearing. The spider darted behind the tree trunk. Mirabelle, Jane and Yvonne drew close together again. Two metres away, Second whistled. The women jumped, but the whistle was a signal for both men to grin stagily, pull their balls out of their pockets, shuffle into a softshoe routine, and resume juggling.

In spite of her outrage, Yvonne doubled over in laughter. They didn't know how ridiculous they looked. The top edge of her paper dug into her neck. Mirabelle wondered if the men thought that nothing had changed since last night; she suddenly felt angry. Jane yelled, "You two are so boring! Don't you know how boring you are? Balls are boring!"

First and Second glanced at each other and their grins slipped, but they valiantly juggled on.

"Stop it!" Jane yelled.

Mirabelle echoed, "yeah. Stop it."

Yvonne straightened and patted her paper through her shirt. Remembering what the scene had reminded her of, she began conducting *The Blue Danube*. "Da da da da dah dada dah da," she hummed, danced toward the computer three steps, back four. "Come on, *Girls*, it's a party! I always wanted dah da da dah to float down some long curving stairs in a low cut ball gown and into the arms of *The Student Prince* da dah dah dah—"

"So did I," Mirabelle admitted.

Jane blushed. "I always wanted to be the *Sugar Plum Fairy.*"

"But the *Nutcracker* was wooden in the end." Yvonne swooped by, one hand outstretched, the other against her waist.

First and Second stopped juggling in astonished confusion. Yvonne grabbed First as she waltzed past. He shoved his balls in his pockets, reorganized her hands and they danced down the path.

Second looked at Jane. "Guess I can't expect you to dance."

"I studied ballet for eight years. I'm an excellent dancer."

"A dancing turtle?" He laughed, turned to Mirabelle. "Madam, may I have the pleasure?"

"Madam, may *I* have the pleasure?" Jane held out her front flippers to a startled Mirabelle. "*You* may experience the pleasure of wallflowerhood," she tossed to Second. With her front flippers halfway up Mirabelle's legs, Jane guided her down the path. Mirabelle looked back at Second and laughed – with a little guilt and a lot of delight. She placed her hand on Jane's head, stroked her hair.

Now the quintet slid into view like penguins on an ice slip. At the end of *The Blue Danube* Jane formally thanked Mirabelle, winked at her, and swept Yvonne away from First. He started toward Mirabelle. She had just resigned herself to politely dancing with him when she noticed the spider peering around the tree trunk. She held out her arms. It scrabbled over, placed its front two legs in her hands, and they waltzed off to *Tales From The Vienna Woods*. First stood beside Second on the grass.

The quintet shifted from Strauss into *The Skater's Waltz* and then *Some Enchanted Evening*. Yvonne danced with Mirabelle and Jane with the spider. First and Second pretended not to notice. Then Jane, Yvonne, Mirabelle, and the spider joined together and performed variations on a minuet. The penguins played on.

Just when they could dance no longer, a white-clothed table laden with crustless sandwiches, pickles, radishes, petit fours, and a champagne bucket materialized in front of the penguins.

"What a wonderful party!" Mirabelle hugged Yvonne. "It's so wonderful to dance again! My legs love it! I don't think I've ever been so happy!" She hugged Jane around the neck, and, picking up the spider, waltzed toward the table.

Jane and Yvonne grinned at each other, and followed Mirabelle. The spider jumped up and hooked all eight legs around a sausage roll. Yvonne opened the champagne.

"Not a bad spread, Yvonne." Jane crammed down an asparagus and cream cheese sandwich. "An excellent party. It takes me back to my ballet days." She was looking intently at Mirabelle. Mirabelle lowered her eyes and flushed.

"We should have had some stairs so we could have made sweeping descents." Yvonne's hand hovered over the plate of small sandwiches. "It's better in the movies – you can't smell the sweat or hear the heavy breathing. I think I'll devote myself to the staircase in *Gone With The Wind* – or splice that one into *The Student Prince*—"

"Student Princess." Jane was still looking at Mirabelle. The way her eyes were shining – Mirabelle hadn't noticed how beautiful Jane's eyes were, green with brown flecks – she reached for the bottle. "More champagne?" Yvonne and

Jane held out their glasses. "We must have lots of dances, and just for us. This is fun." Mirabelle met Jane's eyes, smiled, looked at Yvonne, then around the grove. "Where are the men?"

"Who cares?" Jane drank, held out her glass for a refill. "Now we can actually offer them some food." Mirabelle dabbed at a spill of champagne on her dress; while dabbing with one hand she could not concentrate on the other. More champagne splashed out of her glass. "Maybe something's happened to them," she persisted.

"Who cares?" Jane repeated, holding her head perfectly steady, hoping to still its sudden fizziness.

Mirabelle stared at the skateboard for some time before she registered: *empty.* "Hey! Where's the computer?"

Yvonne's mouth was full of devilled ham and avocado. She swallowed, nearly choked. "Hey!" She ran to the path, looked up and down, ran toward the trees. "Hey! You guys! Bring back our computer!"

Jane pulled into her shell, her anger building on visions of all the men who'd never listened, all the men who'd hurt her, and Ed, who'd not even noticed for two days she was a turtle— Her whole body was shaking. She stuck her head out, her face contorted and red with rage. "Goddam them! That's what you get for having anything to do with men! You get screwed!" Jane hurled her empty glass against the tree.

Mirabelle started to cry, brushed at the tears, and dropped her glass. Jane threw it against the tree as well. "They tricked us!" Mirabelle's voice was high. "They say they want to look after us and then they steal our computer! That's not fair!" The last word wailed into a high note that shattered the remaining glass. It jumped out of Yvonne's hand. One shard scratched her finger.

"Ow!" She put it in her mouth.

Jane raged, "It's all your fault, Yvonne! I *said* let's get going!"

107

"My fault? Like hell!" She glared back, still sucking her finger.

"You had to stay and have a party!"

"You were enjoying it too! It has nothing to do with the computer!"

Mirabelle draped an arm around Yvonne and looked at Jane. Her voice was teary. "Please don't fight with each other. It's bad enough we've lost our computer—" With sudden, stifling anxiety, she spread her fingers. Relief, they were all there. Yet she'd said, *go away*, she'd said, *no*, hadn't she? Jane was still glaring. Yvonne closed her eyes, sighed deeply. Maybe if she hadn't thought of a party? Maybe she'd got carried away? She unbuttoned her shirt, pulled out the paper, smoothed the corners, the two words. No, what the men had done was not her fault. "Let's not blame each other, Jane. We were too trusting – and we don't need to take it out on each other."

Jane stalked around in a circle, sighing and tsk-ing and smacking her lips. It took her two complete revolutions to see beyond her anger. "You're right. I'm sorry. I'm just so mad. We did let it happen, both times. We shouldn't have let them in the cabin in the first place. We're complete suckers, men burst in and take over and we let them – we don't even stick up for each other!"

"Not all men are mean, not all men trick, some men are nice. My father—"

"Of course all men aren't like that," Yvonne began but Jane cut her off.

"That's irrelevant. Not all men were here, just these men and they were like that. And we let ourselves be –" she paused, then yelled, "fucked!"

Mirabelle smacked her tongue on the roof of her mouth. "I wish you wouldn't use that word. I never let my children." She sighed. "What are we going to do now?"

Jane waddled over to the skateboard, flopped onto it. "We are going to get going, aren't we, Yvonne? And if we catch up with those guys we are going to kill them! Slowly, with great enjoyment, relish even, and they're going to scream and cry and plead for mercy!"

Mirabelle sighed more deeply. Her chest hurt. She looked for the spider, curled up asleep on the now empty plate of sausage rolls. She picked it up, walked over to the path. "I just want you to know all men aren't mean. I'm not a man-hater."

Mirabelle slunk along a few paces in front of Yvonne and Jane. After musing for a while, Mirabelle waited for them to catch up. "I maybe hate these men though."

&

They carried on in increasingly despondent silence. Mirabelle had draped the spider around her neck like a feather boa and she stroked it with webby fingers. Jane's head was half withdrawn, a brooding expression on her face as she rolled along in the middle, again at knee level now the computer was gone.

Tall-reaching cumulus clouds merged and parted so the light was sometimes dim, sometimes bright. Yvonne's head ached from champagne, confusion, depression. Her uterus was tender. She clutched her paper to her breast and squinted as the path before them darkened with cloud shadows, tree shadows. She wanted to sit down and rest, she wanted to sleep, she wanted a fridge – ached for one, cool white interior, comforting hum to fill her ears, time her heartbeat – looked around, but none appeared. Still, her paper was white as a fridge, as blank as enamel, gleaming in the sun. **AM. I.** And the curled hair, still clinging.

She didn't want to think about how the dancing had made her feel: old feelings of dancing free as a child, later feelings of self-consciousness, inadequacy, not knowing the steps. She didn't want to think about whether she'd created the party, or what it meant that things happened if she just thought about them – and sometimes when she wasn't thinking.

She didn't want to think if she was angry the men had stolen the computer, or how she felt about the spider, or about giving birth to paper and disappearing words. No, it wasn't that she didn't want to think, it was that she couldn't think. She didn't have words.

They'd flown away – why? Though she did have **I** and **AM** and was grateful – looked at these straight black lines on the paper, they contained – well, at least all of her—

How many words she had not looked at, did not know, could not use. A burbling, turgid swamp inside her she could not describe, define, separate, know or own because she did not have the words.

A fridge door closing to the side, her eyes pulled to it by tendrils of wanting one seconds ago – looked back to her paper. Words frozen like fridges, words she'd learned to use like mechanical appliances. Where were words that pulsated with her blood? Her words?

She could see pictures, could move into them, could let others see, but she could not paint her pictures with words so they would last. And Jane's insistence that she was creating all the things that had happened, confused her. She felt more as if all the things that had happened were creating her. Thinking about that made her feel – a burbling, turbid swamp.

In the swamp grew a cottonwood with spreading tangled roots. Its branches were full of birds, singing, chattering, calling. She could hear them, could see birds perched on branches, see the word *bird* perched on branches, *crow, robin, starling, finch,* see the words spread wings and fly away, still chattering, *word, word, word.* The leaves of the tree were words too, fluttering in the breeze, and the trunk was made of words, vertical, striated, tightly overlapping.

Yvonne ran to the tree, laid the paper at its base, shinnied up the trunk, scratching herself on the bark-words. But

110

as she got closer to the branches the word-leaves curled off their stems and fell to the ground. She climbed down to scoop up the fallen leaves, but a ground breeze swirled them. She tried to grab them as they floated past, but the words were all blown back to the branches and hung again from their stems. Flapping and rustling, the birds flew back into the tree where they chattered, mocking her attempts. Sobbing with frustration, Yvonne tore at the bark of the trunk, scraping her fingers, breaking a nail, determined to have at least one word. Both hands around a chunk, but it would not yield. The birds chattered more loudly, the leaves rustled, the branches rubbed together. She felt all the words in the world were laughing at her.

Yvonne picked up her paper – at least her two words had not flown into the tree.

Feeling sheepish now, she trudged back to the path where Jane and Mirabelle were patiently waiting. Both gave her looks of sympathy. Which she wasn't sure she wanted.

&

The stream was getting wider and more shallow. The gravel of its banks became earth then rushes and tall grass. Through the trees Yvonne saw the glint of water, wondered if it were the ocean, but could smell no seaweed. She and Mirabelle helped Jane roll the skateboard over roots and around tree trunks, and they stopped on the edge of a mountain tarn, its dark depths surrounded by granite boulders.

Their arrival stirred up ravens that swooped across the lake, wings appearing blacker against the changing light. They croaked metallically, dispersing to trees on the other side. Yvonne waited for them to change into their word; when they didn't, she wasn't sure she was relieved or disappointed. A small bridge crossed the stream above the lake. She and Mirabelle pushed Jane over it to a grassy hollow with three boulders and one tree.

Now the clouds held away from the setting sun and the

last beams recalled the warmth of day. The minute the skateboard stopped, Jane flippered down the bank and into the tarn, cruised deep into the middle, a vee-shaped ripple. Yvonne stripped off her clothes, did not glance at Mirabelle until she had her toes in the water. "Aren't you coming in?" Mirabelle held her arms out. "Will I melt? I've seen spiderwebs after a rainstorm all soggy and matted." "I can spread you to dry. I can blow on you. I can hold you in the wind." Yvonne's tone gently teasing. The spider scuttled down the rock on which Mirabelle had placed it and into the lake. It moved all eight legs together like a half-submerged water skater, turned toward them. "If it can, you can," Yvonne encouraged.

The shock of cold wore off immediately. As they swam apart from each other the water turned pink with the reflection of the sun on the clouds and then gold and back to deep steel blue in shadow. Eventually they swam together.

"This is how we met," Mirabelle said. "At a lake."

"And us." Jane turned to Yvonne. "You found us both at bodies of water. I'm sure it's highly significant."

"You would think that, Jane." Mirabelle touched the turtle's hair, all tight curls now it was wet. Mirabelle flowed with tenderness, remembered her babies' hair damp after baths, ached with a longing that collected and swelled. Her fingers wanted to stay on Jane's hair; she willed them back to her, reluctant spiderfingers.

Jane knew that look, glanced away. Mirabelle was not a turtle. Still, she felt shiftings and creakings as if every plate of her shell were moving in a different direction at once.

Yvonne saw the spider stroking near the shore. The water had slicked its hair to smooth and glistening, but its eyes stuck out on stalks, and the way its mandibles curved made her shudder. Forced herself to look at it. The spider stared back. A thin strand of gold and orange twilight joined their stares, held for seconds, and Jane and Mirabelle were silent. The ravens were silent. No breeze rubbed branches together

112

nor rustled the grass. Only a silent sunbeam marked the joining of their gaze. The clouds shifted, melded into a new formation, the beam vanished.

Yvonne realized she was cold.

They lay higher up the clearing to dry in the last of the sun, then dressed. Mirabelle wandered off, came back shortly with a skirtful of huckleberries. She spread them on a rock and they ate.

When the sun went down the full moon's silver-solid light still made sharp demarcations of shadow. The stars were close and numerous and when Yvonne stared at the smooth water, she could not tell what was tarn and what was sky. She remembered the desert cave, did not now want to trade these skies for wallpaper, said to Jane, "that seems a long time ago." Jane agreed.

The dusk-busy swallows were exchanged for bats dipping between the skies, erasing stars and bits of moonlight as they erased mosquitoes. Mirabelle looked for the spider, but it had found a crevasse in a rock and peered out from there.

No sound but the beeping of bats then, behind them and to the side, a scrunch of steps, clatter of rocks. Yvonne and Jane and Mirabelle stilled their muscles, their breathing, did not turn around, moved only their eyes to each other. The crunching continued, someone walking toward them cautiously, but with no attempt at silence. More feet kicked rocks, squished grass: two someones? A snuffling, breathing, closer and closer.

Yvonne gripped a nearby stone. Mirabelle twisted her fingers together for comfort, felt in her left hand the pressure of the right. Jane slowly retracted into her shell and the spider was motionless in its crevasse.

A snort, a snuffle, a small whinny, and again the world was pulled into its usual creakings and breathings. Yvonne stood up, looked over the rock. Mirabelle unentwined herself, stood up as well. The horse came closer, nostrils flaring for scent, daintily picking its way, planting each hoof with care yet occasionally sparking a small stone. A tall, fine-boned, white mare, dazzling in the moonlight.

Now they could see her ears pricked forward, could see her tail held upright, long hairs individual strands in the moonlight, rippling in the breeze. The mare looked at Yvonne, pricked her ears even more, extended her head. Yvonne stroked the flat smoothness of her cheek. The mare flared her nostrils and breathed a soft greeting. Yvonne inhaled her warm, moist-grassy scent and let the horse breathe her scent. Apparently satisfied, the horse rubbed her head on Yvonne's shoulder, and Yvonne stroked her neck. More soft breath on her face, large warm eyes staring directly into hers. The mare moved around until she was sideways to the rock.

"I think she wants you to ride her," Jane whispered.

Yvonne nodded, and smiled at them.

"Is it safe? A strange horse?" Mirabelle, worried. "Remember the fridges, Yvonne – and the men. Are you sure you should go?"

"This is different. It's safe." Reassuringly, she touched Mirabelle's hair, then Jane's. The mare waited by the rock.

Yvonne climbed up on it, was about to throw her leg over when Jane exclaimed, "take your clothes off first! She's naked so you must be!"

Yvonne paused in the rightness of that. The night air was mild, on the horse she would not be cold. She undressed, folded her clothes and placed them in a pile. Yvonne patted the mare's neck, grabbed a handful of mane, swung her leg over the withers. With this, Jane, Mirabelle, their journey, swimming, her paper and words, even the spider, disappeared for Yvonne. She settled herself, gripped with her thighs and knees, and the huge mare leapt away.

&

Jane and Mirabelle watched until the white of the mare

disappeared into night. Mirabelle fought panic. "What if she never comes back? What'll we do?"

"We'll manage. We'll carry on. Though she'd better come back. She promised to find me the ocean." Jane's tone a thin sheet of steel whose edges could cut. The only way she could keep her voice from trembling.

The spider scuttled up the rock, perched smudge-like on the pile of clothes.

"If it had gone too," Jane added, "we could worry. She'll be back."

"Did she take her paper?"

Jane looked at the pile. "No."

"It's the first time she's left us alone."

"Technically, we're not alone. We're together. You and I."

"You know what I mean." Irritably, anxiously, Mirabelle paced back and forth, clutching each shoulder with the opposite hand in a gesture that was becoming automatic, her arms' length and floppiness controlled.

Jane wanted to comfort Mirabelle, wanted Mirabelle to comfort her, wanted to be close to Mirabelle – if Yvonne could just leave like that— Mirabelle's steps reverberated in her shell, increasing her own anxiety, aloneness. "Come sit down."

"I can't." Back and forth, back and forth. An instant of unbearable longing tore her. "Oh – I wish we could have gone too!"

"Can just see me on a horse!"

Startled, Mirabelle could – a large turtle shell slipping and bouncing on the back of the mare. She smiled at Jane in the darkness, felt a little less tense.

Softly, Jane added, "this is the first day since I turned turtle that I wish I hadn't." Reliving the seconds of swimming close to Mirabelle in the tarn, of their dance. She sighed. She was a turtle.

Mirabelle sat down. She wanted to put her hand on Jane's hair or over her shell near her neck, but didn't. Hard to touch her right now – still worried about Yvonne. But Jane's beautiful eyes, how she'd looked at her at the dance— Mirabelle wasn't sure what a touch would mean – what she wanted it to mean. She stared straight ahead, the rock with Yvonne's pile of clothes and the spider, blackly outlined.

Mirabelle was aware of fatique all through her, throbbing in her new limbs. More had happened in this day than in any day she could remember. "Do you think we could be here without Yvonne? Would have met without Yvonne?"

No answer. Had she offended Jane? Had she gone to sleep? Glanced down. Jane had not replenished her make-up after swimming, her face soft and young and – lovable.

That instant Jane looked up, smiled. Mirabelle saw in her eyes some of what she herself was feeling so intensely. Her heart speeded up. She now reached out and touched Jane's hair, draped her arm across Jane's neck.

Jane moved closer to Mirabelle. "It took me so long to answer because I don't like to think I can't do everything, but I guess it's true. This is Yvonne's story." She laughed, looking toward the paper. "We wouldn't be here without her. She found us."

"The two of you found me, I thought."

"She pulled you out of the water. Of course, I could have done that." Wish I had.

"And the spider, not Yvonne, made me arms and legs."

"True. Although without Yvonne – but there are things we can do without Yvonne." Jane lowered her eyelids, shifted closer.

Mirabelle felt a longing, a loneliness even within this closeness with Jane, thought it was because Yvonne was missing, wanted to be closer to Jane, was scared, thought, my new Red Riding Hood wouldn't be scared, Yvonne's gone off like her on her pony – laughed, told Jane.

Jane said, "so don't you be scared. Bash your fears down with a plastic doll." They both smiled straight ahead.

"Are you ever scared?"

"No." Too quick, she knew. Scanned Mirabelle's face: tenderness, interest. "Oh well, a little bit maybe sometimes. Of being flipped onto my back. Helpless."

Mirabelle nodded. "I felt helpless without arms and legs – helpless is awful." Shuddered. When she spoke again her tone was soft and accepting. "I think you're mighty scared, Jane. That's why you have such a big shell."

"I am not!" Jane's denial whined into silence. Mirabelle waited, watching expressions shade, illuminate Jane's face. Kept her arm around her. Jane started to draw in her head, stopped – wouldn't feel Mirabelle's arm. Instead, she drew in her hind flippers, extended her front ones, flapped her tail. Could she really risk?

"All right, I get scared." Her voice, high and thin, a risk itself. "Am scared. I don't feel lovable – or loving. I'm scared of anyone getting too close – you and Yvonne, this is the closest – scared I can't do anything worthwhile except study but I – don't finish things – never finished anything – except relationships." The unintentional joke made her laugh and harden again.

"Now you know." Jane shriveled back into her shell, its interior surface too distant from her skin. She waited for Mirabelle to scorn her, hit her, flagellate her with words.

The granite boulders were stern and silent shadow humps. No stone clicked, bat swooped, breeze rustled. No small nocturnal animal passed by on business. Only the passage of the moon from one high fence of mountains to the other arranged time like a solo in a waiting concert.

Mirabelle continued stroking Jane's hair, let her fingers drift down to include her forehead, felt the difference between hair and smooth skin, tears on Jane's cheek. Wished Jane had a back, an arm to stroke, a hand to hold. "I'm scared of those things too, Jane," she whispered.

Jane found tears on her cheeks under Mirabelle's touch, glanced at her face – a beautiful face, large warm eyes – tender. Longing? Love? Whatever, it was so kind and so giving Jane's eyes wanted to shut it out – too much – but she willed them open, searched Mirabelle's face.

Mirabelle watched Jane's struggle write expressions in the moonlight. She ached to do whatever she could to ease Jane's pain. Nearly her pain, whatever it was, and apprehension flitted through her, but was banished by love. She placed her other hand on Jane's flipper and stroked it too.

Jane wanted and didn't want to say more, but found she had to, started cautiously. "I watched my father beat my mother." Looked at Mirabelle, nodding, stroking. More tears, Jane blinked. "I wanted to save her, but I couldn't, and then I found I could—"

Tears of their own accord, she couldn't stop them. The wrenching inside tore her apart, tore her from her shell, a knife between her shell and her skin – still, she had to go on. "I waited for my father – to come to my bedroom at night – or if – she was away and—"

No! I can't again! Go away! These tears different from the sobs, couldn't breathe, thick in the back of her throat, choking again, gagging, "– if I – if he – were – satisfied – he – wouldn't beat her."

Mirabelle held Jane's head on her lap while she sobbed, crooned "there, there," wanting to sob, choking, herself. Patted whatever bits of shell her hands could reach.

Still touching Jane, Mirabelle moved around to lie down so she faced her. Stretched her new arms on the ground and placed a hand on each side of Jane's face. Then, without warning, fireworks of rage exploded inside her. She wanted to kill Jane's father. Trembled with that, clasped Jane harder. Her daughter's face flashed by, her son's; the explosion left a trail of fear. She eased her grasp, stroked Jane's hair, cheeks, inching closer so Jane's head was on her shoulder while she sobbed.

Jane subsided, sniffed hard, swallowed. Her throat full of mucous, now from crying. Exhausted, how close she was to Mirabelle, breathing in her ear, been crying in her ear, her

118

shoulder probably damp. Jane swallowed again, breathed the scent of Mirabelle's hair and neck through clogged nostrils. Couldn't open her eyes, was whispering. "First time I've ever done that." Burrowed into Mirabelle's neck, felt so good, never wanted to leave, strong shoulders – but her new arms must be tired. "Different from your father, taking you on trips and telling you stories." Her tone factual, but not hard. Clearer, somehow.

"Oh, that's so awful, Jane. I wish I'd been around to help you." Mirabelle had tears in her voice, on her cheeks.

Jane nodded – surprised. Someone to help? Someone could have helped? She'd never thought of that.

Mirabelle's hair tickled. Jane lifted her head and looked at her. Tried to laugh, did manage a smile. "I wish you had been too." Mirabelle's face, such softness and such strength. "You're helping me now." She cleared her throat. It was hard to say, to acknowledge.

"And me. You help me."

"Each other." Jane put her head back on Mirabelle's shoulder, let the full weight of it rest there, and Mirabelle tilted her head over Jane's. She stroked Jane's soft, springy hair. Each time she did she could feel more through her palm, her fingertips. Now they almost tickled. Jane draped her flipper over Mirabelle's shoulder blade. They listened to each other breathe in unison.

Mirabelle's elbows pressed numbly into the ground and her shoulder sockets ached. She shifted. Jane moved her head, smiled tenderly. Mirabelle sat up and hunched her shoulders. Jane rubbed them with her flipper. The moon had rolled to the other side of the sky, looked harder, colder, and a breeze sprang up. The darkest, deepest time of night. Mirabelle's apprehension returned.

"I wish Yvonne would come back." Pushing with her arms, she wobbled to her feet and looked around. Even the spider was nearly invisible. "But she might not, you know, sometimes people don't. Sometimes they just go away or just." She blinked, pushed a new thumb and finger into the corners of her eyes, but her tears ran faster. She sat down again. Jane dragged herself close, now feeling Mirabelle's pain. Wanting to comfort.

"I knew my father was dying." Jane could barely hear her, stretched her neck out.

"He turned waxy yellow and his bones stuck out. I felt the flesh pass off him, drawn through his pores until the skin draped over each bone in his body like a piece of yellow satin thrown over a straight-backed chair. I knew that was death." Mirabelle shuddered, wiped her tears with her dress. "I didn't want it to be. I was so aching for him to stay, and then for him to come back.

"I could only walk about – to stay still was to acknowledge death – I moved my body and my house and I moved my life, and all the time I was searching for something – a button or a switch – I could press to turn time back to before the yellow satin, to change what happened. I couldn't. I can't."

The emptiness tore at her and she sobbed. Jane rubbed her leg with her flipper. "Will Yvonne return? Is she gone too?" Mirabelle's voice muffled in her arms clasping her knees, a solid back hunched over ephemeral limbs, flesh and gauzy spirit joined.

"Yvonne's not your father," Jane said softly, "she's not dead." Her eyelids squeezed out tears. The stones and grass faded out of focus. Her shell too tight, an itch near her shoulder, eczema perhaps, and tired, too tired to move. She'd sleep where she was tonight.

Mirabelle put her hand on Jane's hair, now it really did tickle her palm. She lay down, guided Jane's head until it rested on her soft breast. Jane tensed, breathed sharply, allowed Mirabelle's hand to guide her again and laid the full weight of her head upon Mirabelle's breast. The spider sat motionless upon the pile of clothes, and the moon continued through its trajectory. Jane and Mirabelle slept.

&

"Hello."

Mirabelle sat up with a start, saw Yvonne nakedly outlined against the pre-dawn sky.

"You're back!" At Mirabelle's voice, Jane lifted her head. Mirabelle struggled to stand. Suddenly breathless, she'd been so afraid. "Where'd you go? What'd you do? What was it like? Oh, I'm so glad to see you!" She threw herself at Yvonne, hugged her as tightly as her arms could, shuddering with relief. Yvonne laughed and hugged back, surprised at Mirabelle's intensity.

"Let her get dressed, Mirabelle, the air's chilly." Jane's tone was soft, but she was poised on the edges of her flippers. She hadn't really doubted that Yvonne would return, still, she was extremely relieved to see her.

Yvonne felt her inner thighs, brushed at them, walked to the water. "I'm filthy," she laughed. "I doubt that horse has ever been groomed." She waded knee-deep and, shivering, washed her legs and hands, turned, dripping. All her motions were slow and careful and calm. Her tone, and even her little laugh, were calm.

Mirabelle sat down again beside Jane, grinned at her, and reached out for her ha – flipper. Couldn't take her eyes off Yvonne. Her feelings moved between ecstasy and awe: she really had come back.

Together they watched Yvonne wash, walk up the hill and dress. They felt calm as well, and drew closer to each other. Jane wondered if she were envious of Yvonne, felt Mirabelle's weight against her, decided she was not. Yvonne's smile however, had something mysterious about it. Jane thought of Madonna's smiles in Renaissance piètas.

When Yvonne had picked up her paper, cradled it like a missed child, and sat beside them, Mirabelle again asked, "where did you go? What did you do? What was it like?"

"We didn't go anywhere in particular, just galloped around. It was glorious." She hugged her paper. Too bad it was over. Too bad the mare had left – would she find her again?

"I didn't know you could ride," Jane was saying.

"I haven't been on a horse in years. Didn't matter though, she was so smooth – but I bet I'll be stiff tomorrow."

Mirabelle and Jane looked at each other. They had both heard her wistfulness, longing. "Come on, Yvonne, tell us what happened."

"I told you. We just galloped about." She frowned in the darkness, felt irritability nagging her – how could she put all those feelings into words?

"You were gone for hours, Yvonne! You can't tell us that a huge mare materializes out of nowhere and you climb on her naked and go thundering off and nothing happens! Something had to happen!"

"What do you mean? What is it you want to have happened?" Yvonne's calmness dissipating in the tense frustration all were beginning to share.

"You must have gone to an enchanted land," Mirabelle prompted, "seen castles and princes and so on. You must have been sent to rescue someone or get wisdom from a witch."

"Naked? You think I'd rescue anyone naked?"

Jane had another thought. "Don't you want to tell us?"

"Sure, but there isn't anything to tell – that I can tell."

Reassured, Jane wanted to help Yvonne, wanted to include her in the closeness of sharing that still lingered between her and Mirabelle. "That mare galloped straight out of some myth – I can't think which one just now – and she came for you. She even waited while you got ready. That's why I told you to take off your clothes, so nothing of this world would impede you."

Yvonne's calm was completely shattered. Could feel her face flushing. Her voice shook. "Oh good grief! I don't know which of you has the wilder imagination!" She glared at Jane and Mirabelle, who exchanged glances, and drew closer together. Jane's flipper stirred under Mirabelle's hand. Yvonne felt suddenly as if she had to defend herself, prove Jane wrong.

"She was just a wild mare, they're thousands of them in these mountains – perhaps she was originally domesticated but she got away. It was strange she wanted me to ride her, but she might have been lonely. It has been known for horses to miss humans. And she stopped when she wanted to and let me off – over there. She's probably back with the herd now. And nothing magical happened – except the magic of galloping through the moonlight on a white mare, she was so sure-footed. You were right, Jane, to tell me to undress, it was wonderful, nothing between her skin and mine – like swimming naked when you've always worn a bathing suit. But no castles, no strange lands, no visions, nothing but the sound of her hoofs and the feel of her between my thighs and the magic of the wind whipping through my hair and the scent of horse – now that's very prosaic!"

Jane was frowning at her in the darkness.

"Don't you believe me?"

"Actually, no."

"No," Mirabelle echoed.

"You are the woman who lived in the fridge. You had a giant spider attach itself to you. You have been chased by fridges and a geologic fault, you found a cabin run by a computer –"

"We all found it!"

"– with a chamber orchestra of penguins, and you accelerated time in the orchard, remember? So when you try to tell us that this most magic-looking thing is prosaic," Jane shook her head. "Everyone knows about horses who gallop away with maidens!"

Yvonne sneered. "Maiden?"

"Oh well," Jane moderated her tone in response to

Yvonne's desperation, but she could not leave her point unfinished. "I don't believe that when a most magic looking thing happens you can say it was ordinary. If nothing happened it's because you weren't ready for it."

"That's possible," Mirabelle offered tentatively. She didn't want Yvonne to feel blamed. "Maybe you didn't say the right words or do the right ritual – like walking through a fairy grove and not seeing the brownie you nearly step on."

"That's to be spelled f-a-e-r-y, Yvonne," Jane added, then instantly regretted it. But why couldn't she admit what – to her – was so obvious? It had to have been a magic experience.

Yvonne sprang up, her paper tight in her arms. "You two make me so mad! Why won't you believe me?" Nearly crying in frustration. "Isn't it enough it was magic as it was? It's glorious to gallop around in the back of beyond on a mare who wants to be ridden, and that I did it naked! I've never felt so free! Isn't that enough? Why do you need it to be more than that? You know," she whirled around, "I think you're both jealous the mare came for me!"

"Nonsense," Jane declared.

"I can just see me riding a horse with these limbs." Mirabelle wafted her left arm delicately.

"No, no, we're very glad you had the opportunity. It's just that in view of your recent history, our credulity is strained by statements of normalcy."

"Not that it's very normal to be approached by a wild mare that wants to be ridden. And that's what I'm saying. It's enough as it is."

A delighted grin stretched Jane's face. "Over-stating! She means over-stating, Mirabelle! It'd be too much if she added more detail, get it?"

"Hell and damn, I did not make that horse appear! I just rode her! You want a goddess, Jane, and you want a queen, Mirabelle. Yes, I decorated the fridge when I was in it, but after I got out all these things have just been happening!"

124

"Ah, the art has overtaken the artist." Jane nodded psuedo-sagely.

"You are really making me mad." Yvonne's voice thick with tears. "I wish I'd never come back."

"Oh no, Yvonne!" Mirabelle struggled up, and grabbed her tightly. "That would be awful! We need you, we want you! We're sorry. We believe you." Hanging on as if she'd never let go. Yvonne felt suffocated. "Shh, Jane, be quiet. It doesn't matter, Yvonne. Whether you're doing this or not, we're happy to be along, aren't we, Jane?"

"Yes."

"And we're glad you had a midnight ride. You can make anything happen you want, we trust you, don't we, Jane?"

"Yes. And I'm sorry if I went too far, Yvonne."

Mirabelle still gripped and patted, trying to soften a stiff Yvonne. "After all, you gave me new arms and legs."

Yvonne breathed out through clenched teeth. "No I didn't, Mirabelle. It was the spider, remember?"

"Oh – that's right, dear," Mirabelle said quickly. "It was the spider."

&

They were so tired they slept until late the next day or the day after. Whenever it was they awakened, Yvonne's watch read four o'clock, but the sun seemed too high overhead and so she set it to one.

In spite of their sleep they were all subdued. The path continued across the rock-strewn plateau and around the base of a mountain. On the other side was another deep tarn which narrowed the path between it and a mountain slope.

Yvonne walked silently, apart from the others. She was not angry, she was hurt they hadn't believed her. She felt alone. Something seemed to have changed between the three of them – as if Jane and Mirabelle shared a bond that excluded her. But she was not displeased to be alone. She pensively held her paper and thought about her words. Mirabelle and Jane exchanged anxious glances as they tried to assess her mood. Jane felt guilty and remorseful, perhaps she'd been too hard on Yvonne. She also wondered if she should have said as much as she had to Mirabelle, although Mirabelle was walking close beside her, and her expression, while concerned, appeared loving. Still, Jane felt very naked, inspite of having taken extra care with her make-up.

Mirabelle didn't know who to worry about – Yvonne or Jane – and wished one of them would speak. She couldn't think of anything to say herself. Besides, these mountains were beginning to look familiar. Hadn't she and Martin and the children been here? Jane had drawn her head into her shell so she could only see her face – what a lot of make-up. Yvonne looked as if she had the weight of the world on her shoulders – an intense frown strained her lips.

Mirabelle sighed and dropped behind to pick up the spider. It settled comfortably in her arms. She could feel its hair tickle her hand, its leg tickle her arm – remembered the feel of Jane's hair last night, had a rush of excitement, anxiety. Sighing again, she bent her head over the spider.

The path wound down between two mountains, and thin pine trees grew more closely together. Gradually it widened, became smoother, then suddenly the skateboard wheels bumped on the edge of pavement. Jane nearly fell off the front. Hoisting herself up, she pulled it over the ridge, plopped back on. Minutes later, a yellow line appeared down the middle. The path had become a road.

Once on the macadam the skateboard skooted faster, but now cars whizzed by and they had to move over to the very edge. Motorists stared at two women, a spider and a giant turtle on wheels. Some laughed and pointed; some honked. One cruised so near that its wheel brushed Jane's flipper. "Hey!" she shouted, feeling even more naked under these stares. She pulled herself into her shell until her flipper-tips strained to reach the pavement.

126

Yvonne and Mirabelle drew closer to her. All three looked at each other, looked at the traffic. "This is awful! Can't we find another way?" Mirabelle asked.

Yvonne examined the trees on each side, the path and mountains behind them. "There's nothing but where we've been and this road going on."

"We could go through the forest," Jane suggested. But even she, this low down, could see there were no gaps between the trees.

"We need Little Red Riding Hood's woodcutter." That just popped out; Mirabelle felt silly. But Yvonne and Jane grinned, including each other as well as her.

Another car slowed, its passengers staring and laughing. It accelerated and they coughed in the exhaust fumes. "If we had some money," Jane muttered, her eyes smarting, "we could buy a truck. Create us some money, Yvonne. Make us a money tree over there. You can do it, governments make money out of nothing all the time, deficit financing." She winked at Yvonne's glare.

Jane rolled along on the paved shoulder, Mirabelle and Yvonne walking on the gravel beside her. All three were again united and, in spite of the stares and honks, they felt better.

Then Mirabelle started lagging behind. Yvonne asked, "getting tired?"

"Oh no." Mirabelle smiled, but her expression was abstracted and worried. She hurried to catch up, but, minutes later, was falling behind again.

"What's wrong?"

"Nothing." She sighed. "Oh well, my house is just over there. I think I should go home. I really miss my family."

"Leave us?" Pangs of shock stopped Jane abruptly. "How can you leave us? We haven't finished our journey!"

"Maybe I have," Mirabelle answered sadly. "I have arms and legs now – thanks to the spider," she added to Yvonne. "My family needs me." She couldn't look at Jane.

Yvonne saw Mirabelle's desolation, Jane's anguish. She was

not feeling anything herself – maybe it was convenient to not have words. She raised including eyebrows at Jane. "How about if we come with you to see them?"

"Sure, you go along – check out her fridge. If it's big enough you can stay too, I can continue by myself, can't be very far to the ocean now." Jane didn't like pouting, but the alternatives were rage or tears. At that moment, she hated Mirabelle for even thinking she could leave – her. She paddled the skateboard off with dignity.

Yvonne watched her roll away, turned back to Mirabelle, felt torn. Yet she understood Mirabelle's longing. An image of John and Janet curled up eating popcorn she'd just made. Felt her own longing, the loneliness she'd felt on the path back there, looked back there.

Yvonne hurried to catch up. Jane's face was tight and drawn and anguished. Tear tracks carved mascara paths down her cheeks. "If we go to Mirabelle's house, we won't be separated," Yvonne whispered. "It's something she has to do, doesn't mean she wants to leave us."

Jane smacked her tongue disbelievingly. "Oh sure." But she ducked inside to remove the tears before Mirabelle caught up.

Mirabelle said apologetically to the headless shell, "I'm sorry, Jane. It's something I have to do – it's my duty. Besides, I miss them."

Jane's head reappeared, make-up restored. She smiled tightly, used her academic tone. "It's fine, Mirabelle. Excuse my little display." Yvonne did not believe her, watched confusion pass over Mirabelle's face.

But Mirabelle could not linger on that. The mountains here, this road, familiar. She had to get home.

"We used to go up in the hills to collect wildflowers this time of year, Martin loves pressing wildflowers, he's an amateur botanist." Yvonne felt an ache at the wistfulness in her face, her tone. "It was so wonderful, the children running around playing tag, Martin bent over looking for new species, and I set out the food. We always had chicken and potato salad and coleslaw and croissants and pecan pie, never just sandwiches, we were so happy, all of us." Mirabelle's voice trailed off in a smile of memory. She lifted the spider from her shoulders and set it on the ground. Jane felt very hungry, thought it was for food.

The road curved into a crescent with curbs and sidewalks. A large sign announced: *Happy Valley Subdivision, Quality Single Family Dwellings For The Discerning Buyer.* Fifteen houses, either split level, bungalow or two storey, were equally spaced from the sidewalk and each other. Each house had a garage with double doors dominating the front, and a spreading juniper under the living room window.

Mirabelle grinned at Yvonne and Jane. They'd bought the house when the subdivision was new, hadn't had much money then, Dick a toddler. She'd been pregnant with Sally, so Martin did the painting to save five hundred dollars. Amazing how the cherry tree had grown, could see it over the roof now – she'd planted it the second spring. Sally? Dick? She buzzed with anxiety – had she been away too long?

Jane's morass of feelings that she'd tried to cover up, even to herself, scummed into depression. How could Mirabelle live in a subdivision? Want to go back? Be, right now, radiating excitement? Jane hated subdivisions. When she was studying Social Planning, after Midwifery, but before Theology, she'd written a paper on subdivisions, called *The Dead End Street: A Metaphor For The Nuclear Family.* She felt not just abandoned by Mirabelle, but also betrayed.

Yvonne realized she wished they were going to her house. But it didn't exist – it was sand. Wasn't it? Should she be going back? Could she – across that desert? What had happened to Martin and Janet and John? Mirabelle's longing became hers.

"Oh look what they've done! Aren't they wonderful? And there they are!" Mirabelle grabbed Yvonne's arm and pointed. Halfway down the right side of the street a banner swung from the eaves of a bungalow: *Welcome Home, Mum!* in large black letters. Under it on the front stoop sat a man, a boy, and a girl. The girl had an orange cat on her lap, and the man's left arm draped the neck of a collie.

Mirabelle quickened her pace. "Hello!" she yelled. "I'm back! There they are, see?" she added unnecessarily to Yvonne and Jane. "Spot and Puff are there too, see? Hello!" She stumbled into a run, her arms flailing awkwardly at her sides.

Spot wagged his tail and barked welcomingly at the sound of her voice. Martin, Dick and Sally stood up, shaded their eyes with their hands. Past the Smiths' house, the Wongs', across the LeBlancs' grass – Spot clamped his tail down, backed behind Martin, and resumed barking – now ferociously.

"Spot! Don't you know me?"

"Shut up," Martin said to him, but half-heartedly. Spot whined and slunk around the corner of the house, his tail still clamped tightly for protection.

"What's wrong with him?" Mirabelle asked, but didn't spare much attention. So wonderful to see her family. She beamed and rushed over, such a relief. They all looked fine – though Dick and Sally were taller than she remembered and Sally had had her hair cut – had Martin put on weight? She held her arms out, not knowing whom to hug first.

Martin and Dick were staring at her, their auburn hair, freckled faces so much the same. Sally more like her. She shrank back, her eyes large with horror. "Where'd you get those gross arms?" Her voice quivered in disgust.

Mirabelle's smiled wobbled. Weren't they pleased to see her? "From the spider." She turned to acknowledge it, to introduce Yvonne and Jane. "Puff! No!"

The cat crouched in pounce position three feet away from the spider, his ears flattened against his head, his tail tip twitching. He wriggled his hindquarters menacingly.

The spider poised on the tips of all eight legs, preparing

to jump. Its hair bristled as did Puff's fur, doubling both their normal sizes. The spider's eyes were fixed on the cat's.

Mirabelle bobbled and stumbled across the grass, scooped up the spider and held it over her head. Sally tried to collect Puff, but the cat spat and pushed off with his hind legs. He missed the spider, landed on Mirabelle's chest and clawed at her dress to hang on. The spider twisted in Mirabelle's hands. Its legs flailed the air. She lost her balance under the combined wriggling weight and stumbled backwards until she tripped over the flowerbed and sat down. Hard. The spider leapt out of her hands and turned to face Puff, but Sally managed to grab him and hold on. She ran to the house, shoved the cat inside and banged the door closed. The spider galloped across the yard and up the drainpipe, up the roof and up the chimney where it perched on the edge like a blob of soot.

"Are you all right?" Jane paddled closer, but the skateboard wheels stuck in the grass. Yvonne ran over to Mirabelle, held out a hand to help her up. Martin and Dick had not moved.

"I guess so. Thanks." Mirabelle brushed the back of her dress, pushed at her hair. Her hand left a smudge of dirt on her cheek. She felt desperate. If her family weren't glad to see her –? Brushing the front of her dress, she crossed back to Martin and Dick. Sally came down the stairs.

"Some homecoming," Jane whispered to Yvonne.

&

"These are my friends," Mirabelle introduced, "Jane and Yvonne. This is Martin, and Sally, and Dick." She felt hurt and angry, then embarrassed as she watched her children turn to Martin for direction. "Where are your manners? Say hello to my friends," she whispered to Sally and Dick.

With that, Mirabelle glanced back at Jane – and saw her as her family must – a huge green turtle with red hair –

131

remembered how peculiar she'd first thought Jane. And the spider. Yvonne at least looked normal. Was she asking too much, that they be polite? No, she wasn't. Then Mirabelle flushed – did she look as peculiar to her family with her new arms and legs as Jane did? If so, she couldn't expect them not to be disgusted, could she?

Yvonne felt Mirabelle's confusion and, smiling, quickly held out her hand to Martin. "How do you do?" He shook it.

She passed it to Sally, to Dick. They both shook it. Sally echoed, "how do you do?" Dick pulled his ear and scuffed his toe on the grass. Addressing it, he mumbled, "hello."

Jane decided to be included. "Hello! I'm so pleased to meet you. I've heard a lot about you." She used her warmest, most gracious tone, the one she kept for cocktail parties and new department heads.

"You talk!" Dick stared at her directly, disbelievingly.

"I certainly do – quite a lot, your mother thinks." She smiled reassuringly at Mirabelle, was rewarded with a flicker of gratitude.

"Does the spider talk too?" Dick asked. From under long lashes, he peeked at his mother.

An engaging boy, Jane thought, that adolescent gangliness, he'll have Mirabelle's height. Sally has her eyes, looks as confused as her mother – nothing for it, Jane decided, but to carry on. Though she wasn't sure about Martin, still, she'd probably been to more cocktail parties than all of them together.

Jane laughed. "No, no, not the spider. It's definitely the silent majority – of our group, that is."

Everyone except Martin turned to look up at the chimney. The spider still there. Martin had his eyes full with Jane, Yvonne clutching a considerable amount of bent-cornered paper, and his wife.

"You've got dirt on your face." Martin pulled out his handkerchief. "Let me." Mirabelle held still, smiling, as he dabbed at it. Relief pushed away her desperation. She kissed him on the cheek. He didn't kiss her back, but tentatively patted her shoulder, looking over it at Jane and Yvonne.

Yvonne was relieved he didn't look like her Martin, surprised to realize she'd half-expected that. Her Martin was thin and wiry, with dark hair and a moustache. She wished for Mirabelle's sake this Martin was more welcoming – though at least he'd finally said something – would her Martin welcome her? Still, families were families and children, children – an intense longing for hers tore her. Then she heard John's voice: aw Mum, you're crazy – was that what Sally was thinking about Mirabelle?

"How are you kids? How's school?" Mirabelle looked at Dick and reached out to stroke Sally's hair, but Sally shrank from the grey-pink finger tendrils.

"It's summer holidays." Her tone left no doubt she thought her mother cretin-brained. She patted her own hair – either straightening what Mirabelle had intended to muss or continuing her mother's gesture for herself. She looked at her distrustfully. "How come you don't know that?"

Mirabelle battled down hurt and let surprise keep her tone light. "Is it? I could have sworn it was still spring. We must have lost track of time. Don't you," she looked at Yvonne and Jane, "think it's still spring?"

They were equally surprised. Jane said, consideringly, "late spring."

Yvonne looked at her watch. "Yes, indeed. I'd have it spring myself."

"It's really August twenty-third." Martin had to clear his throat. Mirabelle glanced apprehensively at the accusing spots of red on his cheeks. His eyes glittered as well.

"August twenty-third," Yvonne repeated ruminatively. Her watch said the fifteenth. Of something. She pulled out the stem to set it to Martin's date, then pushed it back in. Who knew about *really*? The fifteenth was fine. And if today weren't the fifteenth, some day soon would be.

Mirabelle turned to Sally and Dick. "You must think I've

133

been gone a long time!"

"You have," they accused simultaneously.

Dick came closer. "I miss your egg sandwiches – Dad won't make them right."

Sally said, "I worried about you. I was going to help you." She sounded very grown up – and very young.

Mirabelle smiled in great relief – they weren't too disgusted, they didn't hate her – and put an arm around each of them. Sally started to pull away, then relented. She rested against her mother. Mirabelle leaned her head on Sally's.

Martin snapped, "you left in the middle of April!"

A knife flew through the air, then another and another, jack knives and pen knives, sabres, épees, kitchen knives of every sort, a Swiss army knife, a pair of scissors, and a thin serrated Oriental saw. Jane screamed and pulled herself into her shell.

"Duck!" Yvonne shouted, hunching her shoulders. The scissors cut through the air toward her paper. Remembering the childhood game, Yvonne made a fist, shook it four times, and the scissors fell to the ground. But the game did nothing with knives.

"Into the house! Quick!" Mirabelle grabbed Sally's and Dick's hands and stumbled up the steps, Martin right behind them. Yvonne glanced at Jane's shell perched on the skateboard. Deciding she was well protected, Yvonne followed the family.

But the knives flowed in the door and windows and through the walls as if the house were made of cards. They pulled out the couch and crouched behind it, their backs to the mirrored tile wall. Mirabelle had time for one glance at Yvonne across the children's heads, was reassured about Jane. The knives zoomed in like guided missiles and buried themselves in the stuffing of the couch. Some scraped against the springs with the sound of fingernails on a chalkboard.

When it was quiet again, Martin stood up cautiously. "What was all that?"

134

Yvonne stood up as well. Her paper unharmed. "I think it was you." He gave her a disgruntled, disbelieving frown. Mirabelle, Sally, and Dick emerged, shaking. Sally clung to her mother. Dick looked from her to his father to the knives, out the window. "I'll check if the turtle's okay." He escaped.

Mirabelle hugged Sally and watched the knives shiver in the couch to the door's reverberation. She agreed that the knives' were Martin's doing, but didn't want to; she almost wanted them to be Yvonne's.

The knives cut Martin's silence. He slammed the couch back into place. One knife clattered to the floor. Sally smothered a shriek in Mirabelle's neck. Martin looked at his daughter as if he'd forgotten she was there and controlled himself. His now pale face emphasized each freckle, but his eyes still glittered. Arms akimbo, he planted his feet apart in a firm stance. "Okay, Mirabelle, what's going on? Where did you get those arms and legs?"

"The spider spun them for me."

"A spider spun them? Uh huh. Tell me another one."

"I can't. That's the only one." His contemptuous sarcasm always scared her. She moved Sally's head to her other side so her daughter wouldn't hear her fast-beating heart.

"Some arms and legs! They're a ridiculous colour, and you can't even control them! They're much too long! You're right about one thing, they're spidery!"

She would not cry. If she looked at Yvonne she might scream. She stared at Martin in silence. How dare he ricicule what the spider had spun!

"But Mum," Sally's voice was muffled. She raised her head. "We were going to look after you, right Dad?"

Martin heard Sally's pleading tone. Pleas always chastened him and gave him a focus. Shoving his hands in his pockets, he began pacing. "Right. I'm going to look after you. I've got a wheelchair, a bed that goes up and down, I've made a ramp to the back door, and I've even applied for your disability pension!''

Mirabelle frowned at him in confusion. She gave Sally a squeeze, backed to a chair, and sat down. Yvonne perched gingerly on the arm of the couch. This was a familiar Martin pacing back and forth, so was the sarcastic one. Why was she confused?

''We were going to get you artifical arms and legs,'' Sally added, ''they look like real ones. What are they called, Dad? Prosthetics? And I was going to help you put them on.'' She pouted the last in disappointed importance.

Mirabelle placed both hands on the arms of the chair, crossed her right leg over her left. Celebrating the pressure on her left knee, the fabric under her palms, she smiled at her husband and daughter. ''Isn't it wonderful you don't have to do that now? Isn't it wonderful the spider did it instead? These ones I can feel, look at the blood in them – that's my blood – that's what makes them sort of pink! I'll never give these ones away!'' Yvonne wanted to yell, rejoice with her, please! She clamped her lips together.

Martin stopped in front of Mirabelle, pulled his hands from his pockets and held them out, fingers downspread. ''But what am I going to do? I want to look after you!''

''I'm sorry to disappoint you, dear.'' Puzzled, Mirabelle frowned. How was she such a disappointment?

''Yeah, I mean,'' Sally broke in desperately, ''you don't even look like my mum any more!''

''You don't sound the same. There's a different tone to your voice.'' Martin ran his hands through his hair. ''Are you sure you're you? You haven't gone crazy because of her –'' he jerked his head toward Yvonne, ''– and a turtle? Carrying a huge spider, of all things!''

He paced to the fireplace, shoved his hands in his pockets again, turned back, said reasonably, ''have a nice hot bath and a good sleep and we'll talk about it in the morning. I'll bring you hot chocolate in bed.''

Out of confusion, defeat. ''I thought you'd be pleased I

had arms and legs again.'' Mirabelle knew she had tears in her voice, in her eyes, hated them, but she wasn't very strong, was she? She did need looking after, didn't she? Martin made very good hot chocolate.

"Of course I'm pleased." He held his palms up and out, moved them back and forth, erasing motions.

"Sure." Sally started to nod in concurrence, but her head shook back and forth in denial.

Not pleased. They were not pleased. It was a revelation. Mirabelle looked at Yvonne, clutching her paper to her breasts, her lips tightly clamped as if she were keeping her words to herself. Mirabelle remembered Yvonne giving birth, being close with Jane in the night, remembered the skateboard, no arms, no legs – First and Second, the feel of the spider in her arms, telling the new Red Riding Hood story—

"I am more me than I've ever been,'' Mirabelle announced, "and I don't just mean arms and legs. I don't have to depend on anyone else to blow my nose, to –'' She gathered strength, this one was for Jane, "– to wipe my ass!'' Martin and Sally gasped; Yvonne bit her cheeks to keep from smiling. "I thought you'd be pleased not to have to look after me, what a drag!"

"Not a drag. I want to do it. I'm good at it." Now he was pleading.

"I want to look after myself." Mirabelle paused, hearing that. A truth. Her truth. She'd never said it before. She looked at Martin. "I need to look after myself. And if I can't do it here—"

"You didn't do a very good job the first time."

His truth about her? She looked into his eyes: sadness, hurt, rage, somewhere love?

"No, I didn't. I looked after everyone else, as you are." His hand made a dismissing motion. "I'm going to do a better job this time. It's not everyone who gets a second chance—"

"Takes." They all turned to Yvonne, serious and intent.

"Takes a second chance. Or takes a chance, period. Maybe chances are like that, unexpected gifts."

"Maybe." But the possibility of agreement was cancelled by a sneer around Martin's mouth. "What about you, anyway? Do you have a family? What are they doing?"

Yvonne's wince scored triumph for him. He turned back to Mirabelle. "What about your family? And the wheelchair and prosthetics and disability pension, they're all tax deductible. Not that that matters, of course. But what about us?"

"I don't know. I thought you'd be glad to see me whole again. If you're not—" She looked at Yvonne.

"I'm pleased to see you, Mum. I'm glad you're all right, it's just that you're different. Why don't you do as Dad said, have a bath and go to bed. We'll get used to you."

Mirabelle put her hands to her face. Her shoulders shook. Yvonne crossed to her and put her arms around her. She leaned against Yvonne's breast, trying to stifle her sobs. A great pain tore at her. If they wouldn't let her look after herself, she couldn't help to look after them. She'd disintegrate again, have to stay in bed forever.

"Oh Christ!" Martin actually tore his hair. Tears were the ultimate plea. "I'm sorry, Mirabelle, of course we want you home, it's just a shock, you must admit. I suppose I can get a refund on the wheelchair." He sounded dubious.

Mirabelle sighed deeply, looked up and Yvonne backed away. "It's no good, Martin. I'd forgotten how you need to look after me. But it's the wrong sort of looking after. I'm sorry I didn't pay attention to how I'd upset you. But I'd better continue with Yvonne and Jane."

"Oh no, don't leave, Mum!" Sally hugged her, buried her face in her chest. "Just tell us how you want to be looked after!"

Mirabelle patted her back and stroked her hair. Sally glanced up with teary eyes, buried her face again. Mirabelle expanded with love and sadness. As soon as she could, she'd help Sally, and Dick. She whispered into Sally's hair, "the way to help me is to let me learn how to look after myself. That's what you can do – it's just for a while. I'll be back."

Dick opened the front door, yelled importantly, "Mum? Jane wants you and Yvonne to come out! She's too big to fit in our house." Dick saw Sally's back, and his mother's tears. "What's wrong?"

"Mum's leaving again," Sally mumbled. She sat up, brushed her face.

Mirabelle lifted herself from the chair, floated across to Dick, put her arms around him. "Just for a while, honey, and not until I show you how I make egg sandwiches."

Mirabelle and Dick emerged first, then Yvonne and Sally. Martin trailed out last. Jane was planted expectantly at the foot of the stairs. "Do you know what they have? Our computer!" She added, directly to Mirabelle, anxiously searching her face, "I hope I'm not disturbing you?"

Mirabelle still had her arm around Dick. She smiled at Jane, shook her head. "Your timing's fine."

Jane grinned, shivering inside her shell with joy. In spite of Mirabelle's red and swollen eyes, tears still on her cheeks, Jane's apprehensions vanished. Mirabelle was looking at her as she had in the night.

Dick turned to his dad. "She has my skateboard, but I said she could keep it since you got me a new one." Mirabelle smiled. Jane had apparently made a friend for life. "And that computer you found is hers!"

"Computer?" Martin pinched his lips, ran his fingers through his hair, smoothed it with his palms. "What makes you think so, Son?"

"Because of the way you found it!" He punched at the air in delighted excitement at having solved a mystery.

"Could be anyone's. There are lots of computers. What kind was yours?" Martin rubbed his hands together briskly and looked from Jane to Yvonne.

Dick frowned. "It's hers, Dad! She says two guys stole it. Those guys who ditched it when you offered them a ride, and they took off into the bush, remember? – well, they're thieves! That makes us – ?'' he turned to Jane.

''Receivers of stolen property.''

''Yeah,'' Dick finished.

''Could be coincidence.''

''Oh, Dad!'' Mirabelle could almost feel Dick's frustration. Sally came to her brother's support. ''Maybe Dick's right, Dad. Anyway, what difference does it make?''

''There's no proof. Possession is nine-tenths of the law. I checked this computer over and cleaned it, hooked it up. We've been enjoying it.'' His children stared at him. Yvonne and Jane stared at him. His wife was staring from their children to him. ''Oh, what the hell. You might be right. Take it.'' Martin spun around, stomped back into the house.

Yvonne and Sally loaded the computer on the skateboard while Mirabelle took Dick to the kitchen and showed him how much dill and paprika she put in egg sandwiches.

Outside again, Mirabelle hugged Sally and Dick. Martin came onto the porch, but did not descend the steps. He crossed his arms. Jane thought he looked like a guard at the castle gate.

Yvonne requested of Dick and Sally, ''would you please phone 567-1234 and speak to my children? Their names are John and Janet. Tell them you've seen me, that I'm all right. Tell them I love them and miss them.'' She blinked back tears. ''Tell them – well, you know.'' Sally nodded reassuringly. Yvonne smiled. ''You and they might become friends, you never know.''

Mirabelle hugged Dick and Sally once more and they both hugged her back. She took a step toward Martin on the porch. At the last moment would he rush down the stairs and throw his arms around her? She smiled, tentatively. Martin did not return it. No, of course he wouldn't. Her step faltered as she turned away.

The spider took an enormous leap off the eavestrough, and landed on her shoulder. She jumped as it landed, then reached up and patted it. One of its legs touched her cheek, a gesture of comfort?

Yvonne took her hand. Mirabelle felt Yvonne's warmth, the pressure as she squeezed. Jane was leading the way. At the end of the walk, all three looked back. Sally and Dick waved. Behind them, Martin had two corners of the banner unfastened already.

&

Jane waddled down the street under her own power. Yvonne pushed the computer on the skateboard, keeping one hand on her paper. With a last squeeze, she'd let go of Mirabelle's arm; Mirabelle now stroked the spider. At the end of the subdivision, she glanced back but could no longer see even the cherry tree. Her voice was bleak and wistful. "I feel like I'm just starting our journey – or beginning it again."

"Maybe that's what journeys are," Jane said, "a series of starts – like lines are a series of points."

She grinned at the road in front of her with the ecstasy of getting away, all three of them, and the spider. Under her cocktail party tone and throughout Dick's interest in how she had become a turtle, and why, and what it was really like, Jane had been battling the horror that she and Yvonne might have to continue to the ocean without Mirabelle. Jane had been glad that her bulk made entry into the house impossible, what she'd seen of the outside had terrified her – a stifling environment, no wonder Mirabelle's legs and arms had fallen off. Still, she did have nice children, especially that Dick – he'd really cared that she hadn't always been a turtle – but now she didn't have to worry about what they'd do if Mirabelle stayed. She was right here beside her. Where she belonged.

Jane grinned again, nearly burbling with ecstasy, wholeness, remembered how abandoned she'd felt earlier – she

141

caught her breath as something inside her tore as gently and softly as ripping tissue – she loved Mirabelle.

Jane gasped, flushed, felt sweat on her forehead, slowed just a bit and looked up at Mirabelle. Love. Yes, she loved Yvonne too, very much, but she loved Mirabelle. With honest precision, Jane corrected herself. She was in love with Mirabelle. And was amazed.

Yvonne pushed the computer and stared at her paper on top of it. She couldn't sort out how she felt about Mirabelle's family – her family – Sally phones up, Janet answers – you've seen my mum? She's okay? Oh great! Run after her and tell her to come back, we can build a new house, tell her we're fine too, we're all awake now and we've been camping out and the sand's all gone – no, we've moved to an oasis – no, there never was a desert, she's crazy—

Sally phones up and she and Dick and John and Janet do become friends, and the Martins do as well, and we all live together somewhere, Jane and the spider too—

But Mirabelle's Martin had not rejoiced about her new arms and legs. Her Martin had not awakened – Yvonne sighed and frowned, looked up from her paper. The three of them continuing on – the four of them, she corrected. The spider stared at her from Mirabelle's shoulder. The same expression as when she'd given birth. Each time their eyes locked she could allow the gaze to continue longer.

Now she looked past her few remaining tendrils of repulsion right into the spider's deep eyes – enlarging and drawing her into the dark, through the darkness to things waving, wavering, and bits of light way down in the darkness—

She caught her toe in a crack, stumbled, righted herself without damage, but their gazes had unlocked and her vision was pulled to the wider view: the whole spider riding regally on Mirabelle's shoulder.

She treats you like a pet, but I know you're something other, Yvonne thought to it.

The spider crossed its two front legs in acknowledgement,

then shifted closer to Mirabelle. Yvonne followed the motion and saw tears on her cheek.

Mirabelle's shoulders slumped and her feet dragged. Yvonne stopped and patted Mirabelle's back compassionately. "It's hard."

Mirabelle sobbed the desolation that swamped her. Jane reached out from all her love and, touching Mirabelle's knee, guided her to rest against her shell. Yvonne crouched down and wrapped her arms around her. Mirabelle wept – why couldn't things be different? She was a failure – had she tried hard enough? Maybe she should go back – but – she couldn't. Like death, it was like death, her father, now her family, her comfort, hopes, and dreams – but no one had died – she should go back, try harder – the wheelchair, bed, hot chocolate, looking after – they didn't understand.

"Oh Mirabelle." She heard Jane's voice – thick, choking, did she hurt too, like this? Mirabelle looked up, saw Jane's compassion, love – blurred again by her own, discovered a place in her not touched – but touched around the edges of that place— What would she do without Jane? Without Yvonne? The spider? Mirabelle hung on to all three, and cried.

Eventually she was staring at her hands loosely upturned in her lap. She blinked her vision clearer, curled her fingers inward. Fine crease lines and rudimentary nails, half-moons at the quick, as if she'd just stopped biting them. And her hands were curled in her lap – couldn't have a lap without legs. Dirty feet, a darker line where the nails were growing. She wiggled her toes, looked up. Yvonne's face, round blue eyes, she'd never noticed just how blue they were, a deep dark blue just now, but sometimes, weren't they turquoise? When Yvonne smiled – tenderly, like this, some lines drew into dimples – Mirabelle felt bathed by her smile. And Jane, her brow wrinkled fiercely with – concern, Mirabelle suppposed. Sometimes she could laugh at Jane's fierceness, it covered so much else, and so much propelled her into fierceness – she wouldn't have her any other way. Or Yvonne. Or the spider. Mirabelle tilted her head so she could stroke it with her cheek, rest some of her weight upon it—

"Well, *girls,* you better help me up. I've got a bit stuck."

Jane, Yvonne, and Mirabelle all grinned. Yvonne threw her arms around Mirabelle in a great hug, then pulled her to her feet. Jane could just reach her free hand. She kissed it.

Mirabelle's breath vibrated with the intensity, the power of that kiss. She looked down, expecting to see the mark of Jane's two lips tattooed on the back of her hand – the kiss spreading outward now, like waves from the center of a mysterious pool, up her arm, warming her blood as it throbbed through the new vessels. Mirabelle smiled, and laid the kissed hand upon Jane's hair.

All of them felt so close their energy swelled and grew until Yvonne could see it – a shimmering, dancing rainbow of colours weaving around them. As they moved on, Yvonne looked back and saw trails of rainbow following them down the street.

&

The road climbed uphill and Jane wished she could ride, but the skateboard with computer was heavy enough for Yvonne and Mirabelle to push. The number of cars increased, each gearing down as it came abreast and soon they were choking in exhaust fumes. As they neared the crest of the hill they heard faint music.

The road did not follow the hill down the other side as they'd expected, but sloped to bisect a grassy plateau. To the right a travelling fair had been set up, to the left a car park. As they stood on the shoulder of the road, the miasma of car fumes became that of popcorn, fried onions, cotton candy and axle grease. Tents for side shows, a small ferris wheel creaking and swinging through its arc, a roller coaster, and spinning rides that stayed on the ground. Music groaned and wheezed mechanically, louder, then suddenly stopping. The air was fractured with silence in the second it took the player to rest – or change tapes.

Above the flag-decorated fair floated an enormous balloon, rainbow-coloured, the yellow melding into orange, into red, into purple, blue and green. It bobbed in the breeze and tugged at its guy ropes, then settled at the whim of the wind. The balloon was a rainbow over all the fair, dwarfing all the fair, making the basket beneath appear to be the pot at the end of the rainbow.

While waiting for Jane, Yvonne and Mirabelle took a few steps forward to have a better look. The spider jumped down from Mirabelle's shoulder, but neither noticed in their surprise at a fair. Jane screamed. Yvonne's and Mirabelle's attention snapped back with a suddeness that curled up their intestines.

Four men had thrown a net over Jane, lifting it so she was turned upside down. Jane had retreated completely into her shell except for one back leg. Her flipper was caught in a hole. She screamed again, a high-pitched noise that echoed and was dulled by the chamber of her shell. The men hoisted her up, exposing her lighter green belly shell. Screams of fear to fear and pain as her flipper twisted forty-five degrees.

"Hey! You can't do that!" Yvonne and Mirabelle charged toward them. "Put her down!"

One of the men laughed. "What do you mean, we can't do that? We done it so you little ladies just carry on. We'll treat this here turtle well."

They were big and burly, with missing teeth and beer bellies, greasy hair, and bulging, shifting muscles under their tee-shirts. Jane was a huge turtle, yet it seemed that each of the men could hoist her alone.

"Thanks for bringing us this here turtle. You come see it any time you want! Admission's three-fifty."

Mirabelle yelled, "we'll get the Police! This is kidnapping!"

Yvonne could hardly speak. "You can't do this!"

"Yeah? Wanna bet?" A disinterested tone. "Out here, the only Bill of rights is the bill of might, right, Bill?" He sounded as if that was an old joke.

"Right," Bill sneered.

"Don't worry, Jane, we'll save you, and whatever you do, don't say anything!" Mirabelle wrung her hands.

"You hear that, Bill? They think it talks! We should exhibit them too!"

The smallest man looked at Yvonne and Mirabelle, shook his head. "Naw. A giant turtle's enough, though—" He leered lasciviously.

Yvonne glanced around for the spider, could not see it. She clasped her hands together, kept the quaver out of her voice. "Look, that's a special turtle, we're taking her to the ocean! You must let her go! Find another turtle, this one'll cause trouble, she doesn't like being locked up!"

The men just laughed, hoisted Jane on their backs and started down the slope to the fair. Yvonne ran after them, pummeled the last man in the kidney area with her fists, but he backhanded her to the ground as if brushing away a fly. "At least fix her flipper, you're hurting her!"

Yvonne watched Jane bob upside down the hill. She felt a searing, cramping, tearing deep inside her, felt the pain of Jane's twisted flipper in her foot, lay where she was, crying hot, hurting, gasping sobs. Mirabelle was vomiting on the other side of the computer.

Eventually they sat on the dry, brown grass and grasped each other's hands. Yvonne shivered with terror. "I've never felt so powerless! Oh, poor Jane! What'll we do?"

Mirabelle couldn't say anything, she couldn't believe it. Jane here one minute and the next captured. What if they killed her? Tortured her? Her flipper all twisted— Mirabelle shivered and gagged.

The spider scuttled to the women, poised on the tip of its feet and leapt onto Mirabelle's chest. "Oof", she gasped, stroking its hairy back. The spider looked at Yvonne.

She glared back. It should have done something – bit the men – or something. "Where were you when we needed you?" she hissed.

"Hiding," Mirabelle immediately defended. "It might have been captured too. Smart spider."

Yvonne shivered again. She looked at the spider, into its eyes, but they were not entrances now. Still, Mirabelle was right. Yvonne whispered "sorry" to the spider, then added, "I guess it isn't strong enough to run off with Jane the way it rescued me from the fridges."

The spider moved around so it could look at the fair. Yvonne sighed. Mirabelle echoed it. So, it seemed from the stillness of its head, did the spider. Yvonne had to do something.

She closed her eyes, re-placed herself and Mirabelle on the crest of the hill waiting for Jane, and brought the men back, but again they netted Jane, again her flipper twisted, again she shrieked.

Yvonne yelled: "no! Go away! Stop it!" But, unlike the doctors and the nurse, the men did not vanish at her command. They just laughed, again brushed Yvonne away and carried their captive down the hill.

The calliope sounded harsh and discordant. The odour of popcorn, fried onions and cotton candy smelled nauseating. The shrieks and screams and sight of people being twisted and swung and jerked on the various rides were terrifying. Above, the sun lingered hot in a long twilight. Only the rainbow balloon hovered unchanged, bobbing and tugging at the conspiracy of breeze and guy ropes.

Yvonne sighed again and stood up. "I'll go find out where they've put Jane. You stay here with the computer and spider."

"I'm coming with you! We shouldn't be separated! Besides, I have to know what's happened to Jane, even if—" Her stomach heaved again, but this time she controlled it. She placed the spider on the ground and stood up as well.

147

"We'll hide the computer in the woods – if we can't free Jane, who cares what happens to it. The spider will stay – maybe."

They wheeled the skateboard behind a thimbleberry bush and looked at the spider. "Stay." Mirabelle intended the imperative, but the word curved into the interrogative.

&

The closer Yvonne and Mirabelle came to the fairgrounds, the more apprehension slowed their steps. Mirabelle stumbled and her fingers floated as they had when she first was learning to control them. Yvonne brushed sweat off her clammy forehead. She looped her right arm through Mirabelle's left, grabbed her fingers as they floated by and, placing Mirabelle's right hand on top of her arm, kept her left hand over it. Mirabelle glanced her appreciation for the help – and the comfort; Yvonne's lips a straight line over tight jaws.

They passed through the gate in the midst of a crowd and managed not to pay admission. Neither questioned her right to do so, although they walked a few metres before Mirabelle stopped anticipating the hand of authority on her shoulder. At the merry-go-round they halted to reconnoiter.

People lined up everywhere – for the rides, the computerized games, the shooting gallery, cotton candy and corn on the cob. Past the games arcade were the sideshows: the five hundred pound man, the bearded lady, the sword swallower, the midget, the cow with five legs. Yvonne pulled Mirabelle that way, pushing through the crowd – "excuse me, excuse me," expecting – hoping, dreading – over each curtained entry to see a sign: *Turtle Lady*.

At the end of the row of sideshows near a hamburger stand they halted again, looked at each other. Mirabelle's eyes were enormous with terror. Yvonne tried not to panic. They disentangled their arms, grasped each other's waists. A man glared, and whispered something to his wife. Yvonne felt like pummeling him to the ground. She heard Jane's caustic voice: you have a problem with people touching? Yvonne felt tears approaching, said aloud, "Jane's not here."

"No." Mirabelle tightened her grasp. She'd seen the man's look too, had glared back, now felt as lost as Yvonne sounded.

"Step right up, folks! Winners quaranteed! Three chances for a dollar!" People pushed by, jostling them, a child rubbed its cotton candy across Mirabelle's legs and Yvonne's jeans, teenagers stopped to kiss. The noise of barkers, of music, of people yelling hurt Mirabelle's ears.

"There! They've got the animals over there!"

"Jane's not an animal!" Yvonne glared indignantly.

"I know that! But they don't. And they don't have her in the sideshows." She glared back. "Don't take your fear out on me."

Yvonne glanced away, bit her lip, nodded sorry.

Arms still around each other's waist, they pushed through the crowd toward the row of cages.

Next to the *Serpent* (a large garter snake), and the *Albino Bear Of Borneo* (a depressed polar bear), they found a cage advertising *A Giant Turtle From The Depths Of The Sargasso Sea, The Only Survivor From Atlantis*. In the exact middle was the huge grey-green hump of Jane, every part of her clamped tightly into her shell. "Is it dead?" a child asked. A man prodded Jane with a stick. "Come on, you lazy thing, get up!" Someone else said, "what a rip-off! Put an empty shell in a cage and call it a turtle!"

Yvonne flared, "don't poke her! You'll hurt her!" The man with the stick didn't hear, but those close by turned to look. A woman tut-tutted disapprovingly. The child stuck a contemplative finger in its mouth.

"Shh." Keeping a cautioning arm around Yvonne, Mirabelle shouldered through the crowd until they were pressed against the bars. Only the back of the cage was solid, the sides and top were barred. Jane had no protection from the sun or from the sightseers. In one corner was a large dish containing limp, brown lettuce, a bent carrot, and kernels of dry dog food. Beside it a battered water dish grew green scum.

Mirabelle, hot and breathless, suffocated by the crowd, wanted to scream in the panic of claustrophobia. Jane must be suffocating, sweltering in her shell. An immense rage filled her – Let her out! Get her out! – was she screaming? She put each hand on a bar and shook them: solid steel, an inch thick. Slumped against them – what could they do? Jane hated being helpless. Her shell not moving – how long could she stay inside? Tears ran down Mirabelle's face. She couldn't move to wipe them. Jane's kiss – through blurring tears she focussed on her hand, felt the warmth and pressure of Jane's lips, and knew how much she loved her.

A woman saw her tears. "There, there, dear, it is awful what they do to animals, but this turtle doesn't know – it's probably quite happy."

Mirabelle glared at her simpering, fatuous face, and backed away with as much dignity as she could muster.

Yvonne had been studying the door of the cage. A hasp and a large padlock. Below that, another hasp with a combination lock. Discouragingly impervious. At Mirabelle's tug Yvonne backed out of the crowd too. Silently, with linked arms, they walked down the row of cages until they reached the last one – a scruffy bald eagle who glared at them balefully. They again walked the row of cages, slowing at Jane's.

"What are we going to do? She must be sweltering." Mirabelle wrung her hands. "If they do think it's only a shell on display, they could really hurt her to make her move."

"Maybe we can file through the bars – but not until dark. We just have to wait."

"We can't wait! What if she suffocates?" Mirabelle's eyes a panicked deer's. "She doesn't even know what's happened to us or if we can get her out – she'll be hopeless! Terrified!

150

Let's find the owners and explain to them."

Yvonne shook her head. "Anyone who has those men working for him wouldn't be sympathetic. There must be tools around here – maybe a rasp?"

A vacant park bench. Yvonne led Mirabelle to it. Their view of Jane was blocked by the crowd swirling by. Yvonne remembered Jane in the desert, how afraid she'd been of boiling to death. If she could get to Jane, if she could give her a drink. She could do nothing, at least until the fair closed for the night. She put her arm around Mirabelle's shoulder and patted it to comfort them both.

Later, Yvonne said bitterly, "fair. You're the one who wanted things to be fair. Here's your fair."

"I didn't mean this sort of fair – and it sure isn't fair to have Jane captured," Mirabelle trembled, felt like vomiting again.

"An unfair." Yvonne trampled a styrofoam cup, kicked at a half-eaten corncob. "A sleazy unfair. Glamour and glitter from a distance and rotten close-up. Come on, let's go back to the hill." Pulled Mirabelle to her feet. They both looked over at the hump of Jane in the cage. Mirabelle sent a silent message: we'll get you out, somehow. Slowly they dragged back toward the sideshows.

Yvonne grabbed Mirabelle's arm. "Look at that! Would you believe it!"

Under a banner proclaiming them to be *The World's Greatest Jugglers* were First and Second, tossing, twirling, throwing, catching, bobbing, bending, their bodies, their balls, their sticks.

&

Yvonne pushed through the crowd until she was in the first row. Mirabelle never wanted to see these men again but, reluctantly, she followed. When the jugglers had finished their act and straightened from their bows, the writing on

151

their tee-shirts was legible. First's read: *Men Have Rights Too* and Second's: *Balls Are Best.*

"We meet again," Yvonne stated, each word separated and flat. She wanted to hurl the words at them like stones, struggled to control herself.

First had waxed the ends of his moustache. Behind it his face paled, then reddened with shock and embarrassment. Second belligerently stuck out his jaw, and his fringe of blonde beard looked like a clothes brush. Both darted glances at each other then to the back of the stage, checking ways of escape.

"I am totally disgusted with your behaviour!" Yvonne's whole body quivered with anger.

"So am I – skipping out after you said you were going to protect us!" Mirabelle's voice hovered around high C. "That wasn't fair and then to steal our computer!"

"What was the point of staying?" First leapt in defensively. "You were laughing at us! And you didn't even dance with us!"

"That's no excuse to steal!" Yvonne said.

"You didn't want to take us seriously."

"We take what you did very seriously. You broke your word to us and you stole our computer." Mirabelle nodded in agreement and put her arm through Yvonne's.

"The pleasure of wallflowerhood," Second sneered. "That was humiliating!" He turned abruptly, walked a few steps, crossed his arms, turned back.

First had his feet planted firmly on the stage. He tossed a ball from one hand to the other, looked over their heads. "We offered to teach you. We offered to protect you."

"We didn't want to be taught or protected. And that's no excuse to steal! I'm getting even angrier that you won't take responsibility for what you did!" Yvonne's face was red. Mirabelle could feel her shaking.

First put his hands in his pockets. Thrusting his pelvis forward, he rocked back on his heels and shrugged. "That's the way it is." His tone sulky. Still looking over their heads.

Yvonne stared at him, at Second scooping up balls and sticks from the stage. Embarrassed, he avoided their eyes. "Uh huh, I can see that's the way it is. In which case, we had better get going." She put her arm around Mirabelle's waist.

The crowd had dispersed, leaving trampled grass littered with torn hamburger wrappers, candy apple sticks, cigarette butts. As they walked away, Yvonne's anger slumped into heavy frustration and hopelessness.

Mirabelle squeezed her waist. "I'm proud of you, Yvonne, the way you confronted them."

"Oh, what was the point?" she mumbled.

"The point was you did all you could do – and me too! I confronted them too!" She squeezed Yvonne's waist again.

Yvonne frowned. "I guess you're right. Though I did hope they'd apologize – or at least acknowledge – it's so disappointing." She sighed.

"Yeah," Mirabelle agreed in a whisper, thinking of Martin.

"Wait a minute!" They were nearly at the gate when First and Second caught up with them. Second gripped First's upper arm. Both looked chastened and embarrassed. "We're really sorry. We're not used to – um – being treated like this. Give us another chance."

Yvonne's anger flashed again. She wheeled around. "Why should we?" But she was struck by the sincerity on their faces, in their body postures – they actually looked different – First's tone had been candid, if a little churlish.

"No reason you have to," Second admitted. "But we think you're the sort of girls who might."

"Women," Mirabelle corrected. Jane's absence jabbed her.

"Women." Second agreed. First nodded.

Yvonne considered. Their tones and attitudes had changed, but her anger had left her raw. Still, she and Jane and Mirabelle had had other chances—

First was looking around. "Where's your friend – the turtle?"

Yvonne saw on Mirabelle's face her desire to tell them, felt her increased agitation. She looked at the men, First did appear genuinely interested. She bit her lip, offered hesitantly, "down there." Paused again. "In a cage on exhibit. Some men captured her."

"Not Tom and Dick and Bill and Harry? They're rough bastards! What are you going to do?" Second asked.

Mirabelle brushed sudden tears away. "We were trying to figure that out when we saw you."

"We'll help." First reached out toward Yvonne's arm, then, hesitating, he rubbed the back of his neck.

"It's okay." Yvonne still uncertain – though Second did say women and First didn't grab her.

"Please. We want to help." First's forehead wrinkled with worry.

Second elaborated, "those guys are mean through and through. And we've been learning the fair's routine."

Yvonne flicked her eyes to Mirabelle, saw increasing acquiescence. She looked back to the men and straightened her shoulders. "How do we know you'll really help? How do we know you're not tricking us – that you won't take over – or take off?"

"You have to trust us," Second said.

Yvonne stared at him. Slowly she shook her head. "No. We don't." The *No* hung in the air while she and Mirabelle searched the men's faces. Nothing but dismay and concern.

Yvonne took Mirabelle's arm and steered her a few paces away. "What do you think?"

"If they know the routine – I'm so scared for Jane." She closed her eyes and a sob caught in her throat.

Yvonne put her arm around her, guided her back. Her tone was grave as she said to First and Second, "we accept your help. Together we'll get Jane out."

Then she and Mirabelle led the men up the hill.

154

"Another computer!" Second exclaimed. "My god, are you in the business?"

Mirabelle had wrapped herself in her arms. Now, in spite of her fear for Jane, she smiled. "It's the same one. You ran away too fast. That was my husband – he was going to offer you a ride."

"No kidding! We thought it was the police – anyway we felt pretty stupid about it later." He shuffled in embarrassment.

With resignation, Yvonne realized that was probably the extent of Second's – or First's – apology, and raised her eyebrow in acknowledgement. Behind him, she saw the spider up a pine tree disguised as a squirrel hole, dark and round against the trunk.

First had been staring at the computer. "Shall we see if it has a program to free turtles?"

"Need to plug it in." Mirabelle tightened her arms. Such a buzz of anxiety about Jane, about the men, she might explode. "No current bushes here."

Second pulled a small square object out of his pocket. "A converter. I can light up my balls for night juggling. It's stupendous, all those balls glowing and when I take them in my hands looks like they disappear. I can be a real magician that way –" his tone faltered and his face flushed with embarrassment. They were all staring at him, Yvonne disdainfully. He started to whistle, jiggled the converter as if he were about to throw it in the air, then looked sheepishly at Yvonne and Mirabelle. "Uh huh, well," he mumbled and, bending down, attached the converter to the computer cord. First switched the computer on, typed: free turtle, list.

For a minute the computer was blank, then print rolled up its screen.

To free turtles from locked cages wait until dark then:
1 turn key in lock

2 cut through lock
3 file lock off
4 bend bars of cage
5 shrink turtle (cross-reference shrinking turtles)
6 lift cage bars out of cage floor
7 lift cage top off cage bars
8 melt cage bars with bar solvent (cross-reference bar solvent)
9 make wax impression of key hole, cut key
10 politely ask cage owner to let turtle out

"What obvious suggestions!" Yvonne said in disgust. "Why have we been carting this computer around? Ask the owner indeed. I can just hear me – please Bill open Jane's cage!"

"Give it a chance, Yvonne." Mirabelle reached toward the keyboard, but her hand appeared unfamiliar in that position and she withdrew it. She could feel her heart beating, pumping blood through her new veins.

"She's right," First agreed. "These are fine computer suggestions. We just have to choose which one is appropriate."

"Could grind up bar solvent, I suppose." Yvonne's apprehension had returned. She wanted to rush down the hill and free Jane immediately, even if she had to forcibly tear the bars apart. Yet she was so tired all her feelings came out as irritation.

"Let me finish. You said one lock was a combination?" First typed more instructions. They bent forward to read.

Common combinations for Canadian locks (for American, Japanese or Arabic locks, cross-reference locks, other countries) subset, common combinations for locks on turtle cages, and the computer listed only three: *24-6-19; 3-58-72; 61-16-6.*

"That's better," Yvonne admitted. "We can try those but we still have to get the other lock off."

The lingering twilight had now totally faded and the fair sparkled multi-coloured below them, reflecting off the

156

underbelly of the balloon. Headlights of cars made a parade away. Soon even the lights of the roller coaster and ferris wheel were extinguished.

Yvonne and Mirabelle, First and Second, loaded the computer on the skateboard. The spider leapt from the tree to the top of the computer and sprawled in Jane's accustomed place. Mirabelle stroked it. First and Second stayed a metre away.

Feeling their way in the dark, they started down the hill. Yvonne pushed the computer, the spider riding regally. Half-way down, she said, "we need to plan what to do if we meet those men."

"They're usually drunk by now and playing poker," First replied.

"Then we'll circle around with the skateboard until we're behind the cages."

"We'll go the front way and check for the security guard."

"Jane," Mirabelle whispered when they were near the second cage, then louder, "Jane!"

"Shh," Yvonne cautioned. Rumbly voices, the bobbing approach of a flashlight. The spider pulled in its legs and held absolutely still. Yvonne undid her shirt buttons, put her paper next to her skin, buttoned up again, felt the paper warming. She and Mirabelle crouched over the computer. The flashlight stopped, held steady, voices rumbled on. Then the light moved away, trailing the scrunch of footsteps with it.

"Yvonne? Mirabelle?" They looked at each other, hardly breathing, but the low voice was First's. "Pays to be a juggler sometimes. I got the guard's keys. So we just have to find the right combination." He proudly fitted the key in the padlock, unlocked and removed it.

"Jane!" Mirabelle whispered.

A dark shape lifted off the floor, oozed toward her voice. "About time! This is the worst thing that's ever happened! Get me out! Get me out!"

Yvonne tried the combinations. Her hands fumbled and she spun past the number. Taking deep breaths to calm herself, she tried again, pulled. The lock didn't budge. She tried that combination again, to be sure. She could hear everyone's breathing; it increased her tension. Jane moaned, tried not to say "hurry!"

Yvonne looked at the second set of numbers. So hard to read even with light from a lamp post. Creak – around once, around twice, to the third number – pulled. The lock came undone. She twisted and slipped it off, pulled the hasp away. The door swung open. First and Second grabbed Jane and heaved her out. "Oh thank heavens!" Mirabelle put her arms around Jane's neck, kissed her cheeks, forehead, made her wet with her tears.

"Oh Mirabelle –" Jane couldn't speak; trembling shook her whole shell. She swallowed desperately, couldn't believe she was out – dreaming? But Mirabelle, her face all wet, and Yvonne stroking her hair, her shell – she was really out? "Let's get away from this hellhole! We can cry later. What are these two doing here?"

"They've been helping us. Free the others too, First," Yvonne ordered, but it was Second who took the key. The snake slithered out and the eagle flapped wings rusty with disuse, but the bear continued to sit in the middle of its cage, front paws splayed like an awkward cat.

"Too used to captivity," Second said. "We'll leave its door open. And what are you going to do now?" He had to lengthen his stride to keep up; Yvonne was hurrying so the computer rattled on the skateboard and threatened to overturn. The spider clung to its bouncing surface with all eight legs outspread.

"We're taking off," Yvonne stated, "in that." She came to a stop by the basket of the balloon.

&

The clear plastic basket was much bigger close up – three

158

metres across – and the balloon towered above them three storeys high. The yellow nylon ropes were as thick as Yvonne's wrist. She climbed in, turned to First to hand her the computer. Out of the dark the spider drew its legs together and sprang onto the edge, a piece of night unfolding. It scuttled down the side and hid behind the bags of briquets. Yvonne let her breath out in relief. If the spider jumped in without hesitation, her decision was correct.

Mirabelle tilted her head back to look at the extent of the balloon, sighed, and climbed in too. But Jane shook her head. "You're not getting me in that! I just got out of one trap!"

"Come on, Jane, you said you nearly got your pilot's licence before you went into nursing."

"That's why you won't get me in there!"

"The ocean, Jane, remember?" Yvonne's quiet tone covered sparks, a bank of thunderheads in front of a storm. "Hurry up, before the guard comes back."

"What about us?" Second demanded.

"What do you mean, 'what about us'?"

"We want to come too."

Second's voice was pleading. In the light from the distant lamp his eyes shone with anxiety. Yvonne looked at First's tense mouth. She softened her tone. "There isn't room for six."

"Five."

"Six. The spider."

"I'll stay behind," Jane offered.

"No you won't. Get in. Now."

Jane blinked. Unusual for Yvonne to command, at least directly. But she was as terrified of heights as she was of cages. The grip of her previous fear increased with the anticipated one. She shook her head, and backed away, struggling not to cry, to scream.

"Oh, Jane!" Yvonne fought down her exasperation. Each time they'd had to start again, Jane had complained. In the oasis, at the cabin. Yvonne felt all the surfaces of her skin prickle with her earlier anger, terror, fatigue – had to get away. Immediately. Before the men sobered up, or lurched out and discovered them. Didn't the others recognize the danger?

"Jane, you have to get in. We have to get away. Now." Yvonne watched Jane shake her head.

Climbing out of the basket, Yvonne walked over and crouched down so their faces were only inches apart. She could see Jane's terror, knew how hard this was. Touched Jane's hair. "You saw the spider leap in. You trust the spider. It hasn't led us into danger." Yvonne withdrew her hand, stood up, hardened her voice again. "Jane, you have to get in. They'll put you back in the cage and throw away the key this time!" She rubbed her hands, whirled around. "Mirabelle, *you* speak to her!"

Mirabelle leaned over the basket. "Please, Jane. She's right. It won't be so bad."

Jane closed her eyes and they could see heart-wrenching lines pull her face. She felt as if she were being led to the scaffold – hadn't she spent enough time there already? How long must this torture continue? Her throat closed against panic. What difference did it make – a balloon or cage? "Okay," she tried to say, and choked, coughed. But her flippers had no strength – no bones. She muttered resignedly, "hoist me up, then."

Mirabelle shook a bag of briquets onto the hibachi, buried cubes of firestarter. "Anybody got a match?" First held out a lighter.

"It's going to take forever to heat the air in the balloon with just a hibachi," he muttered sullenly.

Yvonne scowled at him. "It's a double hibachi." The balloon was practically airborne with her impatience. She erased her scowl with a smile at Second. "Would you contribute your converter?"

He put his hand over his pocket and blurted, "how am

I supposed to light my balls?'' His lower lip stuck out as he glared at her. His eyes shifted to Mirabelle at the hibachi, then upward to the extent of balloon. ''Oh well!'' His tone was sullen as he handed it to her. ''How come we can't go? How come we help you and then you send us away?''

Yvonne climbed into the basket, turned to him, to First. They stood together, their faces wistful and lost. She touched Second's shoulder. ''This is a women-only trip.''

''Why does it have to be? We won't get in your way!'' She heard his anguish, and her eyes teared in response, but she continued to shake her head. A crack grew down Second, spread into little lines, a ceramic container whose glaze had crazed. All could feel his pain escaping.

Mirabelle had moved to lean beside Yvonne. ''I'm sorry it hurts you. We've appreciated your help getting Jane out, and perhaps another trip won't be women-only.''

First put his arm around Second's shoulder, clasped him hard. ''Don't worry about us. We'll be fine.'' He gently punched Second's diaphragm.

''Stiff upper lip brigade?'' Yvonne smiled to acknowledge his attempt, and that he knew it was an attempt, and that she respected it. She placed both hands on the lip of the basket. ''Please phone the Martins.'' She recited her phone number and Mirabelle's. ''Tell them that – we're all – just going on – that we all have to – go on, okay?''

First scuffed his toe in the dirt, Second blew his breath through loose lips. ''Okay,'' they said together. First placed his foot on the skateboard, wheeled it in a circle. ''You want this?''

''Leave it. We're operating on the barter system – something from one place ends up in another.'' Impatiently, Yvonne looked up at the balloon beginning to swell and tug at its ropes. The coals glowed; Mirabelle shook more briquets on top.

First had wheeled away on the skateboard; now he returned with a pail. ''Take some water. Hate to think of you setting the thing on fire!'' He laughed, looked at Second, wheeled closer to Yvonne. "Seriously, Second and I, we, well, respect you. We want you to succeed, whatever you're doing and we will tell the Martins for you." He was looking up at her.

She put her arms around him, gave him a hug. "Thanks, *boys*. We appreciate your help. We might see you again."

"Yeah, you might." Second tried to smile. He hugged her then hugged Mirabelle.

The balloon was tugging to be off, its vibrating ropes making the basket dance. First and Second loosed the guy ropes from their pegs, threw them in the basket. Mirabelle caught and coiled them. The balloon lifted slowly into the dark sky, then faster and faster. Yvonne and Mirabelle waved until First's and Second's faces became disembodied, fading spots of light.

&

"Now we're together again!" Mirabelle sat cross-legged opposite Yvonne who was staring intently at the computer. Jane lay with her flippers spread-eagled, clamped to the floor, head completely in her shell, but Mirabelle knew she'd heard. Looked from Jane to Yvonne, back to Jane – knew she was grinning and probably looked silly. For now, the four of them being together and away from the horrible fair – the unfair – was enough. Yvonne turned and saw Mirabelle's teeth in the glow from the hibachi coals – had to grin too, in spite of her concern that she didn't know enough about computers to make this one work.

Jane's shell created an echo chamber for her occasional moans. Mirabelle slid over and stroked her flipper, looking at the large round basket. It was clear plastic cast in one mold, a half sphere, slightly flattened on the bottom. The yellow nylon ropes threaded through eyes in the plastic were the only supports. She could see in all directions at once.

The balloon above them blocked stars as it drifted, and long ago she'd watched the lights of the unfair disappear. The star-speckled sky ended in darker jagged mountains; occasionally a glacier gleamed in the starlight. Completely silent. The current of air was so slight the ropes didn't thrum. She, Jane, Yvonne, and the spider hung suspended between sky and earth.

Mirabelle remembered the Salvation Army bubble, remembered how she'd felt looking at her old finger lying among the dollar bills; now all of her was lying in a bubble, now all of her was donated to – something, some cause. She looked at Yvonne's back still tensed over the computer and wanted to voice this thought – it was gone before she could. Yet she was whole, not in parts, lying in this bubble. Could feel her fingers when she patted and stroked Jane's flipper.

Looking between the ropes, face pressed to the plexiglas, Mirabelle almost believed that she had surpassed dependence on any aid to flight, was flying by her own power, her own will. She thought she could climb onto the edge of the basket and launch forth, gliding with out-held arms. And not plummet to smash on those white mountain peaks.

Mirabelle let go of Jane's flipper. She placed her hands on the rim of the sphere as if to hoist herself over, but a sudden wind hit her face hard, tore at her hair. She half-turned, saw the balloon above and Jane a dark lump moaning softly, the glow of the briquets in the hibachi, and Yvonne crouched over the green-faced computer. Mirabelle touched a rope, felt its firmness, the reality of the rim under her hand, and the reasoning part of her mind knew she could not launch forth by herself. For a moment she felt intensely disappointed. Then her previous joy returned and she sat down again and, draping her arm over Jane's shell, stared through the plastic side.

Under her arm, Jane's shell trembled. Mirabelle reached out to stroke her hair; none was available. "Jane? How are you? Won't you come out?"

At the sound of Mirabelle's voice Jane tightened her muscles. She felt her flippertip touching Mirabelle's leg. Scared, terrified – this jelly feeling was terror – nothing she could do – nothing she'd been able to do in the cage, nothing she could do now. Helpless. Helpless was terrifying. Jane closed her eyes even more tightly – aching already, had been for days – and whimpered. Helpless. Terrified. The words went round and round in her shell full of jelly – would die soon, maybe not soon enough, would die of terror, of helplessness. Mirabelle's voice penetrated – "Jane! Come out. Please!"

Jane shook her head, shaking her whole shell. How could she come out? She whimpered, moaned. "Jane? Please!" Mirabelle didn't understand, no one understood, help me, help me—

Mirabelle's voice from long, long ago – *Wish I'd been there to help you* – *You're helping me now*—

Jane leaned toward her, warmth of leg against her flipper. Moaning, she inched her jaw out, her neck. Through clogged nostrils, she inhaled the scent of Mirabelle, registered the coolness of the air, Mirabelle's touch on her hair.

Plopped her head in Mirabelle's warm lap, the relief of that, rested the full weight of her head, let crying take her over.

Mirabelle smoothed her hair, wishing she could smooth Jane's pain. Yvonne slid over from the computer, and held Jane's flipper. Her heart ached with each of Jane's wrenching sobs.

Jane gulped and gasped and began to mumble, "I was so scared. So helpless – my father used to lock me in my room and I couldn't get out and my mother'd lock me out of the house and I had no where to go. They could have done anything to me in that cage and I couldn't have prevented it—"

With a violent wretching motion, Jane tore her head from Mirabelle's lap, tore her flipper out of Yvonne's hand. Eyes still tightly closed, she vomited black lumps, some round and pebbly, some large and jagged, vomited, vomited, vomited. A pile of petrified rocks. Coal in the bottom of the basket.

When she was done, her whole body slumped and only her shell kept her up. Every muscle ached. Mirabelle guided her head back onto her lap and Yvonne again caressed her flipper.

Later, Jane said, "Did you have to have me captured? Couldn't you have had the men try and not succeed? Or at the very least couldn't you have got me out sooner? Why'd you take weeks?"

Yvonne's surprise coloured her voice. "It was just one afternoon. We had to wait till dark. And we had nothing to do with your capture – except we couldn't stop it!"

"It's your story, Yvonne." Jane felt angry and confused. "You got out of the fridge, you have the magic teeth, you found the spider, us."

"Yes, but you'd already turned into a turtle, and Mirabelle's arms and legs had already fallen off. I had nothing to do with that," Yvonne defended.

The only way Mirabelle could now tell Jane was still crying was by the dampness of her skirt. She continued to stroke her hair.

"Oh Jane," Yvonne softened. "I didn't want you to be scared – or us. We were scared too, it was awful! But I didn't plan that – I didn't even know the men were there or that Mirabelle and I'd be powerless to stop them."

Mirabelle smoothed Jane's hair. Her voice and hair a woman's – "don't be scared any more. You're not helpless now. We're all looking after each other."

"Yeah? If you'd really been looking after me, I wouldn't have been captured!" Jane's word's blaming, but her tone not. Yvonne and Mirabelle recognized a small child's confusion.

Yvonne said, "there're some things other people can't do – we got you out, that's all we could do."

"I couldn't do anything myself." A residual sob.

"No, you couldn't, Jane. You were helpless. You needed us to get you out."

Mirabelle shifted Jane's head in her lap. "You keep saying this is Yvonne's story, Jane, but we're all responsible. It's all our story."

"Yeah!" Yvonne had a rush of excitement, felt her paper against her skin. "We each have our own story, and I can only make mine happen – that's why I couldn't stop those men capturing Jane the way I could make the doctors vanish! We're each making our own stories happen!" She stood up, shifted her paper against her skin. Her excitement grew with the thought. "And we're telling our stories as they happen – and telling our stories becomes our shared story, and so we're the people in the stories and the tellers and the listeners all at once! And telling our stories, and listening to them, and being in them changes us so there's always more story – which is ultimately *the* story! It's like mirrors on and on getting smaller but never disappearing as long as they're enough mirrors!" Yvonne grinned. It was finally clear to her. But Mirabelle was frowning in total confusion.

"That's not the right analogy," Jane interrupted, her voice still teary. "Because with mirrors the only change is the size of the reflection. There's no distortion of image or chance to go in different directions, or chance for things to just happen – like my being captured – if you *really* didn't plan that for an artistic effect in your story?"

"No, I didn't," Yvonne reassured. Jane seemed to believe her. Mirabelle decided she wouldn't pursue the discussion. It was clear to them, if not to her. She didn't really care.

"How about now? Is this balloon going to work? Did you know we'd be going off in it?" Jane was asking.

"No – not until we had to get away." Yvonne added, "the longer we go on, the clearer some things become. When I got out of the fridge I didn't have a clue what was going to happen, didn't know I was going to meet you, certainly

166

didn't know about Mirabelle, but now I'm pretty sure we will get to the ocean."

"Good," Jane said. Mirabelle felt a wave of sadness, swallowed and closed her eyes against a picture of Jane swimming away, heard Jane add, "though I wish you'd stuck to ground transportation."

"Now the computer's hooked up. All we have to do is add two briquets when it beeps." Yvonne sat down beside them, laughed. "The computer's in charge, it's looking after us."

"That's not true," Mirabelle denied. "You programmed it."

"If we run out of briquets," Jane said later, "we can burn my coal."

&

Yvonne and Mirabelle saw the sun ball up between two peaks. Jane still had her eyes closed. They watched the world beneath them be coloured out of haze and drifting cloud as light inched down the mountains until each tree on their slopes and in the valleys between was drawn into relief, and the rivers and the lakes turned blue and sparkling.

Over this scene moved a round shadow, crinkled now and then by mountains: the balloon. The sun shone through the basket so it looked as if they were floating unattached beneath the ballon, the ropes too thin to cast a shadow at such a distance. Yvonne checked back and forth between the basket and the shadow picture, wondering if they were really there, or here, or anywhere. Suspended in a transparent basket of light.

As the sun rose it shrank into a spot of hot gold and the basket collected rays and almost glowed itself, a second sun. Yvonne and Mirabelle leaned over the edge to cool their perspiring faces. On the floor where Jane was lying there was no breeze.

167

"Clear plastic is not the material to make these baskets from," Jane declared. Her head was fully extended, as were her limbs, chin resting on the floor. The muscles of her eyes hurt from keeping them closed. Every so often they popped open of their own necessity and she stared straight ahead until a cloud crossing her vision reminded her of the distance to the ground and she forced them closed again.

"What I wouldn't give for an old-fashioned wicker basket. No foresight, whoever made this, even coloured plastic'd cut some of the heat. I'm going to come to a boil in my shell, watch for steam, would you. Plastic, the folk material of this century, highly over-rated, I bet the owners're glad we took this inferno off their hands, at least my cage was cooler."

"Stop complaining, Jane!" Mirabelle was unaccustomedly sharp. "So it's hot, talking about it makes it hotter. Treat this as an adventure." She was sprawled on her back, legs stretched out, separated, across Jane's shell. On either side her arms were turned upward, veins vulnerably visible at elbow and wrist.

"I'm tired of adventure. I want a nice cool ocean, lots of seaweed, especially kelp leaves, the part that floats on top of the water, a forest of kelp and I'll dive down that long thick strand they attach themselves by and I'll swim between the kelp. I'll do flipflops and somersaults and weave in and out of the kelp stalks and when I'm hungry I'll swim up to the top and eat the leaves."

"Ugh! Those slimy brown things? They're the colour of cod liver oil!" Mirabelle wrinkled her lip.

"Yum," Jane said with a small smile.

"What else will you do in the ocean?" Yvonne had been watching the spider position itself on a rope. Moving its back legs, preliminary to spinning.

"I'll find some other turtles and learn to be a turtle. It won't matter what I do as long as it's turtlish. I'll belong. That's what's important. I've never felt I belonged anywhere. I've tried practically everything, nursing and universities and business, flying planes, scuba diving, travelling, loving—"

"Women?" Yvonne asked. Jane's lids snapped open in surprise.

"We all love women. Our mothers." Mirabelle's tone was English games-mistressy, spritely and efficient. She picked at the spot on her dress, but her blood was throbbing in her wrists and elbows. She couldn't, but wanted to, look at Jane.

"Not what I assume you meant," Jane said to Yvonne. Then, "yes."

"How was it for you, loving a woman?"

Jane stretched, relaxed each flipper in turn, closed her eyes. Her mascara had smeared in the heat and darkly filled sagging pouches under her eyes. She looked old in her sadness and fatigue, young in her vulnerability and fear – not, Yvonne thought, ageless, but all ages at once.

"It was wonderful in the beginning, the closest I've ever come to feeling right – that I belonged – I thought I'd really found the answer, I bought all the clichés, we'd be together forever, a rose-covered cottage. We did live together four years, but no roses." She laughed. "Though we did have a rhododendron. I thought we'd never leave each other, but then," Jane's face tightened into wrinkles of defeat, "it went sour, the way of all relationships."

"How?" Yvonne prompted after a minute.

"Oh, we changed and grew apart. She was working and I was studying and – I did everything I could to make it work – and she did too, I think. Then she found someone else, and we still tried to make it work, but at the last I began to wonder how I ever could have loved her even while I still was—" A single tear bisected the darkness of Jane's mascara smear. When she resumed talking, her voice was as hard as her shell.

"I don't do well with loving. I've tried a number of times and I've concluded that I am not meant to be part of an intimate relationship. So I will find a herd of turtles and belong there. Intimacy is not a criterion of success for turtles."

"You shouldn't give up, Jane. Maybe she wasn't the right woman." Mirabelle glanced down again when she saw Jane looking at her.

"It doesn't matter. It is no longer a possiblity for me." And you better remember that, Turtle! In love – hah! The others saw her sneer and didn't know what it meant. Mirabelle felt a pain in her stomach, hoped Jane wasn't sneering at her.

"But, Jane, you belong with us, don't you feel you do?" Mirabelle was amazed at her persistence, hoped they weren't thinking she meant anything more than she meant, whatever that was, but she loved Jane so much.

"More than I have ever belonged before, but it's too late now. I'm not a woman, I'm a turtle!" She looked directly at Mirabelle.

"And I'm going to be the best turtle I can. I'll study how they do it. Maybe this time I'll finish the course." Jane's laugh was a choked-off, bitter sneer. She couldn't continue looking at Mirabelle, could feel intensely her agitation. Jane drew in her front flippers. Nothing she could do about it, she'd be leaving as soon as they got to the ocean.

Jane looked at Yvonne. "And you? Have you ever loved a woman?"

"There weren't any in the fridge. But I –"

&

A small vee of Canada geese to Yvonne's left, dark against the sun, their harsh and constant honking like sonar. She watched them for a minute – what had she been about to say?

Then she was with the geese, not flying exactly, not soaring, just being perhaps, horizontal in the air like them, and they made room for her in their vee. Could see the earth below, and wasn't scared, could roll and soar and move at whim through all dimensions. In her mind, like theirs, were motion, feathers, friendship, no words, and images she'd never seen before. Back-ground and foreground changed places so she saw sharp insects on fuzzy trees, but it wasn't really like that – it was all motion, direction; insects on trees whether she was upside down or sideways. All was right way up and all that mattered was the wind.

She saw Jane and Mirabelle and the busy spider in the plexiglas basket which shot sunbeams back to the sun through the vee of geese, through herself. In the basket Mirabelle put a hand up to grasp its lip. Yvonne felt the solidity of that while she flew with the geese.

Now saw herself in the basket looking toward the geese, and her glances met in awareness of each other, of the shapes of herself. Awareness was a beam of energy projecting itself yet also receiving projections, holographed. Walking on this beam were three women. The awareness widened and slid down until they were walking on the crest of a hill. Beside them were birch trees just budding and under all the trees like fallen curls of bark were trilliums, small-growing among the spiky blades of grass. Three cardinals flashed from tree to tree and over all the sky was blue.

Yvonne with the geese knew the outside women walked here because of the middle woman: she was the middle woman. She linked arms with the women on either side and said, "I love you. You are my friends."

What was she doing soaring alone out here just now? Why had the geese called her – why had she called the geese – just now? She saw what she wanted: in the basket, took Mirabelle's hand and reached out her other to touch Jane's hair, said, "I love you. You are my friends."

Yvonne with the geese began to fall, couldn't fly for long without support. A thud near her heart, her diaphragm, jerked her wings, her arms, and her breath caught in her chest. The walking women blurred and faded and the five geese veered away, shrank into a black speck that was lost against the sun.

"I love you," she repeated. "Both of you. I love you."
"And we love you." Mirabelle hugged her, Jane patted her thigh with her flipper. Yvonne felt stiff in Mirabelle's arms, hoped she didn't feel stiff to Mirabelle, hoped Mirabelle didn't think she didn't want to be hugged. But she wasn't used to it, and it was scary. There had been no hugs in the fridge. Through the softness of their breasts, Mirabelle's heart beat against hers, and around her she felt the flesh-filled webbiness of Mirabelle's arms, slightly cooler, weaker, more ephemeral than the torso against which she allowed herself to relax.

"I love you! I really love you!" Yvonne shouted it and laughed and felt the glory of loving. "It's glorious to love you!" She threw her head back, laughing even more. She hugged Mirabelle harder, hugged Jane's neck and then around her shell, feeling as if she had so many lost hugs to give and to receive.

Later, she remembered. "Did you see the geese?"

"What geese?" Jane and Mirabelle asked.

She tried to joke. "Just part of my story, I guess. Written with invisible ink."

The spider had finished spinning a tarpaulin. Under it the air cooled and they sat in muted light. The spider, exhausted, dropped from the lip of the basket. Mirabelle bent to pick it up, but Yvonne said, "let me". She reached out from the overflow of love for Jane and Mirabelle, from the fullness of their love, and scooped up the spider. She kept her eyes closed at first, but its hair and legs were softer than she'd thought. She held it in her arms, at first gingerly, then drew it to her breast, opened her eyes and swallowed hard. The spider lay still, its eyestalks flaccid, all its legs curled in exhaustion like a lover or tired baby. Yvonne put her lips to its mouthparts and gave it the drink she'd denied it in the desert long ago. She gave drinks to Jane and Mirabelle as well, and, released from sacrifice to the sun by the spider's tarpaulin, one by one, in fullness, they fell asleep.

&

They awoke to the beep of the computer. The sun was still high. Puffs of cloud broke off from the horizon – the tops of mountains popped like corn – and floated free until meeting other clouds to join. Mirabelle untangled herself, fed the hibachi more briquets. The spider stretched its legs; Yvonne laughed at the tickling sensation.

"I wonder what the spider's story is," Jane mused.

Yvonne stroked its hair, then they all watched it amble to the bag of briquets. "Maybe you can't know what others' stories are except for what you see of them or they tell you – "

"I wish the spider could," Mirabelle laughed.

" – or how they affect your own story." Yvonne had been looking around. Now she interrupted herself to stare intently through the clear floor. "The mountains are flattening," she announced.

Ahead, it looked as if someone had sliced the white tops off the peaks, rolled them into brown lumps of dough and, farther on, flattened them completely. Yvonne jumped up, leaned over the lip of the basket, shaded her eyes. "We're going the wrong way! We're into the Prairies!"

Mirabelle jumped up as well. The basket lurched in response to her shift and Jane had to dig her flippers in to keep from sliding. "Now I'll never get to the ocean! We forgot about prevailing winds!"

"Don't panic," Yvonne said.

"There's always the Atlantic," Mirabelle added.

"That's too far! Turn us around, Yvonne, somehow!"

The basket and the balloon pulsated with their agitation and the lumpy, rolling, brown earth shrank beneath them as the balloon lifted in the heat of their anxiety.

"Where the hell's the rudder on this thing?"

"Pull on a rope, that should turn us around!"

"Put it down right now, we have to get out, we can walk!"

"We don't have any control! We might crash!"

They all shouted at once, rushed from one side to the other. Mirabelle tripped over Jane and landed on Yvonne but no one paid attention. The more they panicked the more the basket swayed and the more it swayed the more out of control they felt. The spider perched on the bag of briquets and rotated its eyes in response to their rushing, shouting. Then, simultaneously they all said, "calm down, let's not panic, stand still, we need to think."

They took deep breaths while they looked up to the balloon, back to the mountains, ahead to the flat horizon. As they calmed, the balloon lost the altitude their excess heat had generated.

"Okay." Yvonne wriggled the tension out of her shoulders. "It's not a matter of life and death. We don't have to do any thing right away."

The spider relaxed into a smaller black lump, began combing the hair on its legs. Mirabelle placed her elbows on the edge of the basket, chin in her hands. Jane sighed, waddled around in a circle like a dog about to settle.

Yvonne stared at the computer. "Too bad my programing is so elementary, too bad computer work wasn't among your occupations, Jane."

"Actually," Mirabelle turned hesitantly, "I was a programer before I got pregnant – course I've forgotten most of it and computers are so sophisticated now."

"Why didn't you say so before – when we had to free Jane – or even when I hooked it up to the hibachi?"

Mirabelle shrugged. "I thought you'd be better at it than I – and that First and Second would. Men know things like computers."

Yvonne clapped her on the shoulder. "Sure don't trust your abilities, do you?"

In front of the keyboard Mirabelle said, "it might take me a while to figure this out and I'm not sure I can do it at all."

"Do your best," Jane encouraged.

Mirabelle thought, I wonder what that is – my best.

&

"I wonder what that is," Yvonne said shortly. Mirabelle started, certain she'd voiced her thought, but Yvonne was pointing to something that snaked between the basket and the ground. On a road it could have been a speeding truck; higher up it could have been a streamlined blimp. It seemed to copy exactly the bumps and dips in the earth's surface, a giant pencil tracing a scene already drawn. It moved fast, maintaining a constant distance of a few hundred metres above the highest point of land. Colourless metal reflected the sun, and its progress over and around the brown hills made Yvonne think of wasted, sterile land, no people and no growth.

"It's a guided missile," Mirabelle read off the computer screen.

"Really?" Yvonne continued to watch. "I thought missiles were bigger. Is there someone in it, a pilot?"

Mirabelle typed, waited. "No. It's pre-programed."

"To do what?"

"To carry warheads to targets within a 2,500 kilometre range."

"Really?" Yvonne repeated, suddenly afraid. "We don't like this thing, do we?"

"Emphatically not!" Jane said. "We have enough ways of dying already!"

"Can you do something about it, Mirabelle?" Yvonne asked. "Jam its program or something?"

Mirabelle gazed into space for a minute, began typing. Yvonne and Jane kept their eyes on the missile, its elongated shadow zooming beside it on the ground, constant, dark and ominous. Suddenly its shadow shrank to a spot, hovered, then elongated the other way as the missile adopted a course ninety degrees to its previous one. Yvonne put her hands over her ears. Jane pulled halfway into her shell. The missile was coming straight at them, its nose growing large through the bottom of the basket.

"Hey!" Yvonne shouted.

"Ahhhh!" Jane screamed.

At the final second, the missile swung up and around them. A thump and the basket swayed. Jane slithered across the floor, Yvonne grabbed the rim for support and the spider slid off the briquets. As the missile swung past, its stabilizing fin touched the widest part of the balloon. The nylon shrivelled apart like skin from a surgical incision. With a great whine the missile tore into the sky. As its noise receded they were left listening to the hiss of air escaping from the balloon.

Yvonne and Jane and Mirabelle stayed absolutely still, gasping breath into shocked lungs. They stared at each other's terrified eyes and open mouths. Reading realization of their imminent crash on each other's faces, they didn't shriek or scream as earlier. Now panic seemed superfluous, as if it could only fill a space defined by hope. Nor did any of them look down, though they had to force themselves not to – looking down would entrance them into counting out their last seconds, prohibiting the choice of any other action.

With one accord, they looked up at the balloon. The tear was only in the nylon. None of the ropes had been severed. But the first pressure of deflation forced the hole larger. The whine of escaping air changed to a steady moan as the balloon continued to shrivel, causing dips and valleys, long creases in the rainbow. Blue overlapped green that disturbed yellow, a jag in the continuum.

Yvonne yanked the spiderweb tarpaulin, stuffed it in her vest, grabbed a rope, and climbed onto the rim of the basket. She forced herself to not look anywhere but up, forced herself to not think, forced unaccustomed muscles to work. Hand over hand she shinnied up, feet around the rope to steady herself. Stopped just under the tear. Mirabelle and Jane held their breath, terrified she might fall before they did. Yvonne a continuation of the balloon's flapping edges, arm muscles quivering with pain and effort. She had to let go with one hand to get out the patch, could not allow herself to think she could not do it. But her legs trembled more. The shaking was transferred to the basket, which swayed and dipped. Jane dug in her flippers. Mirabelle grabbed the rope to steady it. But now the shaking of the basket sent waves up to meet the trembles coming down. Yvonne twisted around and around, a trapeze artist without a net, had no more strength for hanging on.

A movement parallel to her, the spider scrambling up. It leapt onto her head, reached down and pulled the web out of her vest. The rope snaked by Yvonne's feet again. She arched her torso and hooked her feet around it, pulled herself back until she was suspended over the basket. Still her arms screamed. Pressing the rope to her body with elbows and arms, she grabbed a corner of the web with two fingers. The spider took the other end in its mouth and leapt to the adjacent rope. Together they stretched the web up to the hole, stretched more than she thought she ever could. Together the spider and she draped the web over the hole, pasted it on.

Yvonne let herself slip down. Mirabelle caught her pant leg, guided her foot into the basket, caught all of her as she collapsed. The palms of Yvonne's hands stung as she tried to uncurl her fingers. Her leg and arm muscles cramped. She screamed with the pain. Mirabelle grabbed two limbs at a time and pulled them straight, again and again. When the cramps subsided, Yvonne lay in the bottom of the basket and trembled now from terror as well as exhaustion.

Jane threw briquets on the hibachi, blew on them, almost willed them to burn, and the spider ran around the perimeter of the patch as if gluing it on. All three peered up, half-expecting to see the patch peel loose and float away like a wet bandaid. But it held, and slowly the balloon's rainbow rippled and spread, erasing the jag across its colours. It tugged against the ropes and slowly they stopped falling, hovered fifty metres above the ground, and then began to lift.

Curled up in the bottom of the basket, Yvonne could now look down. Dully, with no energy left to be grateful, she watched the ground recede. Every part of her body shrieked with agony. Through her half-curled fingers she could see abrasions reddening her palms.

Among all the aches, she focussed on a familiar one, struggled to sit up. But she could not undo the buttons on her shirt. Asked Mirabelle to, and when she had, had to ask her to take out the paper. Mirabelle tenderly laid it across her arms. The paper was mangled and crumpled, getting dirty. Many corners were bent and some were torn. Down the middle was an indentation – the rope crease. But the words were still intact. Yvonne blew on them and brushed them with the back of her hand – **I Am**.

Mirabelle sat down and put her arms around Yvonne. "That was the bravest thing anyone has ever done. Thank you, Yvonne." Her voice choked and her eyes shone with grateful, admiring tears.

"Oh well." About to say, wasn't anything, don't mention it, but stopped herself. Still, she blushed.

Jane said, "you saved our lives. Thank you." She massaged Yvonne's calves with her flippers, then laughed. "When it comes to the intersections of our stories, I'm glad you're along."

Yvonne smiled – "Ow." Even her face muscles hurt. "We should all thank the spider."

Watching them from the briquets again, its sides heaving. As they turned, it slowly and sedately marched over to them. "Thank you, Spider," they said, reverently.

It climbed onto Yvonne's leg and its warmth released the tension in those muscles. Even Mirabelle felt too in awe to pick it up or stroke it. For minutes the spider crouched, legs

178

folded at the joints into right angles, eyes rotating from one woman to the other. Then it leapt onto Mirabelle's chest. She made her arms into a cradle and it snuggled down and went to sleep. Yvonne wished it had stayed on her.

Mirabelle looked from Jane to Yvonne. Tears wound silently down her cheeks. "I'm so sorry. I forgot about us when I programed the missile's trajectory. It could have gone right through the basket. I could have killed us all. Even just by tearing the balloon. I could have killed us." Her face as grey as her arms and legs.

They looked up: the spider web as rounded with air as the rest of the balloon.

Jane pushed Mirabelle's hair off her forehead. "You made an error. The missile could have killed us, but it didn't. Don't keep torturing yourself."

"Where did you send it?" Yvonne asked.

Mirabelle drew a shuddering breath. "Space. I set the distance to infinity. It should burn up or go into orbit."

Jane glared. "All it is is one missile! There're thousands of others! We can't get rid of them all, and even if we did they'd still build more! It makes me furious!"

Mirabelle's hands were poised over the spider like wet dishcloths. But instead of wringing them she asked mildly, "do you feel helpless? You always get mad when you do."

Jane felt a wrenching inside her, tears sting her eyes. She closed them, breathed deeply. "That's true." She waddled around in the space between the computer, the hibachi and briquets, the pail of water, and her lumps of coal. Her flippers stiffened. She hissed, "I refuse to feel helpless!"

Mirabelle looked up from her fingers combing the hair on the spider's back. Yvonne opened her eyes. Her legs were straight out and her hands curled loosely at her sides. Jane blinked, looked away. They'd seen her quivering – they'd heard her crying.

"I mean helpless about missiles. And things I can try to do something about." Yvonne closed her eyes. Mirabelle's fingers resumed combing. In a minute, Jane added, with a devious smile, "I wonder what they'll say when the missile doesn't come back?"

&

Consulting the weather program on the computer, Mirabelle discovered a west-flowing current higher up. They loaded briquets on the hibachi and watched the spiderweb patch anxiously, not knowing how much stress it could stand. But its edges clung to the nylon and, except for a non-rainbow greyness, the patch could have been part of the original balloon.

Up here, three or four thousand metres, they felt cold in the thin air. Mirabelle had on only a tee-shirt dress, Yvonne jeans, a shirt, and vest. They sat as close as possible, arms around each other, trying not to shiver, and the spider sprawled across their legs.

Jane, in her shell, was the warmest. But she felt restless, irritable, wanting to pout and throw things. She sighed and heaved about as much as she could in her shell, twitching her fippers and tail, biting her lips.

In a while she stuck her head out and derided, "you look silly wound up in each other's arms like a couple of Victorian schoolgirls! And the spider looks like a lap rug!"

Yvonne tightened her arm around Mirabelle. "Doesn't feel silly, feels good. You could join us, then you wouldn't be looking at us. Besides, it keeps us warm."

"Hard to cuddle a turtle," Mirabelle said sleepily.

"I don't need any cuddling, thank you, and I'm not cold." Jane scratched the top of her head on the edge of her shell, but couldn't reach the itch where her armpit would have been. Wasn't getting eczema, was she? Is that what was wrong?

"We don't want to leave you out."

Under Yvonne's gaze, Jane lidded her eyes. "I don't feel

left out. I don't need anyone, never have. You two can have each other." But she had a pang of anger, of – sadness?

"I get it," Yvonne said. "You think I love Mirabelle more than you and she loves me more than you. You're jealous!"

"I am not!" Jane itched all over. Her shell too tight – do turtles shed like snakes? "Anyway, you'll have each other when I've gone into the ocean, so it's better this way."

"What way?" Mirabelle asked. Here was Jane being fierce again. Mirabelle hoped it was because she didn't want to leave them – her.

"You know!" Fierce and snappish.

"I don't. You mean with Yvonne and me together and you over there? You come over here and that'll be even better. We want you."

"I'm not cold."

"Jane, come here." Exasperation and a pleading command in Yvonne's voice. Slowly, reluctantly, with protestations of not being cold, not being jealous, not being lonely, Jane eventually laid her head across their thighs and let them stroke her hair.

"It's so hard to cuddle you," Mirabelle said, with longing. "You've got that great shell in the way. I wish you had a hand I could hold." She touched the edge of the shell. "I wish you weren't a turtle."

"So do I." Jane hadn't intended to say that. It hovered for all of them to hear. And re-hear. The admission echoed within her shell, scaring her. She stuck her chin out belligerently. "But I am! I turned into a turtle and I am a turtle!" How do turtles show affection?

Yvonne laughed. "Oh well, we love you anyway, Jane – you great big turtle!"

For some reason, that made Jane feel immensely sad, alone and full of longing. She wanted to cry, scream, lie as close as she could to Mirabelle. Instead, she breathed out some of the feeling and closed her eyes.

Mirabelle wound her fingers dreamily in Jane's hair. "I'd

like us to stay together forever. Our children could come to us and we'd go to them, but we'd always be together, the three of us." She glanced up. Jane's eyes closed but the spider was staring at her. "The four of us," she corrected, stroking it. "I wasn't forgetting you."

&

Yvonne, Mirabelle, Jane and the spider languished in the transparent semi-sphere of the basket, all energy pressed out of them by the sun and thin air. Draped around each other, Yvonne and Mirabelle dozed. Jane kept her flipper in Mirabelle's hand and peered through the bottom of the basket.

White-peaked mountains cruised by beneath them, and brown and purple valleys with long skinny glinting lakes or rivers, then rolling beige uplands that folded into more mountains. Thick mist like clouds fallen into valleys swirled up to blend the sky and land. Jane saw a line that flattened mist and mountains. The line grew out of dark into purple and then blue.

"The ocean!" Jane yelled. "Wake up!"

Her word drew the expanse of blue beneath them into ripples, drew the ripples into waves, the waves into shadings of blue-turquoise, cerulean, royal – and a deep, impenetrable green. Her word drew white caps on top of the swells like miniaturized mountain peaks, became audible slaps when the white caps broke.

"The ocean! Do you hear it?"

Yvonne and Mirabelle put their attention in their ears, thought perhaps they could hear it, wanted to hear it because Jane wanted them to.

Jane blew on the bottom of the basket, polished it with her flipper, peered through. Her face, her shell, had the redhead's blotchiness of excitement and her tail snapped back and forth. Jane could hear the ocean. Not just the surface slap of white caps but the swells as well, and way down, the undulations as water sought the dips and ridges of the ocean floor. She could hear the rubbing and shifting of seaweed, of kelp strands, the bubbling of fish food-searching, the scrabbling of crabs on rock, she could hear the small motions of a barnacle's palp.

The munificence below overcame her terror of the balloon's height. The closer she got to her goal, the more difficult, the more terrifying – and now she had to fall.

Yet the ocean before her with all its sounds – and now black humps to the right. Whales, she thought, creating white vees like arrows pointing toward them. Not whales. "Turtles! Over there! Put me down! Right now!" Jane waddled back and forth, taking up all the space, and her tail lashed with excitement.

Yvonne and Mirabelle exchanged glances, raised eyebrows and shrugged, then did as Jane directed. Yvonne pulled the air control cord. The balloon started to deflate. Mirabelle heaved the remaining bags of briquets, the hibachi overboard. Jane, with one last shout, "turtles!", pulled all of herself into her shell so she did not have to watch their descent.

Released from the west-flowing current, the balloon hit one below, was buffeted east, then north, tipped and swung. The balloon's motion was in their stomachs. Gravity forced through the soles of their feet, their orifices, up through their viscera, forcing all of them into their chests, their throats. They had to open their mouths to let the pressure out.

The basket met the water with a knee-aching, teeth-clamping shock, bounced, tipped and threw them from side to side, into each other and rebounding off. Eventually it settled, a rocking motion that grew gentler as the basket and the ocean accepted each other. The deflated balloon trailed on the waves, a multi-coloured ship's anchor, attached by the few yellow ropes. Their transparent vessel was transformed from a balloon basket into a coracle that bobbed up and down in the swell.

Jane stuck out her head, her flippers. "We made it! We're on the ocean! Help me up! Shove me over the edge! Wait for me!" to a group of turtles swimming by. "Oh hurry, hurry! I have to go!" Desperate and imperative.

In slow motion to Jane, Yvonne and Mirabelle lifted each side of her shell, hoisted her to the lip. "Okay, good-bye," Yvonne said, letting Jane drop ungently into the water.

The ocean captured Jane, washed away all memory so she did not say *good-bye* or *thank you* or *see you later*, but hit the water, submerged, surfaced, yelled again, "wait for me! I'm a turtle too!" paddled her flippers after the humps eighty metres away heading out to sea.

With the sudden loss of Jane's 250 pounds the coracle bobbed and swayed in a crazy dance. Yvonne and Mirabelle hung on to the rim, afraid they might fall over too. As their boat settled, the silence around them expanded and pressed on their slumped shoulders, filling lines and crevasses the pain of loss was etching in their faces. Mirabelle stammered, "how could she leave so fast? She could at least have said good-bye!"

Her words at a distance from Yvonne who had found a spot of ocean to stare at, to watch the swell move through that spot, to wonder if any waves would form white caps in the exact centre of her spot. Blinked, focussed farther away. "She's going to have to move some to catch up, they're not waiting."

"Who cares?" Mirabelle's breath caught into sobs. Yvonne put her arm around her, kissed her neck, wiped the tears off her cheek with the back of her hand. "How could she do this to us? After all we've been through – just leave like that – how could she?"

"She had to. Find some turtles, be the same as something." Yvonne had prickles in her eyes, blinked hard, and the blinking felt like little moths against Mirabelle's cheek.

"Yes but leaving us – we love her – not even good-bye."
"Just loving or being loved isn't enough – and really loving someone is letting her go. We've known from the beginning Jane would leave when we got to the ocean—"

Mirabelle pulled away. On her face was such hurt and sorrow Yvonne couldn't stand to look, but reached for her again. Mirabelle shouted, "don't you care? You're just dishing up worn out words, they don't help! Don't you have any feelings? How could she leave?" The words keened out to hurt Yvonne's ears, drove that pain deep into her brain and down through all of her until her pain resonated with the sound of Mirabelle's and filled the space in both of them that Jane's presence had occupied.

Mirabelle sniffed, wiped her nose on her sleeve. "We need some tissue." Still leaning against Yvonne, still encircled by her arms, she put her hands on the edge of the basket and stared in the direction Jane had taken. West. The sun a glowing ball only two fingers above the horizon.

Yvonne put her hand over Mirabelle's, asked softly, "would you give an arm or a leg now if it'd bring Jane back?"

Mirabelle closed heavy, swollen eyes. "That's a dirty question. Once I would have. I would have given anything, everything." She stretched her fingers, felt Yvonne's move too. "Now – I guess not," whispering, "now I guess some sacrifices are too great. I guess I can't destroy myself for someone else no matter how I love her."

Yvonne squeezed her hand. Both stared at the long carpet of light that led to the sun, seeing, or hoping they saw, solid humps that could be turtles, and Jane among them, greeting and being greeted.

As the sun was eaten by the horizon, it became the other half of the semi-sphere they occupied. Yvonne felt as if she and Mirabelle were objects being drawn toward the sun by the power parts have to be made whole. They sat still, their hands joined, and the spider lay still with its legs curled. The coracle rocked and occasionally a larger wave made a

185

wet slapping noise as it passed beneath them.

The rocking motion moved the world they looked at, blurred the edges of the fading red carpet between them and the sun, and the blurring of their vision became the smudging of the sunset. Gold streaks appeared among the red, then purple and iridescent poignant blues.

All of them that was aware had gone out from their eyes and joined the fading colours, wished to hold them longer, drink them all before they disappeared. Their awareness going out of their eyes pulled up their longing, their sadness, happiness and fear, pulled up their breath so their chests hardly lifted, pulled up their moisture and filmed the awareness with quiet little tears.

The colours faded downwards, becoming one bright line at the end of the ocean and their eyelids lowered on top of the tears. The loss of light was the loss of Jane. The dark behind their eyelids became the dark of the sky above one horizontal crack and they felt the pressure of the darkness driving the light down, down into or beyond the ocean, into or beyond themselves. The darkness drove them through, drove through them, to a place beneath the coracle, and the light was in a place beneath the ocean.

&

Through the shining bottom of the coracle they could see the sea and light was all around. A motion caught their vision, at first in the air and then the ocean: the spider, falling or jumping.

Yvonne realized now she had seen it leap up to the lip, pause there, poised, its legs folded like eight right angles, then, having paused, push off from the basket into the air, fall through the air into the ocean, fall through the ocean. Her eyes followed it downward, a black object shrinking in her vision, a black speck spiraling like something thrown overboard, used up, discarded.

"What did it do that for, jump overboard?" Mirabelle

186

started to struggle up, but Yvonne grabbed her arm, pointed through the bottom of the boat again. "Look."

All the moonlight, all the starlight had collected on the bottom of the ocean. They could see each piece of seaweed, long strands of kelp, into hidden crevasses, caves with undulating denizens. They could see the hidden colours of the ocean past moving fish and squid and fleshy octopus. They could see their spider now, a metre across at least, all legs as it had been in the desert by the rose, but bigger now, having had to grow in the magnification of water.

The spider moved its head around, looking for something, crossed their field of vision with a graceful, flowing motion that caused the plants to wave as they parted. Where the spider halted now they could see the edge of a deep cavern, a black hole, an entrance to another world. The spider drew in its legs, poised to leap, looked like it would stay still there, just there, for only one infinitesimal fraction of all time.

Yvonne sprang up – she had only that much time. Had to go where the spider went, she knew that now, knew that the spider had been leading her here, was waiting for her, and would not wait for long.

She climbed over the lip of the coracle and dropped into the water. Her skin tingled, shriveled and the cold drew out her breath so a vacuum was created in her lungs, and she could not feel her toes, her feet. To Mirabelle, her face mirrored some luminous intensity as water chilled her blood, drove it deep into her inner caverns, and the luminous intensity was other worldly.

They looked at each other, feeling a unison beyond words. Mirabelle scared, alone in the basket, Yvonne treading water, desperate to get to the spider, knowing she had to go alone yet wishing Mirabelle could come. Mirabelle ached to say don't go, don't leave me, but was prevented by Yvonne's urgency, the shining of her face. Yvonne saw her tears, knew how hard her leaving was for Mirabelle, but the spider might not wait. Mirabelle leaned over the edge of the basket, her face torn with another loss, and held out her hand. Yvonne reached up and squeezed it, took three deep breaths and dove.

&

Down she went, pulled by the gravity of the ocean floor. All around her she could feel the water. Could feel the water in her body, in her cells, wanting to join with the outside water. Her tissues – the substance of her – felt suspended between the inside and the outside pressure. Not pain, but equal balance. Yvonne rejoiced in it as the ocean floor pulled her faster and harder. Grasses brushed her sides, her arms, her hands touched rocks.

Past mountains half as tall as those she'd ballooned over, down past grasses the size of trees, branched like trees, down past hills of rocks and sediment, some with caves, past fish, anenomes and starfish purple as a bruise, barnacles as long as her thumb: these waved their palps as she dove by.

Colours everywhere, greens, browns, oranges, even yellow stripes, and every shade of blue from brilliant turquoise to thick and secretive cobalt. Down past eyeless fish which swam by scent and feel, plants she'd never seen, dark as northern spruce at night. Awed, almost overwhelmed with awe, Yvonne was pulled past the lowest craggy humps of rock. She put out her hands to stop herself from jarring on the ocean floor, but thick water swirled, cushioning her arrival.

Yvonne pushed herself upright to look around. As she did, she involuntarily took a breath. She felt her lungs expand—

Breathing under water!

Opened her mouth, breathed in, out, through it and her nostrils – water? air? poured in – no matter, she could breathe!

Knew she wasn't creating this alone, but couldn't think about it: there was the spider still poised on the ledge.

Pushing past rocks, she floated over and reached out her hand to the spider; she would go where it would lead. Her fingers wrapped around its water-sleek and now familiar hair. The spider turned its eyes to hers. A long look, quiet, steady. Other looks: the first one in the desert, the birthing look, the look from Mirabelle's shoulder – now the spider's eyes were filmed. Her gaze dropped momentarily. A wisp of sadness. She re-focussed, trying to see in the spider's eyes, far in to waving, wavering? And to light? The spider's eyes were filmed.

The spider turned its head, began to pull away. Yvonne followed the feeling of its hair under her fingers, looked where the spider was looking. A crack in the ocean floor, half a metre wide, and light escaping from it so grasses on either side waved darkly, backlit. Another world. Now Yvonne knew what she'd seen in the spider's eyes before. Her awe increased again, consuming any sadness.

Another world. A crevasse like her desert abyss, but this one full of light – white light, no, coloured, containing all the colours, a light too bright to look at, no, a light just right, illuminating everything. Yvonne stepped forward, excited, trembling, about to have to shade her eyes, but the light changed, blue now, rosy, green? – the ultimate light, ultimate time, intimate place – here I see, here I know, here I find—

Could not quite see yet, not quite past the thickly waving sea grasses, not quite into the crack. Could see only enough light, feel only enough intensity, enough thrill escaping from the crack to set her thrilling too, her heart and lungs and stomach and skin, all her water within. She had to go with the spider, be with the spider, wherever was beyond this crack in the ocean floor—

The spider turned to her again, another long look that held her still. This time with awe she felt confusion. Stared into the spider's eyes, searching, turned to the crack in the ocean floor, searching—

189

The spider shifted its body toward her so she felt all its weight and pressure as in a hug, but the motion shoved her backwards. She put a foot behind to regain balance, and as she did, the spider bunched its legs and leapt into the crack. Instantaneously, Yvonne registered how light was extinguished by the spider's body, how its legs and eyestalks and individual hairs glowed with their own luminosity. She regained her balance and stepped forward to follow. The plates of the ocean floor shifted. The crack closed up. The light disappeared.

Half-swam, half-ran to where she'd last seen the light – nothing. Desperately, not wanting to believe it, she pried at the rocks and tried to scrape the mud away – had to be there somewhere, the entrance to the other world, the spider.

Nothing. Dark now, the last trace of that light fading from her eyes, a terrifying, stultifying, oppressive dark. And the tickle of mud, of fishes, the felt presence of ominous shapes.

Alone. No spider. No other world. How could the spider show her it and then not let her enter?

Yvonne screamed! Screamed! Every lost, abandoned, horrible, rejected, grief-filled, angry, frustrated and disappointed feeling she had ever felt. Screamed!

The screams left her mouth in rising bubbles of air that mixed with air escaped from the other world.

Now the one shift necessary to close up the crack set others in motion. The floor trembled and rumbled, rocks fell down, ledges grew up, the increasing turbulence jarred her, terrified her –

could no longer breathe under water.

– catapulted her halfway to the surface.

Pushed upward, following the stream of bubbles from her scream, responding to the pain in her lungs, her ears, her throat, kicked hard, upward to the air so far above, its imperative through all of her, she had burned away her body fluids and the water on her skin was first an irritation, then an

190

agony, her mouth about to open to be filled with water. Broke the surface, gulped great mouthfuls of air, how could she have been breathing under water? All around her bubbles of her scream broke the surface with popping sounds, and floated on the surface of the water, closer and closer, drawn to her. They touched her body, clung to it all over like oil in water. She felt she'd grown a new layer of skin. She turned and saw the basket, a moon, bobbing on the waterline, round and coolly lit, and Mirabelle waving, yelling. The woman in the moon. Fatigue through all of Yvonne, coldness of the ocean in her bones, no energy, no strength. Her new layer of skin weighed her down.

Mirabelle pulling on the balloon, a rainbow slick on the water – oh. The ropes. Yvonne kicked her legs, they barely moved, paddled with her hands. All she wanted to do was put her head in the ocean and sleep.

A touch to her fingers. She grabbed at the rope, missed, grabbed again, her fingers could not feel or clasp. With her teeth, her elbows, she pulled it closer. Hand over hand, kicking slowly, every movement a series of pains, Yvonne approached the coracle. Its sides towered above her. Mirabelle grinning, crying, looking joyful and afraid, leaned over the rim, held out her hands. Yvonne tried to lift hers, so heavy, could Mirabelle? Were her arms strong enough?

Mirabelle felt Yvonne's fingers – cadaverously cold. Her own blood began to chill. She grasped Yvonne's wrist and pulled. Could Yvonne get her footing on the slippery plastic basket? Pulled more. She wished the spider were there to help. Her breath caught in a sob with the effort, with no spider. Yvonne grabbed Mirabelle's forearm, walked her feet up the basket. It started to spin away. Both knew they would not be able to do this again. Mirabelle heaved and Yvonne leapt. Backing up, and up, Mirabelle wouldn't let go. Her arms would have to come out of the sockets first. She hauled Yvonne up the side, over the lip.

They both toppled onto the floor of the basket. Mirabelle

took Yvonne in her arms and kissed her face all over. Cold-shrivelled, wrinkled – Mirabelle didn't care. She hadn't ever expected to see her again. For some minutes they lay panting, gulping. Yvonne's shivers became shakes that set the basket rattling. Mirabelle took the wet clothes off Yvonne and rubbed her with her dress. Wrung out the shirt, jeans, vest, and spread them to dry, delighting in domestic tasks. Yvonne wrapped herself in her paper, curled up again, and slowly her shivers subsided. Mirabelle held her in her arms against her warmth and together they lay in the bottom of the basket, Mirabelle waiting until Yvonne could talk.

&

The moon drew the light from beyond the ocean back into itself, becoming smaller, denser, contained again and waiting. As the moonlight was drawn away the stars stung more brightly in sky and ocean, now thorns of light or fire sparks from another world. Yvonne and Mirabelle saw how the moonlight on the ocean had fractured into starlight and the way the light had changed was the way that time had changed.

Mirabelle, her arms wrapped around Yvonne, her head on her shoulder, said, "was that Heaven that you saw the spider go into and it's in the ocean, not the sky?"

Yvonne sighed. All of her ached, but her chest contained the greatest ache. She looked up at the stars, over the water; they blurred with tears. "I've lost the spider. I've lost the magic. Even Jane."

"You said Jane had to go. Maybe the spider had to go too. Though I was so hoping you'd bring it back." Mirabelle didn't know which loss was worse – Jane or the spider – couldn't measure them – at least Yvonne was back. Yes, the loss of Jane was worse.

Hot, burning tears creased Mirabelle's cheeks. Her mouth sagged open and she breathed out her pain, kept wiping her

192

cheeks and nose with her hand. Jane, Spider.

She curled one leg, rubbed her shin with her hand, felt hair, bristly like stubble after shaving. Rubbed more, pulled up her other leg, hair on it as well. She smiled through her tears in the starlight, tightened her arm around Yvonne's shoulder, wanting to share this with her as some small reassurance.

Behind her eyes Yvonne kept seeing the spider poised and leaping, poised and leaping, out of the basket, into the crack, poised and leaping somewhere she couldn't go. Fine for Mirabelle she had arms and legs. Fine for Jane, she'd found the ocean. What about her? The spider poised and leapt, the magic gone, her words gone, what good was paper now? How to survive? Why to survive? Standing with the spider under water, she'd not needed air to breathe. She could survive in strange places with the spider – could not breathe when it had leapt – left her – deserted her.

The spider had followed her from the desert, was her spider, had gone where she had led, behind her, with her, and now when she'd been willing to follow it – it hadn't waited, hadn't wanted her, had taken its magic, gone into a place of magic, left her out.

"Why wouldn't it let me go too? Let me stay with it? Stay with me?" She banged her fists on the basket. "It could at least have let me see!"

Yvonne's cry was lost in a great crackling. The sky behind them lit up with such colours the balloon could have been shredded and uplifted to hang there. Yvonne looked up, felt the northern lights raging for her, shouted encouragement and shook her fists as well. As they raged, she calmed and heard the power in the sky, sometimes noisy with little statics, sometimes booming thunder. Colours bounced and danced and drew them close, retreated and pushed them far.

As she listened, she took into herself the colours of the sky – pinks and oranges, purples, whites and gold – and they mingled with the colours she'd seen under the ocean. She had seen them, had seen the light from the crack in the ocean, had seen the spider disappear, could see it and see it and see it again. Yvonne laughed. She had seen what it was that she could see – and her skin felt smooth with the bubbles of her scream. These bubbles contained air from the other world – and her teeth turned into ice cubes before she'd met the spider. She had some magic too – not as much as the spider, but her own.

She laughed again, threw her arms out and her head back. As large as the sky and ocean together, large enough to have all these colours in her. Mirabelle had never heard Yvonne laugh so joyously. Had to laugh as well. There she was, throwing her arms out to the sky as if inviting it into her. Her hair stuck out too, salt water thickened into a bush. Jeans filthy, shirt sleeve torn, and her paper padded her abdomen into early pregnancy. Mirabelle looked at Yvonne's face and loved it, laughing, open, such joy – though so many more lines and wrinkles.

Still laughing, Yvonne held out her hands. Mirabelle grabbed them and they began to dance, bending and twisting in rhythm with the northern lights. As they danced they were covered with the lights themselves, laughing and loving them on each other. Their dancing flickered in the borealis, the sea a mirror for them and the lights to dance upon.

Under the silence of the sky they heard a little voice, "wait for me! Wait for me!" The northern lights held still. Yvonne and Mirabelle leaned over the edge and peered into the sea. Each held her breath in case it wasn't true, and their eyes grew large and round, searching the surface of the sea. The voice again, faint and watery, "Yvonne! Mirabelle! Wait for me!"

"Jane! It's Jane! She's come back!" Mirabelle grabbed Yvonne's arm and shook it, jumped up and down.

Yvonne shaded her eyes with her hand as if that gesture would help, looked at all the ripples in the sea, all the shadings of the sea. Hard to see anything, the water moved and the lights flashed on it – was that –?

A small, dark speck and lighter splashes all around it: Jane's swimming head and a trail of phosphorescence.

Now Yvonne clutched Mirabelle too. Jane's progress was so slow, much slower than her leaving, her swimming not so strong and she not so big.

Yvonne frowned. "Something's different?"

"Yeah," Mirabelle whispered. "Do you think –?" Felt Yvonne nod. "– she's lost her –?"

"Shell?" Yvonne risked a quick glance at Mirabelle. Hands folded prayer-position between her breasts. On her face delight and love and worry.

Yvonne located the wash of phosphorescence again. Now Jane's alternating strokes were creating wheels of light to either side.

Mirabelle wrung her hands and shook them. "Come on, Jane! Not much farther!" To Yvonne, "can we do anything to get to her?"

"Nothing I can think of. Except wait." She yelled, "it's okay, Jane, you'll make it!"

They waited, watching Jane's imperceptible progress, holding their breath to help her, wishing the coracle would drift toward her, hoping it would not drift the other way. Then she was two metres away, then one, then exhaustedly flailing her last strokes to them.

Yvonne grabbed Jane's left arm and Mirabelle her right. They hauled up. Jane, dead weight heavy, slithered up the slippery sides and fell, shivering, into their arms. Mirabelle gathered her to her, surprisingly small and thin for someone who had had such a heavy shell. Yvonne sat down beside Mirabelle and they warmed Jane in their laps.

Only by her red hair did they recognize her, and even it was frizzy, too long to hold its perm. The water had washed away all her make-up. How wan and swollen her face from the battering of her journey. The nostrils of her prominent

195

nose were pinched, and her skin blue-tinged with cold. Her breasts with shrivelled nipples barely moved, breathing too quietly. Yvonne rubbed her arms, her legs, and Mirabelle wiped her dry with the hem of her skirt. They held her close while the aurora borealis splayed them with orange and purple light. Slowly their warmth sank into Jane so her colour changed from pale grey-blue to slightly pink again, and above her, Yvonne and Mirabelle grinned at each other.

&

Jane opened her eyes, focussed her friends' faces out of shapes against the northern lights, and her eyes brimmed with all the water she'd swum through. Tears fell down her cheeks, into her mouth and along her neck. Yvonne and Mirabelle hugged her and Mirabelle wiped Jane's tears with the hem of her skirt. Jane gasped for breath. As she did, she felt a pain stab her, a stitch under her breastbone. The stitch grew into a tearing sensation that stretched all the length of her, consuming her: the pain of another shell breaking apart inside her. She shrieked, sobbed, tried to breathe against the pain. As it lessened, she felt a flowing from one side of her to the other, of something warm and golden. Heat spread through her, soothing the jagged edges where her inside shell had been.

Jane lay in their arms for a long time, wondering at the golden flowing. She stroked Yvonne's arm with one hand, Mirabelle's with the other. Smiled, and they noticed, through her drying tears, the calm smoothness of her face. Her cheeks sloped away from their bones so her face seemed closer to them and not so pinched.

She cleared her throat and whispered, "those turtles wouldn't wait for me. I kept swimming after them, yelling for them to wait. At first it felt so good in the ocean, at first I knew I was where I had to be, but then I started missing you so much." Jane rubbed their arms again, and shuddered. "I wondered what I was doing, leaving you – still, I kept on trying to catch up, thinking that's what I had to do, since I was a turtle, but the closer I got to them the more I missed you. I started to feel awful about the way I'd left, not even saying good-bye, not even saying I love you."

On their faces love for her – would they forgive her? She shifted between them, looked at her hands holding theirs, surprised by the familiarity of hers. "I stopped swimming then and looked back for you. When I did, the turtles turned around and spread out. There I was surrounded by turtles, just as I'd thought I'd wanted. I couldn't see you anywhere, so I tried to stop missing you, thinking, well, now I'll really be a turtle. But the other turtles were looking at me as if I were a strange beast, and I could only think I'd never see you again. I started to cry and my shell dissolved, just floated away. I was naked. I had no protection and I was afraid I'd drown. It was so awful. I dove after my shell, but it was too heavy, I couldn't pull it up and I couldn't get under it."

Jane was shaking. Yvonne and Mirabelle each put an arm around her and squeezed her hands. "I realized I'd been all wrong – I did belong with you. I wasn't really a turtle, even though I was tugging on my shell – and then I let it go –" closed her eyes watching her shell sink down, down to the ocean floor-"I asked the turtles to help me, to give me a ride back to you. They just looked at me and swam away." Jane blinked tears. On her face profound sadness.

"I have never felt so alone or so scared in my whole life – ocean everywhere, nothing but ocean. I thought I might as well drown and get it over with, but then I heard this huge noise like a sonic boom, and then the sky lit up."

"The northern lights," Mirabelle whispered.

Jane nodded. "Against them I could see the basket and your dancing, you looked miles away. I started swimming toward you, and yelling. Such a long way. I wanted to be with you right then. I was terrified you wouldn't hear me, that you'd float up into the sky, and I was so cold and tired, I could only keep swimming. I felt so sorry I'd left you, so ashamed, so – sad."

"We were sad too," Mirabelle said. "I'm so glad you came back."

Jane squeezed their hands, then looked around the basket. "Where's the spider? I thought out there, I hoped – if I could get back – maybe the spider can spin me a new shell?"

"The spider is gone. It left after you did. It leapt into the ocean – I went after it. I would have followed it forever, but – it went through into another world and – didn't let me come." Yvonne leaned her cheek on Jane's hair.

"But Jane's returned now. Maybe the spider will too."

Yvonne shook her head. "It won't."

"How do you know? It might," Mirabelle persisted.

"I just know." Her last vision before the ocean quake catapulted her up: the finality of light extinguished by the shifting floor, the spider on the other side forever. She had seen.

Mirabelle had a different thought. "Maybe it just wasn't your time to go there, wherever it is. Maybe that's not your story yet?"

"Maybe." Yvonne smiled, oddly comforted.

Jane mourned, "now I can't ever have a new shell. I'll have to go around like this." Naked in their arms. Small breasts over smaller bumps of rib cage. Fuzzy red hair. Not even any make-up.

"I think you're beautiful, Jane." Mirabelle's voice shy. "Much more beautiful as a woman than a turtle."

Jane twisted to look at her face – so sweet and soft, more lined than when they'd met. And her large eyes – almost blinding in their intensity. Mirabelle's lips curved into the most beautiful smile Jane had ever seen.

"I agree, Jane." Yvonne stroked her thigh. "You don't need a shell."

Jane's shoulders rose, tightened, fell in a sigh. "I wanted

to be a turtle. I felt better, all that protection."

"We'll protect you." Mirabelle brushed her lips against Jane's hair. "A bit."

"I was willing to be a really good turtle."

Yvonne and Mirabelle held the limp, anguished shape of Jane. Mirabelle kissed her hair again, whispered, "you are a really good woman."

Maybe with Mirabelle and Yvonne, Jane thought, that might be more possible than it ever had been. Smiled her love and gratitude up at them. They smiled at her, at each other, and the smiles went on and on, and the sky still blazed. Then Jane began to shiver again so Mirabelle took off her dress and gave it to her. Yvonne gave Mirabelle her shirt and socks, and eventually, wrapped in each other's arms, they fell asleep.

&

When they awoke the sun hung bright over the horizon. The colour of the ocean was the colour of the sky, and the coracle rocked on little ripply waves that topped long swells.

Jane stretched and stood up. Mirabelle's dress hung past her knees, and its colour clashed with her hair. "You know what I want? A chocolate milkshake. Maybe even a chocolate malted milkshake."

"No nice sea salad? No kelp?" Yvonne.

"Not even a seaweed milkshake?" Mirabelle.

"Amazing isn't it? I was craving seaweed and now just the thought of it makes me sick. But I had to find out I suppose." She looked at her arms and legs. "I'm scared. I don't remember what it's like without a shell. I feel horribly naked and vulnerable."

"You are naked and vulnerable," Yvonne retorted, raising her eyebrows. "It's supposed to be the human condition." Jane grimaced and Yvonne laughed.

"I thought you'd be much bigger," Mirabelle stood beside

her, measuring. "About six feet and solid, but you're the smallest of us!"

"Yes, I'm only five-one. Now you see why I needed a shell?" Jane tossed off her embarrassment that accompanied their scrutiny.

"No," Yvonne replied solemnly. "I really don't see. I never have."

Suddenly remembering, Mirabelle shifted her examination from Jane to her own legs. She yelled in dismay, "oh, look! Last night I could feel hair, but look! It's black on one leg and blonde on the other! The spider really goofed!" Jane and Yvonne howled. "It's not funny," she chided, hurt.

"Actually, I think it is," Jane said, then tried to be serious. "But you can always shave your legs, though I hope you don't. It's really wonderful. The spider knew you were unique!"

Yvonne added, "I agree. It's like a tribute to the spider."

Mirabelle mumbled, "mmm" and rubbed the hair both ways, but felt mollified. Perhaps it was unique, perhaps she could wear it like a tribute.

Jane stretched her arms, looked at her old familiar hands. Hadn't seen that scar in ages – slamming her finger in a door – and that one, cutting carrots for a party – was the skin more crepe-like, less elastic? She stood up on her toes, wiggled them, back onto her heels. All felt quite familiar – had she really been a turtle? Shrugged her shoulders, and for an instant, could again feel the weight of her shell. She looked at the ocean all around them, and shuddered. "Okay, Yvonne, what are we going to do now?"

"Why ask me?" Yvonne looked up from her papers. Some sheets wet and crinkled as well as dirty and rope-scarred. "I'm not in charge, remember?"

Jane laughed. "Oops. Old habits etc. I mean, what do you want to do? And you, Mirabelle? Is there land anywhere or are we going to bounce around in this plastic bowl forever?"

"Feels like years since we've had anything to eat,"

Mirabelle said. "I'd like a cheeseburger with my milkshake. Even a drink of water would help."

Yvonne reached over and handed her First's pail. "Here you go, my dear." Mirabelle looked at her in surprise, then took the pail and drank. Yvonne just smiled, resumed smoothing her papers.

"A bath," Jane added. "I want to wash my hair."

"And get some different clothes. We haven't got out of these since the beginning."

"Be nice if a hotel floated by."

Yvonne laughed. "You'd have got stuck in the elevator, Jane, as a turtle – we did have a wonderful cabin though." She happened to look at the computer. Looked again. On its screen was a red and purple tulip.

Mirabelle saw Yvonne notice it. "Oh yes. When I was alone and I didn't think either of you was coming back I re-programed the computer. To keep my mind off how I was feeling." Yvonne and Jane nodded, intrigued. Mirabelle looked bashful. Her eyes were anxious, but she could not control a smirk.

"I erased all that stuff about turtle cages and guided missiles – did you know this computer was capable of guiding one to a target, not just into space? – and well," Mirabelle took a deep breath, and wrung her hands. "I've always grown flowers. Before I lost my arms and legs, I grew roses and chyrsanthemums-I used to win prizes." She looked at Jane and Yvonne earnestly – no, not laughing at her. "Back then I thought tulips were coarse and vulgar and ostentatious, but while you were gone it occurred to me – some flowers have hundreds of tiny petals and can lose some and no one notices, but not tulips. They only have a few. Each petal's important to a tulip. Now I think they're bold flowers, and their petals are so smooth and their colours so bright. I'd love to grow them in shades of red and purple and pink no one's ever seen before." Blushing, she laughed at herself before they could. "Isn't that strange, tulips?"

"No." Jane reached out and gently took her hand. "Not strange, wonderful. Lovable."

Looking at her hand in Jane's, Mirabelle felt the length of time she'd waited for what had seemed impossible. She raised Jane's hand to her lips and returned Jane's earlier kiss. Then she included Yvonne in the brilliance of her smile. "My story could end right now," she whispered, feeling completely happy.

"This might be another beginning coming up." Jane pointed. "Look."

A hundred metres away the ocean met a sandy cove surrounded by arbutus, cedar, fir and hemlock. They could see a path leading out of the cove. Grinning in delight, Jane and Mirabelle squeezed each other's hands.

Yvonne shuffled her papers into a stack, buttoned them under her vest. Had they always been this close to land and hadn't noticed in the moonlight or in this sun? Had their combined longing pulled them to the shore or the shore to them? She had so much to think about – everything that had happened, that kept on happening.

Mirabelle and Jane hauled the balloon into the basket. Without an anchoring drag the basket sped toward the beach, up one side of a swell and down the other, pushed more by the tide than pulled back by the undertow. Smiling, the women watched the land come to them. The ocean breeze blew their hair against their cheeks and the land breeze blew it back.

A wave crunched them onto the sand. They jumped out and pulled the basket up the beach, scraping over the tide line of tangled seaweed, flat arbutus leaves, dead crabs and fir cones. Jane lifted out the computer, its tulip flashing with excitement, and they started toward the path.

&

"Just a minute." Mirabelle ran back to the balloon, pulled

it systematically through her fingers. She frowned, pulled it inch by inch the other way. A slash in the material, its nylon edges melted into keloid lumps. "No spider patch. I thought it might come in handy someday, but it's not there." She stuffed the crumpled, seared balloon into the basket, walked back to the others. "Where did it go?" Yvonne shrugged, Jane shook her head. They looked at each other, then back to the balloon.

The absence of the spider's patch made them miss the spider more, made grief at the loss of might-have-beens expand their chests and close their throats. Yvonne thought of her fridge and blue-striped wallpaper, controllable green stars on the ceiling, thought of the rose in the desert and the spider handing her a word. She held her paper to her breast, stroking it pensively. Mirabelle thought of her finger in the Salvation Army bowl, her children, thought of her new arms and legs, blonde and black haired. Jane thought of her shell and shrugged her shoulders, of the spider's eye-stalks, of Mirabelle's tenderness.

Spontaneous thoughts of the spider leapt into their minds, mingled and formed images. The images overlapped, grew upon each other's, shimmered and solidified.

Near the balloon, all three saw the spider, starkly outlined against the ocean. But each saw it differently: Yvonne as she had at first, behind the rose stem, and at last, leaping into the ocean crack; Mirabelle saw it draped comfortably in her arms, but grown big the way her children had; and Jane saw the spider pasting its web onto the balloon. They stared at it silently, each overwhelmed with awe and gratitude, and grief that it had left them. Yvonne stroked Mirabelle's arm – soft with hair like the spider's. It had taken her so long to touch it. Mirabelle put her hand on Jane's shoulder, felt different to them both without her shell. Jane did something she had never done; threw her arm around Yvonne's waist and squeezed. As the spider faded they found, mixed with grief and loss, joy and reverence.

They turned to contemplate the path. Only a few metres were visible, winding through huge cedars and hemlocks. Speckles of light poked between branches. Crows cawed and squirrels scurried up trunks, and it could have been many paths before except for the poignant mewl of a lone seagull and the salt tang that mixed with the pungency of the sun-pocked forest floor.

Suddenly the air was filled with cacophonous rustlings and flappings and callings that sounded joyously familiar to Yvonne. She whirled around, holding her paper outstretched before her, and looked up, down, to the sides.

"Come on! Oh please! Come on now!" Yvonne begged and wheedled, pleaded and requested, holding her paper this way and that, as if swatting for invisible insects. Jane and Mirabelle realized what she was doing, and held their breath for fear of disturbing what they could not see.

"Here. Here's the paper. Here I am! Come here!" Yvonne twisted this way and that – slowly stopped. Disappointment lengthened her face, slumped her shoulders. She pulled her paper back to her chest with trembling hands. Trying to keep her voice light, bright, she said, "false alarm, I guess."

Jane patted her shoulder sympathetically. Mirabelle was just about to say, that's too bad, when she was distracted by something fluttering on Yvonne's—

"Wait, there's something on your neck." She scratched at it with her nearly-grown fingernail. It fluttered more.

Jane exclaimed, "there's something on your forehead, your cheek."

"Look at your arms!" Mirabelle sounded so excited.

"You're covered in words!" Jane announced. "They're stuck to your skin! All over!"

Yvonne looked at her hands, at her arms – they were covered in words, words of all different colours and sizes and shapes, words in all different sorts of type, script, calligraphy, writing, printing, hieroglyphics, signs and symbols of every kind, she was hirsute with words. She lifted her sleeve, pulled up her jeans, words everywhere, stuck to the new layer of skin. She put her hands over her eyes and burst into grateful, disbelieving, overjoyed sobs mixed with laughter. Words on her palms stuck to words on her cheeks, some changed places, some overlapped others, and some transformed themselves completely.

Mirabelle said, with self-satisfaction, "I told you they'd come back when they needed you!"

"They're not children," Jane retorted.

"I need them – do you think they knew that?" Yvonne's voice still amazed.

Jane shrugged. "Perhaps." Words all over Yvonne, looked as if she could do with a good bath. She laughed. "Well, at least we have reading material. Would you like her left arm, or right, Mirabelle?"

"I suppose anyone can read my face now," Yvonne said. "Like a book!"

"I am taking the balloon," Mirabelle said. "I'll wear it. You never can tell. I saved Martin's wide ties for years then I got ruthless and threw them out and guess what?"

"The next year they were back in style, I know." Jane laughed. "My mother saved string and material and old wax paper that she pressed."

Mirabelle ran back to get the balloon. Yvonne twisted her held out hands, studying those words. Some had transferred to the paper already, without her help. Mirabelle walked back, wrapping the balloon around her.

"You look quite regal," Yvonne commented, looked again. "You know, if anyone asked me I would have sworn your eyes were grey, but they're violet. How odd."

"So they are," Jane agreed. "Equally beautiful, though! And yours, Yvonne, I thought they were light blue, but they're dark, dark cobalt!"

"Yours are a wonderful, warm brown, not green – they're stunning with red hair!"

"I'll have to get completely new make-up to go with

brown eyes." Jane laughed.

"I always wanted purple eyes." Mirabelle adjusted the balloon more comfortably.

"Violet," Jane said.

"Purple."

"Violet."

"Purple. They're my eyes."

SANDY FRANCES DUNCAN was born in Vancouver in 1942. She has lived in Saskatchewan and Ontario and currently lives on Gabriola Island, British Columbia. She worked as a psychologist before turning to fiction writing in 1973. Under the name Frances Duncan she has published books for children and young adults: *Cariboo Runaway, Kap-Sung Ferris, The Toothpaste Genie* and *Finding Home (Guest Soloist)*. She is also the author of *Dragonhunt*.